Shadows
in the Mind

Hemmie Martin

Winter Goose Publishing
2701 Del Paso Road, 130-92
Sacramento, CA 95835

www.wintergoosepublishing.com
Contact Information: info@wintergoosepublishing.com

Shadows in the Mind

First Edition, May 2015

ISBN: 978-1-941058-30-5

Cover Art by Winter Goose Publishing
Typeset by Michelle Lovi

Published in the United States of America

To my mother, Jane
With love

To Shirley

Thank you for reading my

books. I hope you continue

enjoying them.

Best wishes

Chapter One

Wednesday arrived at her mum and stepfather's house at three in the morning, to find every window illuminated. She parked next to Oliver's muddy Land Rover and scrambled out of her car, straight into the house.

"Where are you, Oliver?"

"Up here. She's locked herself in the bathroom."

Dashing up the stairs two by two, she found Oliver leaning against the wall outside the bathroom door. He offered a weak smile, ill disguising the black shadows smudged under his eyes.

"Mum, it's Eva. Let me in please."

Silence.

"When did this start?" she said, turning to him.

"I think things started going downhill when my pottery business slowed down. Three shops have stopped stocking my stuff, so money's tight. I've been a bit down about it and Joan may have absorbed some of my stress."

"You can't blame yourself; these are difficult times. Anything else?"

"She's been distant with me, and her sleep pattern is a nightmare. She sleeps all day and is up all ruddy night."

She could see the strain on his face. He was largely a placid man, with an insurmountable ability to cope with a wife with schizoaffective disorder.

"What about her meds? I thought she was going on the depot injection?" she asked.

"She refused. I became concerned when she began eating less and changing her sleep pattern. I now suspect she's up to her old tricks of hiding her tablets."

Wednesday knocked quietly on the door. "Mum, we want to help you, but we can't unless you let us in."

"You don't want to help me; you want to force those god-awful tablets down me. I know Oliver's been hiding them in my food."

Wednesday sighed, knowing the next move was to call an ambulance and get Joan assessed by a psychiatrist. It was becoming an all too familiar routine.

Twenty minutes later, the ambulance arrived; a crew who had visited the house before. The paramedic remembered Joan, and she remembered him. He coaxed her out of the bathroom and into the ambulance, but she refused to allow Oliver or Wednesday to travel with her.

"I'll drive, Oliver. I'll just go and pack her a bag."

Wednesday wandered into the bedroom, gazing at the disarray. Joan had clearly lost the drive to look after herself or the house, and Oliver had never been that way inclined. She shoved the necessary items into a bag before racing back down.

They drove to the hospital on the periphery of Cambridge, with only the sound of the windscreen wipers breaking the silence. Stopping at traffic lights, Wednesday rubbed the nicotine patch on her arm, willing it to give her an extra dose. At times like these she missed the real thing.

Joan was assessed by the psychiatrist, then sectioned into the new psychiatric unit, The Raven Unit. And that was that. Joan was placed in a room, before Wednesday and Oliver headed back to the car.

"It's the best thing for her," Wednesday said, turning on the engine.

"I know, but it doesn't make it any easier. They're going to force her to take her meds. She'll hate it there."

Wednesday reached out and patted him on his hand. "Let's see if we can tidy the house before she returns. Do it room by room."

Oliver smiled wryly. "We'll have to let Scarlett know."

"Let's wait for a more humane hour of the day."

Wednesday was conscious that in two hours she would be at work; hoping it would be a calm and crime-free day. "Who am I kidding," she muttered.

"How long's your mum been in the unit now?" Lennox asked, pouring hot water into a mug.

"Twenty-eight days. She's now detained under section three for six months. She's so disconnected from the world, they're trying new meds," replied Wednesday, before taking a sip of coffee and screwing up her nose. "I see the Guv hasn't bent to us all whinging about this muck."

"Austerity continues, so he tells us." He paused to cough. "I'm sorry about Joan," he mumbled.

"DI Wednesday and DS Lennox, in my office please," DCI Hunter called across the Incident Room, giving her no time to reply to Lennox.

Digby Hunter beckoned them to sit before checking his computer screen. "There's been a death at The Raven Unit in Cambridge hospital. Do you know it?"

Wednesday sat up straight, burning her throat on the steaming coffee as she swallowed hard. "Yes Guv, we know it," she threw Lennox a glance. "Actually, my mum's there currently."

"Ah, right . . . well it's not your mother. Anyway, all the staff need interviewing, and the patients will require video interviewing with a medical professional present if they're vulnerable. You know the drill, Wednesday, which is why I want you involved, regardless of your mother's situation."

Wednesday hid her burning cheeks behind her coffee mug as they rose to leave.

"You still fancy him, I see," Lennox said, grinning as they walked through the Incident Room.

She jabbed her elbow into his ribs before grabbing her bag from her office. "I'll drive."

"How do you want to play this?" he asked, pulling on his seatbelt.

"I'll introduce us quickly in case they think I'm visiting Mum. It'll be fine." She wondered, however, what impact the death would have on her mother and the other patients.

The now familiar sight of The Raven Unit folded over her stomach as they moved to the front door and pressed the bell.

Inside, the unit smelt of fresh paint, with sounds of pollen-induced sneezing echoing around the sparse corridors. Wednesday made a valiant attempt not to scan around for Joan.

A heavy shroud of silence cocooned the staff milling about the nurses' station. The female nurses smiled discreetly at Lennox, whilst others looked hostile at their very presence.

A young constable stood guard outside the deceased's room. He looked on wide-eyed as a patient hovered nearby.

"She won't bite," said Wednesday on approaching him.

"I might," replied the woman with a sly grin, before moving off.

The site of a body hanging was never an easy image to see; it turned Wednesday's stomach. The lifeless form hung in the ensuite, her feet dangling over the toilet. Her face pale, her eyes semi-open. Doctor Edmond Carter stood near the body, waiting for the photographer to finish. He turned on hearing them arrive.

"I want to get her back to the lab as soon as possible; I believe her presence is causing distress to the other patients." He smiled gently at Wednesday before turning away.

"Is this definitely a suicide?" she asked.

"Won't know for sure until the post mortem. Her mental health may be the main factor."

There was nothing more to do at the present, so they left the scene and headed to the nurses' station. Wednesday asked to see the psychiatrist.

"Doctor Manning's in his office. Just knock," replied a nurse, pointing down the corridor.

Entering his office, they were hit by the contrast to the rest of the unit. The office walls were painted a subtle shade of grey, with glossy-black floating shelves housing academic books, and black framed certificates placed artistically around the walls, giving the room an air of masculine domination.

"Detective Inspector Wednesday and Detective Sergeant Lennox," she said.

"I suppose you want to talk about Susan Roche," he said, stretching out his hand to greet them.

"We'd like to know a bit about her," replied Wednesday, noticing his blond quiff, resembling a frothy wave in a shandy glass.

"She has a diagnosis of bipolar, and was prone to depression. She never mentioned killing herself whilst here, but her husband apparently reported she did at home."

"You don't believe him?"

"All people lie at times, DI Wednesday. It's a case of knowing when and why, and that's not easy to do."

"Why would he lie?"

"Hard to say; living with someone who is mentally ill must be excruciatingly difficult at times. People react differently; I can't predict how an individual will cope with the pressure."

"Are you saying he found it hard?"

"No harder than anyone else, I suppose."

"Did she get on with the staff and patients on the unit?"

"As far as I am aware." He stifled a yawn.

"Is this the first death on this unit?"

"Yes, we've only been open eight months. This was Mrs Roche's second stay with us. Last time was a success, as I'm sure you'll find with Joan Willow," he concluded, eyeing Wednesday with a pointed stare.

She returned eye contact briefly. "We'll get back to you if we have further questions," she said, handing him her card.

She hesitated in the corridor, aware that Joan's room was two doors down. Taking a deep breath, she let the air out slowly before speaking.

"Let's get on and interview the staff."

Chapter 2

Charge Nurse Eric Knight strolled into the family room and sat on the low chair facing the detectives. He leant back, spreading his legs wide, looking Wednesday straight in the eye.

"You were on duty the night shift. How was Susan Roche?" she asked.

"No different than from the previous nights."

"Can you expand on that? Was she depressed, engaged?"

"She'd hit a period of depression, but nothing we couldn't handle. It's bread and butter nursing," he smirked, looking down his hooked nose.

"What about her last few hours?"

"Nothing special to report."

"Did she make any friends in here?"

"She was an introvert; the only person she'd converse with was Joan Willow." He sat forward, cocking his head.

Wednesday kept her eyes focused on his forehead. "Had she spoken with Mrs Willow the day of her death?"

"I've no idea."

"Thank you for your time. If you think of anything else, you can contact me here," she concluded, shakily handing him her card.

Expelling a cleansing breath, she half smiled at Lennox as they awaited the next person. He opened his mouth, but decided to wait.

A nurse tapped on the open door. Wednesday waved her in and pointed to the chair.

"Nurse Karen Reilly," she stated.

"I gather you were working the night shift. When did you last see Susan?"

"I did the medication round at eight. Susan was in the toilet so I left her meds on the bedside table. Her husband said he'd make sure she took them."

"Did you see her after he'd gone?"

Karen Reilly searched the ceiling before answering.

"I don't think so. But someone would have."

"How was the night shift?"

"Hectic. Rene Blower was having a psychotic episode, so we were occupied with her. She required attending to frequently."

"So anyone could have entered Susan Roche's room and you wouldn't have noticed."

"The nights are less staffed than the day shifts. Look, I've said all of this to the first police on the scene."

"I'm just piecing together the hours prior to her death. It's standard procedure."

Karen shrugged, muttering something about wasting time.

"Did Susan have any enemies on the unit?"

"Not that I'm aware of." She yawned theatrically. "When can I go home, it's been a tiring shift?"

Wednesday sighed deliberately loudly. "Take my card in case you think of some other details. Thank you for your time."

She took the card, shoving it in her pocket before leaving the room.

The next person to arrive was Sara Morris, a diminutive, fresh-faced student nurse.

"It was my first experience of a night shift. There's more to do than I anticipated. Not everybody sleeps well at night."

"Were you nurses together at all times?"

"No, we tended to different people at times."

"At what time was Rene Blower's psychotic episode?"

"At twelve forty-five a.m., both Eric and Karen rushed to her room on hearing her screams. I followed to watch; I hadn't seen her having a psychotic episode before."

"So all three of you were occupied, leaving the ward unattended."

Sara blushed, fixing her stare on her ragged nails. "I wasn't there for long, they wanted me to watch the ward."

"You sound rather upset about that."

"I am, I suppose. I wanted to learn." She blushed more furiously. "But I did as I was told, and left them to it."

"Did you go in each patient's room to check on them?"

"No, I just peered through the windows in the doors so as not to disturb them."

"You may have to change that policy. Susan Roche's body had been replaced by pillows in her bed; you saw those instead of her."

Sara's head lowered, letting salty tears drop into her lap. "Am I in trouble?"

"That's up to the NHS enquiry. Did you notice anyone unfamiliar on the unit at visiting time or afterwards?"

Sara shook her head, sobbing quietly.

"Call me on this number if you think of anything else. It may appear insignificant to you, but it may be the jigsaw piece we're looking for."

Sara carefully took the card before wiping her cheeks with the backs of her hands. Wednesday frowned, wrinkling her nose at a familiar smell.

"Do you smoke?" she enquired.

"Yes."

"Do you take cigarette breaks during a shift?"

Sara wrapped her arms across her abdomen, focusing on the floor, and nodded.

"When did you take breaks?"

"My first one was around midnight . . ."

"And the second?" Wednesday said, pushing her through her reluctance.

"Around two a.m.," she broke to swallow a sob.

Irritation bubbled in Wednesday's stomach as she observed Sara trip over her own words.

"Eric came out with me the second time. He told me all about Rene Blower's episode; saying how adept he is at handling such situations."

"So Karen Reilly was left on her own? Is that protocol?"

"We were only just outside the door. Officially, we're supposed to walk off the grounds but that wasn't practical. If Karen needed us, we'd have been there straight away."

Wednesday did not like being lied to, and it also made her wonder what else the staff were lying about. The talk of smoking bristled her desire for one.

As Sara left the room, Wednesday turned to Lennox and suggested he interview her mother before they continue, so it was not constantly gnawing away at the back of her mind.

Chapter 3

Lennox sat in a room waiting for Joan Willow's arrival; the process was taking longer than he anticipated. Finally he heard the sound of shuffling feet accompanied by verbal coaxing.

"This is Joan Willow," announced another student nurse, Tom Lee, as they entered the room. They took their seats, facing the camera sitting on a tripod.

Lennox knew exactly who she was, but refrained from saying so. Joan showed no recognition in her eyes even when he introduced himself.

"I understand you were friends with Susan Roche. Can you tell me about that?"

Joan was picking the skin around her nails, reminding him of one of Wednesday's habits. He pushed thoughts of her far from his mind. Joan's silence was as dense as the bottom of a beer glass, and as tough to break.

"What did you and Susan like to do? Play cards, watch TV?"

"There now God all clear . . ." she whispered.

Lennox was perplexed, looking to the nurse for clarification.

"It's called 'word salad,'" he said, smiling haughtily.

"You mean she's not making any sense," replied Lennox, unimpressed by the young man's over-inflated self-importance.

"I'm not sure how much sense you'll get out of any of them in here."

Lennox clenched his jaw. "Perhaps *you* can tell me a little about their friendship?"

Tom looked towards Joan then back at Lennox.

"Sometimes they just sat in silence, sometimes holding each other's hands, like they were communicating their profound unhappiness telepathically."

"Is that what everybody thought?"

"Some thought they were suppressed lesbians."

"Was there evidence to corroborate that?"

"Not as far as I'm aware. But who knows what goes on in their minds?"

"Did they go into each other's bedrooms?"

"That's not permitted. Patients can only socialise in the family lounge, TV or dining room, or garden."

"Has it been known for patients to break that rule?"

"Not that I'm aware of, but I bet it has. Some of these patients can be quite cunning, you know. They'll run the shower whilst having a crafty fag in the ensuite, then liberally spray deodorant. The smoke detector rats them out, though."

Lennox thanked Joan before Tom escorted her back to her room. It surprised him how seeing her in that state affected him, to the point of feeling sorry for Wednesday, which he knew she would abhor.

Wednesday arrived just as Nurse Angela Rhodes entered with Fiona Campbell, the youngest patient on the unit. She was newly wed to Jordan, and suffered with a delusional disorder, that of delusion of control. Jorden insisted on sitting with her during the interview.

"Did you know Susan Roche?" Wednesday asked.

"I'd seen her around, but never spoken to her," Fiona whispered.

"How come?"

"She was trying to control me."

"How was she doing that?"

"She'd take my thoughts if we were in the same room. At night she'd put thoughts into my head."

"What kind of thoughts did she put in your head?"

"Oh no, you're not tricking me like that. You've brought evil with you, and I won't serve you."

The nurse leant into Fiona and spoke gently. Fiona listened then shook her head, looking to her left. She was transfixed. Jordan reached out, touching her hand briefly.

"I don't want to be here," she whispered.

"I'm sorry," Angela said, "I think that will have to do for now." She stood up, guiding Fiona and her husband towards the door. She turned back to them. "There's no chance of you interviewing Rene Blower today, by the way; she's in a catatonic state."

"We'll see her another day. Anyone else?" Lennox could not help noticing the shape of her calves.

"The men are in group therapy, and can't be disturbed."

Lennox exhaled, turning to Wednesday for advice. He wanted to talk to the nurse for longer. They returned to the car; both thinking about smoking.

Fiona and Jordan Campbell entered the TV room and stared at the blank screen.

"You haven't done anything silly, have you?" Jordan whispered in her ear.

"I'm not sure; I don't remember. Will you help me if I have?"

"Always."

Chapter 4

Wednesday pulled into the station car park. Lennox raced to the court-yard as she continued down into the bowels of the building, with nicotine cravings ravaging her mind.

"Ah just the person, I have some findings for you," declared Edmond, as she entered the pathology laboratory.

"I want to show you the signs of manual strangulation on Susan Roche's neck."

"So it's murder, not suicide. I'd rather you just told me; already feeling a bit peaky," she said, apologetically.

Disappointed, but undeterred, Edmond took a file from his desk and flipped it open.

"There are grip patterns around her neck; haemorrhaging in her neck muscles and her hyoid and thyroid bones are fractured due to squeezing or a downward traction." He paused to sneeze. "The mistake people often make is they think they're disguising strangulation by hanging the corpse, but the dead don't bruise. Blood stops flowing the minute the heart stops."

"More fool them," Wednesday said with a wry smile.

"Also, she remained lying prone after death, as the blood pooled in her back, causing red and purple patchy areas."

"So it's possible she was killed in her bed then moved later."

"I wonder how they moved the ceiling tile without the staff hearing."

"Another patient was having a psychotic episode. The noise she created was the perfect cover."

Edmond made a guttural noise.

"Anyway, any other insightful offerings?" she asked, sensing he was near the end of his report.

"The person needn't have been strong to kill her; her slender neck would have needed nothing more than thirty seconds of pressure. She has petechial haemorrhaging around her eyes, lips, and upper chest, and oedema on her face and tongue."

"So a male or female could have done it."

Edmond nodded. "Sorry I can't be more helpful."

Wednesday smiled, touching his arm; the man she considered to be like a favourite uncle never need apologise.

Mounting the stairs, her thoughts turned to her mother, when she bumped into Lennox coming through the courtyard door.

"You stink," she said, holding her finger under her nose. "I never noticed it when I smoked."

"You might have to start again if we're to continue working together."

"Don't be so unsupportive," she chided.

Lennox breathed a sigh of relief as Wednesday turned off the engine, and Joni Mitchell.

The estate where Susan and Barry Roche lived stood in the less affluent part of Cambridge. Grey-bricked buildings with concrete communal areas, dotted with overflowing bins and roaming dogs, housed clusters of hooded youths sitting on concrete bollards smoking rollups and spitting.

The detectives may have been in an unmarked car, but the youths had a sixth sense. They watched the pair cross the road and stride up to a row of buzzers, entering the building under the watchful eye of the group.

The entrance was stark, with fluorescent lights and rows of gun-metal grey post boxes. Piles of pizza menus and junk mail lay strewn on top of the boxes. Some had wafted onto the floor and were covered with muddy shoe prints.

They chose to walk up the two flights, rather than inhale the acrid aroma of stale urine in the lift. Barry was waiting by his door.

"DI Wednesday, and this is DS Lennox," began Wednesday, holding out her badge. "We're from the Cambridgeshire Major Crime Unit. We're very sorry for your loss. Perhaps we could come in and conduct our questioning in private."

The smell of dog and stale tobacco hit them as soon as they stepped inside the narrow corridor. They squeezed passed his muscle-bound mass, trying valiantly not to touch him. They headed for the room he was pointing to, beyond the poky kitchen.

They found themselves in a lounge diner, with a nicotine-stained ceiling and a layer of dust shrouding the DVD boxes scattered along the windowsill. Over-flowing ashtrays occupied the coffee table and the arm of an armchair, where a black Labrador lay sleeping. Wednesday and Lennox perched on the edge of the dilapidated sofa.

"I'm sorry to inform you, but following further investigation, we now know your wife was murdered."

His face blanched. "Murdered?" Picking up a mug, he took a mouthful of liquid. "I thought her madness had finally finished her off." His voice was strong, belying any grief he may be feeling.

"You do understand, she didn't commit suicide."

"So you say. But who'd want to kill her?"

"That's what we're trying to establish."

Barry slumped into the armchair, running his hand over his smooth head.

"How was she when you last saw her?"

"She was sulky and seemed to hate me. The doctor said I should still visit, but it was a waste of time, if you ask me."

"Was your marriage a happy one?"

He finally looked Wednesday in the eye, briefly. "What's that got to do with anything?"

"It's a routine question."

"She could be a miserable cow, but liked sex, and spending money we hadn't got."

Wednesday nodded, waiting for him to continue, but he just folded his arms, dropping his chin to his chest.

"So not particularly happy."

His face shimmered with sweat. "I suppose not. But have you tried living with a mad person?"

Lennox viewed Wednesday in his peripheral vision. She did not flinch.

"There's no doubting life must have been difficult at times. Do you have any children?" she asked, catching sight of a photo on the wall of Barry and Susan with a young boy.

"We've got a twenty-year-old son, Gavin. He's not here."

"Where is he?"

"Out, his mum's death has hit him hard."

"We'd like to speak with him at some point. What do you do?"

"I'm a builder." He flexed his muscles so the naked lady tattoo on his upper arm waved at them.

"Where were you the night your wife died?"

"I saw her that evening, then I came home. Gavin was here."

"How did she seem?"

"Her usual self. When can I have the funeral?"

"When the second post mortem is completed, things should start moving." She studied his facial expression and body language, but he was giving nothing away.

He caught her looking, and glared.

"If you suspect me you're barking up the wrong tree. Yes I stopped loving her, but I didn't hate her enough to risk going to prison."

"Had she stopped loving you too?" Lennox asked.

"Who knew? I'd stopped expecting any affection, apart from the occasional sex marathon."

Wednesday's shoulders tensed. Lennox looked around the room taking in the disorder and general lack of care, and worried his bedsit was bumbling in the same direction, if he was not vigilant.

"Could you ask Gavin to give us a call?" Wednesday said as she stood.

After they left, Barry picked up the phone and dialled. After a few rings, it went to Ansaphone.

"Where are you, Gavin? I need to speak with you urgently. Call me."

"What did you make of him?" Lennox asked, climbing into the car.

"Clearly likes his bodybuilding. There's certainly a lack of compassion towards Susan. But, that doesn't mean he killed her."

Back at her desk, her mobile alerted her to a text. She checked it and smiled, she had forgotten about the date that evening. She wrote up her report before closing her computer and grabbing her handbag, unaware of Lennox watching her leave.

Chapter 5

Wednesday changed outfits three times, trying to make the right impression. She found herself wishing Scarlett still lived with her.

Wheels crunching on the gravel drive alerted her to his arrival. She gave one last look in the mirror, compounding her dissatisfaction, before heading downstairs.

"Shall we go straight away, or do you want to come in first?" she asked.

"Let's go now, plenty of time to be inside later," Alex replied.

Walking side by side, the backs of their hands brushed against one another as they headed towards The Black Horse.

"Can I have a word?" DCI Hunter said, beckoning Lennox into his office.

Closing the door behind him, Lennox waited behind the chair.

"Sit, I want to talk to you about this Roche case."

Lennox scraped back the chair and sat down.

"You've interview Joan Willow I understand."

"Yes, Guv."

"I want this to be clear; she is just as much a suspect as the other patients in that unit."

"I interviewed her in the same manner. Besides, she didn't recognise me."

"That's all well and good, but have you dismissed her on the grounds of her being Wednesday's mother?"

"Not at all. In fact, she's the only patient on the unit who communicated with Susan Roche, which gives her access to the victim. We believe Susan possibly knew her assailant, as there were no defensive wounds."

"So who does that give you?"

"Barry Roche and any of the staff or patients."

"Is Wednesday aware of this?"

"I'm going to inform her this morning."

"She needs to be aware. I will see her about her visits to her mother when she gets in. Where is she?"

"Usually here by now." Lennox turned, looking through the glass panel, to see her arrive.

"Do you want me to send her in?"

Hunter nodded before picking up his mug and gulping down a mouthful of tepid coffee.

"Guv wants a word," he said to her as she reached her office door.

"I bet I can guess what about."

He gave her a wry smile. "I'm sorry about all of this."

"What do you need to apologise for?"

"For having Joan amongst my list of suspects."

Wednesday folded her arms around her abdomen. "I can see why, I just can't conceive her capable of the act."

Lennox was about to reciprocate, but instead, watched her strut towards Hunter's office.

"I suppose you know what I wish to discuss," he said.

"My mother."

"How are you feeling?"

"On a personal level I worry about the impact the crime will have on her, as well as her safety. But I accept that everyone on the unit is a suspect; Joan Willow included."

"That's honourable, but I will be observing the case closely. Normally, I'd take you off such a case, but your expertise in mental health issues is invaluable. Don't let me down."

"No, Guv." She prepared to leave, when he spoke again.

"One last very important point; when you visit your mother, you're forbidden to discuss the case. I don't want her story skewed by information fed by you."

"Understood." She left his office, red-faced.

"I've organised for us to meet the male patients at The Raven Unit," Lennox said, putting on his coat.

"Great, my day's getting better and better," she sniped.

Chapter 6

Spring rain hammered on the tarmac as they walked towards The Raven Unit. Wednesday thought Lennox looked like the Count in Sesame Street with his collar turned up. He rang the bell announcing their arrival.

The corridor smelt of antiseptic. Nurse Angela Rhodes was waiting for them at the nurses' station. She gave Lennox an open-mouthed smile, ignoring Wednesday completely.

"Back to interview the men," she said, gazing at Lennox from under a canopy of heavily made-up eyelashes. "I'll bring them to you."

"Thank you," replied Wednesday, stepping forward.

Lennox moved away reluctantly and Wednesday noticed.

"You do know it's a cliché, policemen and nurses, don't you?" she whispered.

"You can't blame me."

"Everyone on this unit is potentially a suspect. Remember that."

"She was on the morning shift, not the night."

"It doesn't matter, we have to tread carefully."

They entered the interview suite and positioned the chairs carefully for the video camera.

"Did Hunter ask you to keep an eye on me?" Wednesday asked, rummaging in her handbag for a tissue to blot her rain splattered face.

"Would it matter if he had? I know you're not going to cross the line, but it makes him feel better to think I'm watching over things."

"So he did ask."

"He wants you on this case and he wants us to succeed. You know how he is."

She had no time to reply as a knock at the door announced the first patient.

"This is Eddie Brass," said Angela.

He lumbered towards a chair, diving into it so the chair legs buckled slightly.

Wednesday introduced them and asked if he was happy to talk in front of the nurse. She then went on to explain that they wanted to know what he was doing, what he heard, and what he saw the night of Susan Roche's death.

"I can't remember."

"Do you remember Susan Roche?"

"Yes, she was the opposite of me. She was slim and I'm, well you can see."

"Is there anything else you remember about her? How she interacted with other patients and staff, and how she was when her husband visited?"

Eddie rubbed the stubble on his chin, making a scratching sound that made the hair on Wednesday's neck bristle.

"She got on with most people, except the charge nurse. He didn't like her." He glanced at Angela.

"What makes you say that?"

"I overheard him telling the husband that he shouldn't let her talk to him like that; he said she was too demanding."

"Do you remember what her husband said?"

Eddie rolled his eyes to the ceiling and looked around before shrugging his shoulders.

"How did you get on with her?"

"I found her a bit demeaning; telling me I should lose weight so I'd get a girlfriend. I told her I had an eating disorder and was gay, and she said I was using that as an excuse for being fat and single."

"How did that make you feel?"

"I laughed in her face, which is hard to do when you're depressed."

Wednesday let a smile drift subtly across her lips. "Did Susan argue with anyone the day she died?"

"Not that I recall . . . But as I already said, I don't remember."

"Thank you for your time, Mr Brass. If you do think of anything else, then please do contact me," she said, handing him her card.

As Angela took him away, the detectives stood up and stretched their legs.

"I get the feeling we're not going to find out much from the patients," Lennox said.

"Give it time, every little detail is a small piece of the jigsaw puzzle."

"I'd like some of your conviction."

Wednesday smiled. Angela returned with Melvyn Rollins, bringing with him the stench of stale smoke. Again Wednesday ran through the same statements to ensure he was comfortable.

"I've been highly anxious since being in here, so the night she died, I was pacing the corridor."

"Did you see anyone enter Susan's room?"

"Not . . . Not that I can recall. Anxiety blinds me, if you get what I mean." His knee bounced up and down rapidly, as he squeezed a stress ball in his hand.

"Did you hear anyone arguing with her during the day or preceding days?"

Melvyn's rocking became more pronounced, and was accompanied by a humming sound. Angela leant towards him and put her hand on his arm, making his humming noise increase in volume momentarily.

"I did hear shouting coming from her room, but I don't know what day it was."

"Did you hear Susan's voice?"

"I think so."

"Was the other voice a man or a woman?"

"I think it was a man."

"Did you recognise the voice; think about staff and patients, for example."

Melvyn shoved his glasses up his bulbous nose. He shook his head so tiny particles of dandruff scattered into the atmosphere like miniscule satellites.

"I know I've heard the voice before, but I can't remember who it is. Sorry . . . sorry." His body broke out into a mass of nervous tics, so Angela escorted him back to his room for some peace.

Dave Hyde, the last male patient, took some encouraging to enter the room. He was suffering with paranoid schizophrenia, and was distrusting of everyone around him. A cigarette lodged behind his right ear like a carpenter's pencil.

After several minutes of coaxing, Dave entered but refused to sit down. Wednesday was not fazed but Lennox was less confident about the situation, forcing him to perch on the edge of his seat with a need to be in charge of the interview. Wednesday recognised that.

"I didn't like the woman," he snapped. "She stole my cigarettes."

"How do you know it was her?" Lennox asked.

"The voices told me; they saw her do it."

"Did she smoke?" Lennox asked Angela.

"Of course she fucking did. Why else would she nick mine?" Dave shouted, pulling his hair and glaring at Lennox.

Lennox's heart pounded in his chest, as he caught his breath.

"Did she own up when you asked her?" interjected Wednesday.

"Fuck, no. I wanted to search her room but I heard footsteps in the corridor, and we're not allowed in each other's rooms. I thought I'd go in later when she was watching TV."

"Did she steal cigarettes from anyone else?"

"I don't care about anyone else; they're all fucking loons." And with that, he swaggered out towards the garden for a smoke.

"Will that be all?" Angela asked, in Lennox's direction.

"We'd like to interview the last two morning shift staff; Nurse Joshua Plough and care assistant Doris Smith, please," Wednesday said calmly.

Angela nodded briefly before sashaying down the corridor.

Looking at Lennox, Wednesday raised her eyebrows as he turned the cigarette packet in his coat pocket.

"You wanted to see me. I'm Joshua Plough."

"Thank you for coming. You were on the late shift prior to Susan Roche's death and the early shift after. How did you find the unit in the morning?"

"Staff were shocked by the finding; hanging is a gruesome form of death." He stopped to let the information filter into the room.

"What about changes in the patients?"

"It's a small unit, so the news spread fast. The women appeared shocked, whereas the men were barely bothered."

"Did you hear any rumours banded about?"

"Not that I can think of. No offence, but gossip is the domain of the women in this place."

"Did you notice any difficult relationships between Susan and other patients?"

"Rene Blower was too ill to interact with anyone. Eddie Brass tended to avoid her as he felt even fatter next to her. Dave Hyde tends to keep away from everyone as he thinks they're all out to get him."

"Are you aware he argued with Susan Roche on the day she died? He accused her of stealing his cigarettes."

A red hue erupted over Joshua's face and ears. Clasping his hands together, he kept checking the door and shifting around in his seat.

"Look, I feel bad . . . Dave was pacing around muttering about Susan and his cigarettes. I didn't intervene as he's a paranoid schizophrenic. I thought it was all just fantasy."

"Did you report this to anyone?" Lennox queried.

Joshua looked down at his hands. "I don't believe I did; it was nothing out of the ordinary with Dave. He's quick to move on to another strand of paranoia."

"The NHS is doing their own investigation, so we'll leave it to them to investigate the protocols," Lennox said with a hint of relish.

Joshua left the room, muttering under his breath.

"How about coming back to mine and I'll make us something to eat whilst we run through what we have so far. I bet you've only eaten crap recently," Wednesday suggested.

"You know me too well. I'll take you up on the offer, thanks."

Chapter 7

Lennox parked outside Wednesday's house and grabbed a full packet of cigarettes from the glove compartment, before shoving them into his coat pocket.

Wednesday was already inside, leaving the front door swinging open for him. He had not been there since breaking-up with Scarlett, and was glad of the opportunity to rekindle his acquaintance with it. Her kitchen had always offered him wholesome nourishment and company, both of which had been lacking of late.

"Do you mind?" he asked, brandishing the packet of cigarettes.

"Only if you step outside; I don't want to be tempted," she replied, patting the patch on her arm.

She poured him a beer and a wine for herself, before placing some Lincolnshire sausages in the Aga, and putting some potatoes on to boil.

Lennox blew a cloud of noxious fumes into the damp air. "I miss smoking with you," he called out.

"I hope you're not trying to coerce me back. You're just jealous you're not strong enough to give up."

"I don't want to give up, and I don't want a long life either."

"Oh don't be so melodramatic. As soon as you have the right woman in your life, you'll change your tune."

"There are always plenty of women, but whether I'll ever find the right one, now there's another story . . ."

"What's up with you tonight? Where's your normal joie de vie?"

Lennox shrugged. "How do you cope?"

"With what?"

"With your mother's illness. Just seeing how people are in The Raven Unit, a world you are part of afterhours, I couldn't begin to comprehend. I'm not sure I'd cope."

"Perhaps not. Some people find me aloof, but I'm merely guarding my personal life. It's not been easy since it was revealed at work."

"People still respect you at the station, and so do I."

"Enough now," she blushed, "let's pick over the case."

Lennox took a last drag before crushing the tab end underfoot.

The kitchen was infused with the odour of rosemary, sausages, and onion. Lennox's stomach growled in anticipation. He watched her move about the kitchen with a grace she did not always demonstrate at work.

In the middle of mashing the potatoes, the doorbell rang.

"Get that for me please," she asked.

Striding to the door, he swung it open to find himself face to face with Scarlett.

"Jacob Lennox; fancy seeing you here," she said, stepping inside.

"We're working."

"A little late for working, eh sis?" Scarlett announced, entering the kitchen.

"There's a lot going on currently. Not here to get a journalistic scoop are you?"

"Give me a little credit."

"So you're here to ask about Mum."

"Not really; but how's she doing?"

"What do you think?"

"Precisely why I haven't been there."

Wednesday served a dollop of mash out onto two plates before sliding the tray of sausages out of the Aga.

"Any going spare? I'm famished," Scarlett asked, sitting down opposite Lennox.

"As always."

Wednesday sat at the head of the table, surveying her two surrogate children. She observed them guardedly watching each other, and wondered who would back down first.

"So Jacob, how many women at the station and beyond, have you conquered since we parted?"

"Let's leave that track and move on to more neutral territory," he replied.

"Okay, what leads do you have for the Raven case?"

The look of indignation on their faces made Scarlett tip her head back and laugh loudly. "I'm kidding. Hell, you two are so gullible at times."

Wednesday pushed her plate away, having barely touched her food. "Seeing as we can't discuss work now," she said, looking at Lennox, "I'm off for a shower. Make sure you pull the door hard to lock it when you leave," she said to no one in particular, before heading for the stairs.

"Morning, Boss," Lennox said as Wednesday entered the Incident Room.

"I trust you had a pleasant evening."

"I did thanks, in my *own* bedsit, *alone*."

Wednesday moved towards her office, sensing him close behind.

"May I have a word, in private?" He followed her in, closing the door behind him.

"Why do I sense we're either going to talk about Scarlett or my mum?"

"The latter actually."

Opening up her computer, she waited for him to continue.

"Edmond mentioned that Susan may have known her killer as there were no defensive wounds."

"Go on."

"Apart from her family, the only person who had a rapport with her was Joan."

"I believe that's already been established. What's your point?"

"We have strands of stories from other patients, and I've been trying to draw a timeline this morning. But without clarity of days and times, it's virtually impossible to map it out correctly."

Wednesday spread her hands, demonstrating her frustration.

"I need to interview Joan again to gather more clarity, and I just wanted to give you a heads-up."

"I appreciate your courtesy, although I'm not sure if she'll make more sense even now. However, may I point out that I can't imagine her having the strength to hoist the body up?"

"With respect, the ceiling panels are only made of polystyrene; easy to move. But I admit I can't imagine her moving the body alone."

"I can't imagine her being in cahoots with anyone there. Interview her again. If I stop you it'll only look suspicious."

Lennox gave a half smile. "What will you do?"

"Barry Roche phoned to say his son's home. I'll check him out."

"DI Wednesday, do come in," Barry Roche said on opening the front door onto the dingy corridor. "Gavin's in the kitchen."

Wednesday was in the kitchen in a matter of three strides and found Gavin leaning against the worktop, rolling a cigarette. She was struck by how handsome he was considering both his parents were rather plain.

"I'm sorry about the loss of your mother," she began.

He shrugged, licking the paper before sealing it. Only once he had lit it did he look up and gaze at her with his dove-grey eyes.

"I hear you believe it was murder and not suicide," he said, letting the smoke trail out of his mouth and twist around his face.

"It looked like suicide to begin with, but forensic found the cause of death to be manual strangulation rather than hanging."

Barry walked in, so Gavin moved them to the lounge.

"Get down, Gus," he said to the black Labrador who was sprawled on the sofa. "I always thought she'd commit suicide one day; she was selfish like that."

"How was your relationship with her?"

"Strained at the best of times, but thankfully being at uni kept us apart."

"What are you studying?"

"Art history."

"Where were you the night of your mother's death?"

"I was here. I'd come up to visit my parents."

"Anyone else to corroborate your story?"

"Apart from Dad, no. I know you police always put a family member in the frame, but I can't help more than that."

"More than what?" Barry asked, walking in with a tray of coffees.

"Needing to know where family members were at the time of the victim's death," Wednesday replied.

"Always seems a bit harsh on families trying to grieve, if you ask me," he replied, handing out the mugs.

"Do you like Hockney?" Gavin asked her, nursing the mug between his two hands.

"Not wild about him, why?"

"I like the deconstruction in his paintings; imitates a broken mind, to me."

"I don't see the point of his paintings; any kid could splash paint around," Barry joined in.

"You're such a heathen, Dad. There's a point to everything; you've just got to find it."

Wednesday witnessed the bristling animosity between the pair, and imagined it with the added pressure of Susan being around. The tension must have been unbearable at times.

Chapter 8

Joan Willow was already sitting in the room, waiting for Lennox's arrival. Her unruly hair had been brushed and parted in the wrong place, giving her the air of an infant having her first school photo taken.

Lennox arrived and followed Eric Knight to the room. Eric then sat in a chair in the corner, crossing his arms with an exaggerated gesture.

"We've met before, I'm DS Lennox, and I want to talk to you again about Susan Roche's death, if that's okay."

Joan looked at him questioningly, tilting her head one way and then the other.

"I know you; you're Eva's boyfriend . . . Jason . . . ?"

Lennox blushed furiously. "Jacob Lennox, and I'm just her work colleague."

"You both keep telling me that, but I can see you're both crazy about one another."

Lennox cleared his throat; annoyed at Eric smirking in the corner.

As Joan appeared more lucid than his last visit, he hoped to conduct a more informative interview.

"I understand you were quite close to Susan; she seemed to only like you out of everyone here."

"Yes, we'd become friends. She needed someone to talk to and I'm a good listener."

"Did she ever mention somebody disliking her or frightening her?"

Joan rubbed her hands together as she thought about his question.

"I know she and her husband weren't getting along. And that nurse . . ." She leant in to Lennox and whispered, "Karen Reilly, she didn't like Susan either."

"What makes you say that?"

"Susan said that nurse called her a waste of space when giving her tablets."

"When was this?"

"Why aren't you dating my Eva? Is she not good enough for you?"

"She's my boss, it wouldn't be right."

Joan suddenly closed-up as though someone had cut off the power. Eric gloated in the corner, refusing to move unless summoned. The awkward silence loomed, with only the cacophony of sounds emanating from beyond the door.

Lennox tried to engage her further, but to no avail. He stood up, signalling the end of the interview; desperate to get back to the sane world he knew and trusted. Eric rose slowly to lead her away, as Lennox wandered towards the nurses' station to see if Karen Reilly was on duty. Unfortunately she was on an early shift the next day. Never mind, it could wait.

Darkness descended as Wednesday drove down the dirt track towards Joan and Oliver's house. The tall grasses and weeds brushed the underside of her car as she bounced and juddered along the route. Pulling up next to Oliver's filthy Land Rover, she took a deep breath before going inside.

Mountains of crockery threatening to topple over resided in and around the sink, and unread newspapers acting as doorstops or draft excluders. Oliver looked as dishevelled as his surroundings.

"Fancy a cup of tea?" he asked.

"I think I should make you one," she replied, guiding him to the only clear chair around the table.

"Sorry, love. I can't seem to get myself motivated lately."

She smiled sympathetically before filling the kettle. "How's Mum?"

"A bit perturbed by that woman's death; and frankly so am I. You don't think the murderer will strike again, do you?"

"We're still gathering information. We've yet to find a motive but . . ." She caught herself before revealing too much.

"I know you can't discuss the case but I need reassurance."

"If I thought Mum was at risk I would want her moved. I'm sure she'll be fine."

She could see he was not totally reassured, but accepting of his limited right to demand information.

"When are you going to see her?" he asked, peering intently at her.

"Tomorrow hopefully. Has Scarlett been yet?"

Oliver shook his head. She knew not to press the matter further.

Chapter 9

Through her glass partition, Wednesday watched the female staff surround Lennox, hanging on his every word as though he were a savant. She noticed how he always stood a couple of inches taller when in that situation. Then he disappeared.

When he returned reeking of tobacco, with his breath smelling like an ashtray, Wednesday informed him they were off to interview Nurse Karen Reilly.

"You might want to suck one of these before talking to her," she snapped, throwing a packet of mints at him.

Classical music filtered from the car stereo as she drove to The Raven Unit; her eyes fixed on the road, and hands gripping the steering wheel, turning her hands blotchy.

Karen Reilly saw them approaching, and offered a wintry smile. They congregated in Eric Knight's office.

"It has come to our attention you apparently told Susan Roche she was a waste of space. Would you care to clarify this?" Wednesday asked; the nicotine cravings finally appeasing.

"I don't know who told you that, I've no recollection of saying such a thing. It would be terribly unprofessional."

"Indeed it would, as well as being unnecessarily cruel."

"Is that all you wanted to ask?"

"We know it's not possible to like everyone you come into contact with. When that happens, are you able to push through it, or does it affect your caregiving? I ask, as several people have commented you appeared dismissive of the victim; lacking compassion even," Wednesday said.

Karen stared straight ahead; a red rash accumulating along her neck line. "I'm a nurse, not a robot. I saw the way she treated her husband who was clearly doing the best he could."

"Did her son visit often?"

"Only once or twice. He's at a university in London, I believe."

"How did she treat him?"

"Much the same."

"Did either Barry or Gavin discuss this matter with you?"

"No, I'm not Susan's named nurse. Joshua is; they would talk to him more."

"It doesn't stop you observing people in the family room. Did the husband look upset with his treatment from her?"

Karen shrugged. "No one looks particularly happy to be visiting here," she said, with a withered smile.

"Is Joshua Plough available now?"

"Yes, should I send him in?"

"Please."

Joshua's lanky frame sauntered into the room, his shoulder-length, mousey hair tied back in a ponytail. He sat in a chair, slouching down so the tips of his shoes were almost touching Wednesday's.

"Did Barry Roche ever talk to you about the way his wife treated him or their son?" Lennox asked.

"I'm not sure what you're getting at?" His beard waggled as he spoke.

"Consensus around here is that Susan Roche gave her husband a rough ride, never appreciating all he did for her."

"I see, yeah, she was rather blunt with the old guy, but he never complained to me. He looked rather embarrassed about her behaviour at times."

"What about the son?"

"I think I only met him once. He asked me how long she was likely to be in here."

"How did he seem to you?"

"Distracted by an assignment he said was due in. Seemed a nice guy. It's always a shame when there's a mental health issue in a family." He blushed furiously, tugging on his beard.

"If you think of anything else, then please contact us," he concluded, handing him a card.

With the room empty, Wednesday turned to Lennox.

"I'd like to pop in and see Mum whilst we're here, and I'd like you to come with me to exclude a need for subterfuge."

He was about to challenge her point of view, but she raised her hand before walking off.

Joan was sitting in a chair facing the window, looking at the cherry blossom tree in bloom in the garden. She did not turn at the sound of her daughter's voice, or react to her touch.

She was locked deep in a depressive phase; her eyes impenetrable. Wednesday felt isolated in her world without Joan, but it was a world she had known for most of her life.

Without saying a word, she bent down and kissed her on her forehead before leaving the room with Lennox following closely behind.

Chapter 10

Lennox's voice infiltrated Wednesday's office from across the Incident Room. His free arm gesticulated wildly as he paced around his desk, like a child's wind-up toy.

Everyone in the vicinity strained to catch a word or two, curiosity nipping at their heels. Lennox was unaware of his impact on the team, so before Hunter arrived, Wednesday rushed over to calm the situation.

He did not hear her tapping on the door, or enter and close it softly behind her. When he finally stopped pacing, he halted before her with a wild look in his eyes.

"I've got to go," he snapped before hanging up. "Boss?"

"You're causing quite a stir, what's wrong?"

"That was Lucy. Archie's been arrested and is being held in police cells in Bethnal Green."

"I'm so sorry. What's happened?"

"He was involved in a gang fight over territory. The thing is . . . one boy got stabbed and . . . They're pointing the finger at Archie." His words hit the air like an axe against a tree trunk.

Wednesday was rendered speechless for a few seconds before her brain located the right words. "Go to him, I'll square it with Hunter."

"Thanks, but Lucy has expressly barred me from being near them. They've had to put their wedding on hold and believes I'm probably delighted about that. How little she thinks of me is astounding."

"Go home then, give yourself time to assimilate what's going on."

"If it's all the same with you, I'd rather work; it'll keep my mind occupied. I'll go mad thinking about him in a cell."

Wednesday had never seen his eyes filled with so much fear.

The sound of Hunter clapping his hands together to gather the team broke their silence. She gave Lennox one last questioning look before opening the door and walking out.

"We need to pick up the pace with this Roche case. We don't know whether the killer intends to strike again, or whether Susan Roche was the one and only intended victim." He paused to sip some coffee. "Wednesday and Lennox, I want you two to interview Fiona and Jordan Campbell separately, as well as getting background info from Doctor Harvey Manning as to her capability. Her animosity with the victim is key currently. Arlow and Damlish are to check the backgrounds of all the staff at the unit."

The room broke into a murmur as Hunter left for a meeting. Wednesday noticed the women of the team staring at Lennox, all offering him a shoulder to unburden his woes on.

"Let's get you out of here, I'll drive."

"Do you mind if I do, I'll focus better on the case?"

Lennox's car no longer smelt of pristine leather. Instead, it stank of an overflowing ashtray, which Wednesday found difficult to stomach.

Lennox reached across to the glove compartment then shut it quickly, before starting the engine. Wednesday took one look at his hands gripping the steering wheel tightly then pulled out his packet of cigarettes before offering him one.

"Do you mind?" he queried.

"Just take it."

Jordan Campbell was at work, but had agreed to meet Wednesday and Lennox during his lunch hour.

"I haven't got long," he announced.

"We'll try and keep it short," Lennox replied. "We'd just like to ask you about the animosity your wife had towards Susan Roche."

"You mean the woman who died? I don't think my wife had anything to do with her."

"Your wife believed Susan took her thoughts and replaced them with her own. She said she didn't like being in the same room as her because of that."

"There you go then, they were never together. Fiona has a delusional disorder, doesn't that tell you anything?"

"It must be difficult to live with at times."

"You don't know the half of it."

"Was she ill when you met?"

"What you really mean is did I know she was ill before we got married, then the answer is no. And would I have still married her had I known, the answer would be yes. I love her and would do anything for her."

"Even if she'd committed a crime?"

Jordan looked at Lennox with a fixed gazed. "I'm not sure what you're implying."

"Did it cross your mind that Fiona could have committed the crime?"

"No. She's a sweet woman, who's unfortunate enough to suffer with a mental affliction, but that doesn't make her a killer; that's an archaic point of view."

"We're not suggesting she is. We're looking at everyone on the unit."

"Including Mrs Willow?" he queried, turning to Wednesday.

"Absolutely," she replied.

"I bet if you found out it was her, you'd frame someone else. The mentally ill are vulnerable to something like that happening to them."

"I can reassure you that our investigations are transparent and open," Wednesday said softly.

"From what I've seen and heard, the dead woman was only friendly with Mrs Willow. Nothing is missed on such a small unit."

"If you notice everything, was there something, or someone that sticks out the evening of the murder?"

"No, but the good money's on your mother, DI Wednesday. The fact you're investigating this case is perturbing."

"I work continuously with DS Lennox, and am overseen by my superior, so you can allay your fears."

"We'll see."

"Thank you for your time Mr Campbell," Wednesday said, rising from her seat.

They walked outside to be met by a bank of drizzle. The promising start to the day had turned disappointingly dismal.

"What do you think of him?" Wednesday asked, pulling up her coat collar.

"Freely admitted he'd do anything for her. Perhaps he'd hang a dead body to hide his wife's crime?"

"Totally plausible. Let's go and see what she has to say for herself."

It had not slipped Wednesday's attention that he had kept looking at his watch all morning. His distraction was becoming irritating.

"I can interview her alone if you'd rather stay in the car and smoke," she offered, with a subtle hint of exasperation.

"Even a whole packet wouldn't cut into my stress."

He drove over the speed bumps in the hospital car park rather too quickly, shaking them around in their seats.

"I suggest that when this day is over, you grab an overnight bag and come to mine for dinner and beer. The spare room's made up. It'll do you good, and we don't have to talk if you don't want to."

He pulled on the handbrake, muttering non-committal thanks before getting out.

"What can we do for you today, detectives?" asked Karen Reilly.

"We'd like to have a chat with Fiona Campbell," Wednesday replied.

"You can see her in her room, just take the camcorder. Do you need a member of staff to sit with you?"

"Shouldn't be necessary unless she requests so."

Fiona was sitting in an armchair facing the window. She did not turn to see them; preferring to watch their reflections in the glass.

"How are you feeling today?" Wednesday began.

"However they want me to feel."

"Who are 'they'?"

"The people in here."

"Are you feeling different or perhaps better now that Susan's gone?"

"The others are working on her behalf. Her spirit lingers and guides them."

"But she's dead."

"Death is not the end for people like her." She drifted off momentarily.

"Can you remember anything about the night Susan died?"

Fiona began rocking in her chair, pulling the sleeves of her cardigan over her hands. "The days merge." She bent over in the chair before looking up slowly. "The truth is I can't remember what I did around that time; probably because someone was controlling my mind."

"Was your husband here?"

"He's always here in the evenings. He loves me, but they may get to him if he's not careful."

"Would he help you if you were in trouble?"

"Of course, anything . . ." Fiona shrugged, burying her head in her hands. "I get confused . . . I don't know anything anymore. I'm feeling tired." Rising slowly from the chair, she moved to her bed and lay down, burying her face in the pillow.

"I'm sorry if we've upset you." Wednesday said, tapping Lennox on the shoulder before walking out quietly.

"We need to see the psychiatrist. I don't know enough about her illness to know what she'd be capable of," she said, heading for the nurses' station.

"He isn't here, he's at a departmental meeting," Angela Rhodes advised them. "Can I help you instead?"

"We'd like to know more about Fiona Campbell's diagnosis. Well, to make it more ethical, could you just explain what delusion of control means," Wednesday asked.

"Delusions can be part of a psychotic diagnosis of schizophrenia, psychotic depression, or the manic phase of bi-polar, for example." She looked pointedly at the detectives, one after the other.

"Would someone in such a state of delusions be able to kill?"

"I'm not really qualified to answer that, but I imagine if the person feels threatened enough it's possible. Fear can give a person untold strength, no matter how slight they may be."

"Jordan, I need to see you, please . . . soon," Fiona whispered into the phone.

Chapter 11

"Sling your bag in the spare room. I'll put dinner on," Wednesday commanded.

Tramping up the stairs, Lennox's thoughts returned and crowded his mind now that the work day was over. He pushed against the spare room door and dumped his bag on the floor. The bed looked inviting, but he knew if he lay on it, he would not return downstairs.

Returning to the kitchen, he found an open bottle of beer sitting on the table. Wednesday watched him from the corner of the kitchen, wondering when to speak. As he took a long drink, she thought he might be ready.

"Tell me more about Archie's situation," she asked, putting a couple of lamb chops in the Aga.

He wiped the condensation from the side of the bottle with his thumb. "I got a call from my old station giving me the heads-up about Archie, so when Lucy called I was prepared. It didn't help though, she was fuming."

"It's understandable, she's upset, Jacob."

"I'm upset too." He took another large swig of beer. "I'm also embarrassed. God that sounds like crap when said aloud."

"What's embarrassing you the most?"

"That I'm a detective and Archie's been arrested."

"Anything can happen to anybody. And most of us have a skeleton or two in our cupboards." She looked at him with a wry smile.

"I'm also gut-wrenchingly worried about how he'll cope if he goes into a YOI. There'll be some tough kids in there. Archie's not tough, even though he likes to think he is."

"He'll survive, and you can support him emotionally."

"If he wants me involved."

"Of course he will; he's your son."

Lennox gave a dry laugh. "What do you know about parenting? The other news is Alfie's really excited about Lucy marrying Brian."

"And that worries you?"

"Damn right. Brian's proving to be a competent father where Alfie's concerned."

"Surely it's better they like their step-dad rather than live a miserable existence?"

Lennox rubbed the top of his head, making his hair stand to attention. The silence was only broken by the sound of the beer sloshing around the bottle as he swirled it around.

A while later, Wednesday served the lamb chops with sweet corn and chips, covered in a rich gravy. Lennox hardly touched his plate.

"Do you mind if I smoke?" he asked.

"If you must."

"How long's it been now?"

"Five weeks, but the cravings still hit me hard from time to time."

"They say once a smoker, always a smoker," he said, moving to the back door.

"Thanks for your support."

"*So*, Hunter's having marital difficulties," Lennox said, before letting out a lungful of smoke.

"It's this job. I don't know anyone who has a fulfilling personal life."

"Dave Arlow does. He's got a baby daughter and a happy marriage by all accounts."

"Okay, good for Dave. But that's it for the team. Too many indiscretions in the force in general."

"Talking of which. You once went out with a work colleague, what went on there?"

"That was during my first job. I was young and naive back then."

Lennox blew out the last of the smoke before crushing the tab end underfoot. Returning to the table, he urged her to continue.

"I was a constable and he was a sergeant. We worked many shifts together, and it was during a spell of night shifts that we became close." She paused to sip some wine. "I knew he was married, but he gave me a sob story—you know, *my wife doesn't understand me*—and I fell for it."

"A married man, I am surprised."

She scowled at him. "We'd been having an affair for about three months when his wife came into the station. She found texts from me and demanded to see 'the slut' who was shagging her husband. She made such a racket at reception."

Lennox laughed out loud.

"It's not funny, it gets worse. The duty sergeant brought her into the back. She got away from him and ran into the team room, where Kevin and I were."

Lennox indicated his beer was gone, so she retrieved another one from the fridge and slid it over to him.

"She was screaming wildly, and some helpful sod pointed out that I was 'the slut' in question. I didn't realise everyone knew. I was mortified." Her face was puce with the memories.

"She ran over to me and began slapping and punching me, yelling that I was a 'worthless whore.' The DI had to rescue me, as Kevin had become a simpering coward. I never lived it down and eventually had to leave the team."

"I needed a good laugh," he said, slapping the table with the palm of his hand.

"Yes, well I don't want the story repeating. I only told you to distract you from your woes."

"And now you're dating a toy boy, Alex Green."

"Dating is a strong word. I enjoy his company."

"I think it's a bit more for him. You should see the lustful way he looks at you behind your back."

"My life's too chaotic currently. He's a great distraction, but he's not *the one*."

"Then who is?"

"I haven't met him yet."

After a few hours of watching mindless drivel, she suddenly felt sapped of energy. Bidding him goodnight, she headed upstairs, leaving him with the remote control in one hand, and a whisky in the other.

Stepping out of the shower, she wrapped a towel around her hair and strolled to her bedroom. She heard Lennox pottering around in the kitchen, with the unmistakable aroma of coffee wafting up the stairs.

Throwing on a dark grey suit over a pale pink shirt, she descended just as the doorbell rang.

"Good morning. I thought you'd like some croissant for breakfast," Alex said, brandishing a brown paper bag in front of him.

"How thoughtful, come in."

He followed her into the kitchen, faltering in the doorway.

"Morning, Alex. Fancy some fresh coffee?" enquired Lennox, wearing only a pair of pyjama bottoms.

Alex almost crushed the croissants, but managed to pull through his discomfort, remaining impeccably calm.

"Sorry, I've only brought two," he said, dropping the bag on the table.

"Don't worry, I thrive on coffee and cigarettes."

Wednesday put two plates on the table before sitting down, as Lennox passed the mugs around.

"You two been discussing work until the early hours, eh?" Alex asked, spraying crumbs over the table.

"No, she took pity on me and decided I needed feeding," laughed Lennox.

He was the only one laughing. Wednesday's face prickled with heat, forcing her to stuff the remaining morsel in her mouth. When there were only crumbs left on the plates and dregs in the mugs, she announced it was time to go to work.

Embarrassed by the glut of men around her, she took her own car, preferring the company of Joni.

She had no idea what kind of day awaited her, but her gut was telling her it was going to be bad.

Chapter 12

Digby Hunter clapped his hands, grabbing everyone's attention.

"Let's focus on the motive for Susan Roche's death. DC Damlish, what did you find out?"

"Barry Roche is the sole beneficiary for his wife's life insurance policy, to the sum of seventy-five thousand pounds. That would be enough to clear his twenty-five thousand pounds debt and leave him well provided for."

"DI Wednesday?"

"DS Lennox and I interviewed the patients on the unit. Fiona Campbell believed the victim was controlling her mind, Eddie Brass found the victim to be rude and homophobic, and Dave Hyde believed the victim stole his cigarettes. He also has a police record of GBH against his girlfriend. All of them had motive and opportunity to commit the crime."

"Would Campbell have managed alone?"

"Not sure, but she could have had help from any of the patients aforementioned, or even her husband, who said he'd do anything for her."

"DC Arlow, what did you find?"

"So far, I've found that Charge Nurse Eric Knight is addicted to gambling and has the debts to prove it, but I can't find how that would link to the crime."

"So we have various suspects. I want Wednesday and Lennox to revisit Barry Roche to discuss his financial situation, then move on to the patients again, especially Dave Hyde. Also, find out when the funeral is, I want you to attend. Arlow and Damlish are to continue looking into the staff's backgrounds."

Hunter walked back to his office, closing the door forcefully. A collective sigh echoed across the room.

"I could really do with a smoke," Wednesday confided as she and Lennox walked to his car.

"Are you asking for one, or just thinking aloud?"

"The latter, so don't even show me one."

Barry Roche looked displeased on opening the door.

"We'd like to talk to you. May we come in?" Wednesday asked.

"I don't think I have a choice, do I?"

The flat was just as messy, only instead of piles of tabloid newspapers, glossy car magazines lay open on the floor. Barry pushed a pile in front of the sofa to one side with his foot, leaving room for everyone to sit down. Gus bounded over, and nuzzled Wednesday's thigh.

"We understand you're acquiring a substantial amount of money from your wife's life insurance policy," Wednesday began, stroking the dog.

"So what? Everybody has a life insurance policy in case of events such as these. Susan would have gained had I been the one to die. I'd be silly to kill her for money; it's the first thing you'd think of."

"Nevertheless, the money will come in handy to pay off your debts."

"God, is nothing sacred with you? Why do you have to dig around my personal affairs, when I'm as much of a victim in this case?"

"With murder, we have to explore those close to the victim; the victim often knows their killer."

Barry puffed out his cheeks, folding his arms across his chest, and stared at Wednesday through half-closed eyes. "I got into debt thanks to Susan's spending sprees, so once the debts are paid off, I won't end up in such a bad way ever again."

Wednesday looked around, not sure what the money had been spent on.

"I make no secret of it, detectives, Susan didn't bring much joy into my life, but I wouldn't have had the nerve to kill her." He paused to look at his watch. "I need to get to the funeral parlour to finalise the arrangements."

"When is it?" Lennox asked.

"This Friday at ten. I doubt many people will turn up. She didn't have many friends."

"Is that the same for you?"

"Yes. How could I make friends with Susan around? Even the neighbours were too afraid of her to speak."

The detectives thanked him for his time, grateful of leaving behind the stale, messy environment.

Once at The Raven Unit, they found Dave Hyde in a thunderous mood, gesticulating wildly, and shouting about his ex-girlfriend being a cheating bitch. Eric Knight did not think they would get much out of him.

"He's fixated on his ex; she's the reason he's in here. She really got under his skin; sounded like she had her own issues going. Typical woman," he sneered.

Wednesday bristled, and sensing that, Lennox jumped in.

"You've a record of violence against your ex-girlfriend, Mr Hyde. Have you had any incidents here?"

Eric answered briskly. "He tends to stay out of the way of the others, especially the women. He doesn't tolerate people well, which is why he often doesn't cope in society."

The information made Wednesday think of her mother, and as though reading her mind, Eric chipped in.

"Your mother's been asking after you and your *boyfriend*," he said, pointedly looking at Lennox.

"DS Lennox is a colleague, she often gets confused. We'll pop in and see her after."

Dave continued pacing around, glaring at them, before storming out, closely followed by Eric. The interview was over before it began.

"Shall I wait out here, Boss?"

"For the sake of transparency, I think it's best you come in, on the understanding I'm just having a private and personal conversation with her. Understood?"

Lennox nodded before following her into Joan's bedroom.

"Hi Mum, the nurse said you were looking for me."

Joan looked up, unsure at first of who was talking to her. After a few seconds her face illuminated.

"I saw them kissing, you know."

"You saw who kissing?" Wednesday asked hesitantly, unsure of what Joan was about to divulge.

"Them. They don't know I know. I think they'll be cross with me, but I had to see it, don't you understand?"

Wednesday did not comprehend and neither did Lennox, so he decided to try.

"Were they here on the unit, the two people you saw kissing?"

"Of course they were," she whispered. "He shouldn't be here, but he comes for her."

"Who does, Mrs Willow?"

"My name's Joan."

"Sorry, Joan. What's the name of the man?"

"I don't know him, but he knows me."

"Okay, what about the name of the woman?"

"That nurse . . . can't remember her name . . . Karen, I think."

Now they were getting somewhere. Wednesday let Lennox continue.

"Nurse Karen Reilly. Who was she kissing?"

"How's Scarlett? I haven't seen her for ages. I'm worried for her."

"She's fine, Mum, she's just busy at work."

"As long as she's safe, or they'll bring her in here too." Joan closed her eyes, inhaling deeply, signalling the end of her fragmented conversation.

Lennox tried to extrapolate more details, but she had retreated into her sleepy world.

"What was that all about?" asked Lennox.

"The problem is Mum also suffers hallucinations, so this may be all in her mind. The fact that she doesn't know who the man is may mean she saw Karen Reilly kissing her boyfriend or husband, greeting or parting at the nurses' station."

"I see what you're saying. Still, we should bear it in mind all the same."

Wednesday nodded, craving a cigarette as she always did after seeing Joan.

Just as they reached the exit, a piercing scream echoed down the corridor. The squeaking sound of shoes scrambling on the vinyl floor compounded the racket. Wednesday and Lennox followed the commotion and found themselves outside Dave Hyde's room, where they saw him bearing down on Angela Rhodes, his fleshy hands, like slabs of luncheon meat, wrapped around her neck.

Eric was attempting to release Dave's hands, with no luck, so Lennox moved forward and freed her after a brief struggle.

He pushed Dave back onto the bed and held him there with Eric's assistance, whilst Wednesday hurried to Angela's side.

"Are you okay?"

Angela's face was puce, her eyes watery, and red marks were daubed around her neck. Wednesday guided her out of the room towards the nurses' station, where she sat down, trembling.

Bending forward, Angela coughed, trying to fill her lungs with oxygen. "I'm fine," she said hoarsely. "No need to fuss."

"Do you want him charged with assault?"

"No point, he's not mentally stable. He'll be sorry in a day or two."

Another nurse appeared with a glass of water. She took bird-sips to soothe her traumatised throat. All the while, Wednesday watched the mark on her neck deepen, and decided that photos of the marks may prove useful at a later date. She called the station.

The detectives left the unit, with Wednesday feeling uneasy about leaving Joan in the presence of clearly a dangerous man. She decided she would speak to the psychiatrist to see what could be done.

Chapter 13

It was another day of constant drizzle, befitting a funeral. Funerals were never a joyous task to undertake, and Wednesday found such events sliced straight into her heart.

Standing under a budding tree near the entrance to the church, they watched the smattering of mourners arrive. Barry Roche was right when he said Susan had few friends.

After everyone had entered, the detectives nipped inside and sat in the back pew, looking like plastic gnomes at the Chelsea Flower Show.

The sight of a coffin being carried down the aisle never failed to fold Wednesday's stomach to the point of nausea. The moisture in her eyes always betrayed her, compounding the notion amongst the male colleague that she was too soft for the job at times.

Barry and Gavin Roche followed behind the coffin looking suitably dour. With their eyes cast down, neither of them spotted the detectives.

Wednesday and Lennox scanned the gathering, recognising no one except the grieving men, and Nurse Joshua Plough. It was a sad indictment of a life fraught with mental illness; one was by definition on the periphery of society through people's fear and ignorance.

The hymn, "The Lord is My Shepherd," was sung tunelessly before the vicar said a few words about a woman he clearly did not know well. It all seemed farcical to Wednesday, in a society of so many non-believers.

Sermon and hymns dispensed with, it was time for the coffin to be transported to the burial ground. Barry had explained that his wife was fearful of being burnt alive, hence no cremation. Wednesday thought the idea of being buried alive was far more sinister; but each to their own.

On leaving the church, Gavin caught sight of them and scowled. They gave him a reverend nod, acknowledging his pain, but he just raised his nose in the air.

They kept a broad distance of the burial site, observing the peripheries of the setting. There wasn't a lone figure watching the denouement of his or her plan, and nothing or no one seemed out of place.

After the last clumps of earth were thrown onto the coffin, the few turned to walk away. Gavin spotted them and sprinted in their direction.

"What are you still doing here?" he spat.

"We did let your father know we'd be here," Lennox began. "We like to see who does or doesn't attend the funerals, as part of our investigation."

"I think you're persecuting Dad. I could complain to your boss about this. You've no idea what he went through with Mum. Her madness ruined his life, and now she's still haunting him through death."

"I'm sorry our presence has upset you. You can speak to DCI Hunter if you like, but I assure you this is a routine procedure," Wednesday said softly.

"Whatever," Gavin replied, before striding off after his father who was getting into the awaiting black car.

"He wasn't a happy man," whispered Lennox.

"It's hard having a mother with a mental illness. Let's head back."

The drizzle had developed into stair-rods, stinging their faces. Once inside the car, they wiped droplets from their coats and hair.

"Archie's in a young offenders' institute whilst awaiting his time in court. He's requested I visit him tomorrow," Lennox said, slamming the car into reverse.

"That will be a difficult visit. Is Lucy okay with that?"

"Her views don't count as he's requested it himself. Not sure if he's doing it to embarrass me, or not."

"He might genuinely want to see you, don't be so harsh."

Lennox turned on the heater, blowing warm air onto the windscreen.

"I genuinely feel a failure where he's concerned. The news will soon filter around the station."

"Not if we don't tell anyone."

"We didn't tell anyone about your mum but that eventually got out."

"Point taken."

Turning into the station car park, Lennox cleared his throat and pulled into his parking space. Jamming on the handbrake, he turned to her and took a deep breath.

"Could I ask you a favour?"

"Go on," she replied cautiously.

"I have to drive to Buckinghamshire to see Archie, and I wondered whether . . . well, if you'd come along for the ride? I'd buy you dinner as a thank you."

Wednesday forced herself not to answer straight away, as was customary, choosing instead to say she would think about it. "I have Mum to think of."

"Of course."

The sun shone meekly as Lennox pulled up outside Wednesday's house and hooted the horn. She slid into the passenger seat and pulled on her seatbelt.

"This is very good of you, I appreciate it," he said.

"Yeah well, I'm storing up the IOUs. You'll pay me back one day."

On a long journey such as this, Wednesday would have enjoyed a smoke whilst listening to music. Although the cravings passed after three minutes, they were still intense, and she did not know whether she was strong enough to resist.

"Have you thought about what you're going to say to him?" she asked, wrapping strands of hair around her finger.

"I'll try not to lecture him. I'm sure he's had enough of that already. But I'm not a great conversationalist, that's why I'm glad you'll be there too."

"What," she exclaimed. "There was no mention of that yesterday. I was coming with you for the journey."

"I know, but I managed to get you on the visitors' list. I hope you don't mind."

"I do mind; I mind very much. You could have warned me."

"Sorry, I won't do it again," he smiled.

After being searched and circled by sniffer dogs, Wednesday and Lennox entered the visitors' room, walking over to table forty-two where Archie sat in his bright yellow tabard.

He offered a frosty smile to his father and a suspicious regard to Wednesday.

"I thought you said you weren't his girlfriend."

"Don't be rude," snapped Lennox.

"It's all right, I see where he's coming from. This is as much a surprise to you as it is to me, Archie."

"So why are you here?"

"I'm not quite sure. Ask your dad."

They both looked at him with raised eyebrows.

"I thought Wednesday, sorry, Eva, would help with the awkward silences. We've never been great talkers, you and me."

"You haven't been around much recently."

"Is that your excuse for your behaviour?" He looked briefly at Wednesday.

"I think what your Dad's trying to say, is that he has a very demanding job, and weekends off aren't always guaranteed. But he should have put you first once in a while."

"Easier said than . . . Sorry son, let's start again. How is it in here?"

"How do you think? It stinks. The other boys are stupid, think they're gangsters."

"And what do you think you are?"

"I'm not stupid, that's for sure."

"I beg to differ, Archie. You're in a young offenders' institute, which isn't going to look good on your CV."

"I knew that's all you'd care about."

"That's not true or fair. I worry about your future."

"Are you sure you're not worried what people think of you at work. I bet you're embarrassed as hell."

Wednesday put her hand on Lennox's arm and shook her head gently.

"You requested your dad be here today, Archie. Was there something you wanted to ask him in particular?"

Archie's mouth clamped shut as he sunk further down in the hard chair, folding his arms across his chest.

"Perhaps you'd find it easier to talk to him if I left you two alone."

"Don't bother, you can both leave. Mum was right. This was a waste of time."

"Of course she'd say that, she's . . ."

"Jacob, I think you've said enough. Try and keep positive in here, Archie." She stood up, waiting for Lennox to make a move.

"Keep strong, and try and do some school work, son." That was as positive as he could get as he tried not to sprint out of the oppressive room.

Once outside, Lennox fumbled for the cigarettes in his coat pocket, took one out and lit it. He took a deep drag before noticing Wednesday watching him intently.

"Do you want one?"

"I do, but that's not what I was thinking."

"Spit it out."

"You've got to cut Archie some slack. I believe he knows he's made mistakes. He needs guiding back to the right road, not reversed down the road he took to get here."

"Whatever," he replied, mimicking his son.

It was late evening by the time he pulled up outside Wednesday's house, to find Scarlett sitting in her car on the driveway. Wednesday's heart dipped as she got out of the car and tapped on the window. Scarlett beamed with happiness.

"I needed some company, and I forgot my key. Oh and you're here too, Jacob. Bonus."

Wednesday sighed as the pair followed her inside. She had a feeling they would not be staying for long.

Chapter 14

"So what do you think of the unit?" Eric Knight asked Sara Morris.

"It's all right. The death certainly livened things up," she replied, before sucking hard on her cigarette.

"What kind of nursing do you want to do when you qualify?"

"Private clinic work, where the wealthy and famous go."

"Hoping to find a rich boyfriend with an addiction to painkillers perhaps?"

Sara shrugged, inhaling again and savouring the smoke. "Who do you think killed Mrs Roche?" she asked finally.

"Any one of the patients, except for Rene Blower. Who do you think it was?"

"I'm more for a member of staff."

"Really? Who?"

"I'm watching you all," she said, smiling slyly.

"I'd better watch myself then," he said, crushing the tab end underfoot. "And you had too."

He walked back inside, oblivious as to whether Sara had entered behind him or not. She hurriedly followed, locking the door, and placing the key on top of the door frame.

Wednesday arrived at the station before Lennox, which was unusual. She watched his empty office from her chair, whilst nursing a mug of instant coffee. She turned on the computer to trawl through the list of suspects in the Roche case. No one was standing out to her as the perpetrator, and she knew she was missing vital clues to put the pieces together.

Lennox entered the Incident Room and headed straight for her office.

"Sorry I'm late, Boss," he said, sticking his head around the open door.

"Good evening was it?"

"Interesting, as they always are with Scarlett. Thanks for yesterday, by the way."

Wednesday nodded. "I've arranged for us to visit Doctor Manning at his home this morning. Then we'll see Nurse Angela Rhodes. Ready to leave in ten? I'll drive."

Lennox raced back to make a coffee which he then gulped down, scolding his tongue and throat. He felt he was being punished for the debauchery of the previous night, but it didn't stop a smile from drifting across his face.

Harvey Manning's house was as they expected; a large, double-fronted modern house, with a sweeping paved driveway, and a double garage.

The front door was imposing, with a large elephant-head brass knocker positioned centrally. The door was flanked by two potted olive trees. Lennox took pleasure in rapping the elephant head loudly.

The door was opened by a willowy woman, sporting a blonde precision-cut bob. Her face was fixed with a semi-welcoming smile as she ushered them in.

"I'm Olivia Manning. My husband's in his study," she announced, leading the way. "I don't quite understand the need for you to visit on a Sunday."

"I'm sorry for the inconvenience, but murder enquiries have a speed of their own. We hope not to be here too long," replied Wednesday.

Harvey was sitting in a rust-coloured leather swivel chair behind an ostentatiously carved rosewood desk.

"You do understand, detectives, I can't disclose medical information about individuals," he said tersely.

"We understand. We'd really like information about the illnesses suffered and whether they could potentially lead to violent acts," Wednesday replied.

"It's a misnomer that all people with schizophrenia are violent. It's considered to be the most crippling of mental illnesses, and only a small percentage of those diagnosed can live independently. But anyone could potentially harm another regardless of mental health issues, as I'm sure you're aware. So forgive me if I don't share your view that one of my patients is the murderer."

"Everyone on the unit is currently a suspect," stated Lennox.

"Even me?"

"We're looking at everyone connected to the unit."

Harvey and Lennox locked eye contact.

"What precautions have you put in place at the unit, considering the perpetrator could still be there?" Wednesday asked, slicing through the testosterone in the room.

"Extra staff on each shift, doing rounds every fifteen minutes."

"Will that be enough to ensure the safety of everyone on the unit?"

"Worried about your mother, detective?"

"It would be unnatural not to be."

"I believe so, yes. By the way, your mother has started having nightmares. Was that happening before?"

"Not that I'm aware of. You should ask her husband."

"I will, it's just sometimes people are plagued with nightmares when their unconscious mind is troubled."

Wednesday frowned, balling her fists behind her back. "I don't think I like what you're suggesting."

"You're reading too much into what I'm saying. All I mean is that people can do the strangest of things at times, sometimes without reason. I would have thought you'd know that; you're no stranger to mental health issues."

"Well I am," Lennox chipped in, "and I'd like to know what delusional disorder is exactly."

Harvey turned to face him. "A person suffering with this can believe they are controlled by another force, supernatural or otherwise. They believe they are acting out someone else's thoughts and demands; perhaps even God's."

"Would someone with this forget if they'd done something out of character?"

"Depends on the individual and how powerful their delusions are. Often people have lost their sense of self."

"What about the staff? Any issues there?"

Harvey rocked backwards in his chair. "Nothing springs to mind. I wager it's an outsider."

"The unit was locked and there was no evidence of a break-in," Lennox retorted.

Harvey shrugged his shoulders, pursing his lips.

"Where were you on the night of the murder?"

"At home, working on a research paper."

"A patient was having a psychotic episode. Were you not needed on the unit?" Wednesday asked.

"The patients are written up for PRN—emergency medication—for such incidences. I'm only called if the PRN doesn't work. Now if that's all, I'd like to get on with enjoying my day."

"Thank you for your time. If you think of anything else pertinent, please call us," Wednesday said, handing him a card.

He dropped it into a drawer, slamming it shut.

"One last thing," Wednesday began. "Could your wife corroborate you were here that night?"

"I imagine so."

They walked back into the hallway where Olivia was waiting for them.

"Do you remember where your husband was the night of the murder?" Wednesday asked.

"He was in his study, probably working on something to do with the unit. He's totally dedicated to it. It's his life and passion."

"So I take it you were in all evening too."

"I spend much of my time in the home gym. It's very high-tech, would you like to see it?"

Wednesday declined the offer. Deflated, Olivia let them out.

"I hope you know what you're doing, getting involved with Scarlett again," Wednesday said, switching on the engine.

"Don't start fretting about that again. She knows it's not serious."

Wednesday rolled her eyes before driving off.

"Are you seeing her tonight?"

"Maybe."

"Tread lightly, Jacob. It's a dangerous road you're heading down, and I won't pick up the pieces."

"I hear you, but you needn't worry, it's all in hand."

"I've heard *that* before."

Chapter 15

Lennox drew up outside his flat and pulled on the handbrake. Putting his head back against the headrest, he closed his eyes and enjoyed the confined space and silence, until a tap on the window disturbed him. Opening his eyes, he saw Scarlett looking in on him. He lowered the window.

"I was at a loose end and I thought you might be too," she said coyly.

Lennox was not feeling lonely, but believed if he turned her away, she would go into a major sulk, causing him more hassle in the long run.

Wednesday walked onto The Raven Unit and found her mother sitting in her room, facing the window. The darkening evening meant that all they could see was each other's reflections.

"Hello Mum. How are you doing?"

Joan turned her head slowly. "I hate it here. They're always watching me."

"Who are?"

"Everyone. That Dave Hyde has started blaming me for things going missing from his room. He used to blame Susan."

"What's he saying?"

"If we're in the same room he points at me and says I'm a thief."

"Try and take no notice of him. I'll speak with the staff."

Wednesday watched Joan retreat into her shell.

"Mum, do you remember the night Susan died?"

"Why are you questioning me, I've answered questions already. Your boyfriend asked me."

Wednesday pulled a chair over and sat next to her, putting her hand on her mother's knee.

"Lennox is . . ." Wednesday sighed. "You talked about people kissing on the unit. Can you remember who they were now?"

"That Nurse Karen was kissing a man who wasn't hers."

Wednesday looked towards the door then back at Joan. "Can you remember who he was? Does he stay on the unit?"

Joan rolled her eyes up, tracing cobweb threads that stretched from the ceiling light to the window.

"I can't quite place him."

"So he's not a patient or member of staff. He must be a visitor then."

"Maybe . . ."

"Do you remember what time you saw them kissing?"

"Eva dear, you know time has no meaning in my world. You'd have always been late for school if it wasn't for your dad and then Oliver."

"Have you seen the man again since?"

"I've spent a lot of time in my room or asleep . . . I might have. I don't know. I'll keep an eye out for him, if I can."

Wednesday hated seeing her depressed. It altered her perception of self and others, and it had robbed her of a mother many times.

Placing her hands in a prayer-like position, she contemplated which men would visit the unit. There was Fiona Campbell's husband, Jordan, and Susan's husband, Barry, that she knew of.

Joan had nodded off in the chair, so Wednesday kissed her on the forehead and tiptoed out. Taking a deep breath, she walked to the nurses' station.

Joshua Plough was writing up some notes, and Sara Morris was flicking through a trashy magazine.

"Oh, hi DI . . . Miss Wednesday," she spluttered.

"I know I have my relative's hat on, so to speak, but I still have a detective's mind. Could you tell me who has male visitors apart from Susan Roche, Fiona Campbell, and Joan Willow?"

Joshua looked up and sat back in the chair. "Should I be talking to you about such things?"

"I can come back tomorrow and ask the same question."

He sighed. "Rene Blower's husband, Howard. Melvyn Rollins's best mate also comes." He shuffled through the pages of the visitors' book. "Chris White. And Eddie Brass's brother, Samuel. Hope that helps," he said, closing the book.

"Food for thought, thanks."

"Are visitors suspects now?"

"I'm just exploring all the avenues. Thanks for your help."

As soon as she got in the car she took out her notebook and wrote down their names. Tomorrow she was going to dig deeper.

Lennox held the door open for Wednesday to enter The Raven Unit. They knew Karen Reilly was on duty, and she knew they were coming.

"We can meet in Eric's office, he's not on duty," she said, leading the way.

Lennox noticed the extra wax in her blonde elfin cut. Her hair swirled around her crown and pointed wisps framing her petite face.

"Please don't be affronted by my question, but it came to our attention that you were seen kissing a man on the unit. Could you clarify who that was?" Wednesday asked.

Karen's face contorted as though unsure which expression to show. "Damn right it's none of your business."

"I understand, but if it was your boyfriend there'd be no harm in telling us, would there?"

"He *is* my boyfriend. Satisfied?"

"Does he have a name?"

"Naturally, had it since birth."

Wednesday's eyes narrowed.

"All right," huffed Karen, "I don't want to name him as he's a married man. I don't want to get him into trouble, and I suppose I'm not proud of the fact."

"Is he married to one of the patients?"

Karen stood up, her chest heaving as she tried catching her breath. "If you bloody know who it is, why don't you just tell me his name?"

Lennox looked in Wednesday's direction in anticipation.

"I'm not out to trick you. There are only a few to choose from."

"If I tell you, you're going to put two and two together and come up with five."

"Go on."

"It's Barry Roche."

"I see."

"I knew I'd get that tone from you. You now think he killed her so he could be with me, don't you?"

"That's a plausible motive."

"Well there was no need. She was depressed most of their married life, hence only having one child. He was planning on divorcing her. She was seven years older than him and had become more of a mad mother figure to him."

"Divorce can be messy and expensive, though."

"Why don't you address this issue with him? He'll be able to set you straight. I've got to get on, if that's all."

"That's all for now. Oh, one last thing, was Susan Roche aware of her husband's infidelity?"

"I doubt it." Reilly strode out of the office holding her head high.

"Are you going to tell me how you deduced that nugget of info?" Lennox asked.

"Mum mentioned seeing Reilly kissing a man she recognised from the ward, but not a patient or someone who worked here."

"I remember that from my interview."

"Well, I visited her last night, as her daughter, and the subject cropped up."

"Right." He pushed air through his teeth. "Hunter would want to know that kind of detail, you know."

"I understand your position, but—"

"*But* I don't think he needs to know about your personal visits. You're allowed some privacy, after all."

Smiling at him, she suggested they go and visit Barry Roche.

Climbing into Lennox's car, Wednesday telephoned Barry to advise him of their arrival.

"You've got her killer?" he asked on opening the front door.

"No sir, but we have a few questions to ask you, if we could come in," Wednesday said.

"Can't be long; I've got a job to do in half an hour."

"It's about your relationship with Karen Reilly."

Roche's face blanched as he ushered them quickly inside.

"I'm not sure what you're talking about."

"Karen's already informed us," Lennox said.

They followed him into the lounge where they all sat down. Barry hunched over, his arms cradling his stomach.

"We kept it quiet from you as it would make me look guilty."

"The truth always comes out, so being honest with us would have made you look less guilty."

"You can't possibly suspect me?"

"You have to admit it doesn't look good for you." Lennox stood up, bouncing on the balls of his feet. "With your wife dead, you gain a substantial amount of money, and you get to be with the woman you're having an affair with. That speaks volumes."

"Yes, I know . . . I know. But you have to believe me, I didn't do it."

"We're aware Karen didn't like your wife. Perhaps she found a way to end your misery. Have you ever thought about that?"

Jumping up, Barry paced around. "You're determined to pin this murder on me or people close to me. Where's you evidence?"

"We're piecing it all together," Lennox replied.

"Well don't waste time on me or Karen. The murderer could still be inside, ready to strike again."

"Are you in love with Karen or is it just at the lust stage?"

"What difference does that make?"

"They're two distinct phases in a relationship. The former is serious and the latter is transitional. I hazard a guess that the former rings true to you."

Barry stopped pacing right in front of Lennox.

"You're a man. Can't you see how being married to Susan wasn't fulfilling. She's been in and out of hospital for most of our married life. She's forty-nine, I'm only forty-two, and Karen's only forty, and we have much more in common . . ."

"It does put a new angle on things," replied Wednesday. "I guess it's something that will be in the forefront of our minds from now on."

He clasped his hands together tightly.

"Is your relationship with Karen going to continue?"

"Nothing's changed as far as I'm concerned."

They left him with beads of sweat clinging to every facial crevice, and glistening across his pumped-up neck. Picking up his mobile, he pressed speed dial. When he got the Ansaphone he hung up.

Chapter 16

"You're quiet," Alex stated, putting the drinks on the table.

"Sorry, it's this case. We've got clues here and there, but nothing's adding up to much," Wednesday replied.

The Crazy Duck was full of the usual police crowd, thanks to its proximity to the station. As Alex sat down, Wednesday noticed several younger women giving him the eye. When he caught one of them looking, her cheeks grew pink within seconds.

"You cause quite a stir wherever you go, don't you?" Wednesday mused, with a heavy heart.

"You read too much into things; little details never get passed you."

"I think my work brain never switches off."

"Well drink and mellow those grey cells."

"I really do like you, Alex . . ."

"*But?*"

Wednesday quaffed her drink then coughed a little. "The age difference bothers me too much."

Alex rolled his eyes. "It doesn't bother me."

"When I see younger, prettier, and slimmer women than me, eyeing you up, I'm reminded I'd be in competition with them."

"Nonsense. I've only had eyes for you for some time now. You have to trust me."

"I trust you, I think, but I don't trust other women. A taken man can be such a temptation for some women."

"You have a very warped view of your gender."

"Maybe my view's always been warped. There's a couple in this case. He married an older woman, but ends up having an affair with a younger one. I don't want to be in that situation."

The conversation dried up like a trickling stream in mid-summer. They clutched their drinks like magic potions they hoped harboured the answers to their futures.

"Wednesday and Lennox, I want you to visit Gavin Roche. He's at home currently. Suss out if he knows about his father's affair," Hunter ordered as the pair were making a coffee. He walked off without waiting for a response.

Lennox rolled his eyes. "You look tired. Do you want me to drive?"

Wednesday nodded before blowing on her coffee. "I need a few mouthfuls of this first."

"Heavy night?"

"Not the type you're thinking of."

"You can tell me on the way, if you want," he smiled.

Climbing into his car, she wrinkled up her nose. The scented hanging tree had clearly run out of potency.

"So what's on your mind?"

"I went for a drink with Alex last night, and it was rather awkward."

Switching on the engine he reversed out of the parking space. "And?"

"In the cold light of day it sounds ridiculous, but when I'm with him . . ."

"Not the age issue again."

"It's a big deal for me."

"If you don't mind me saying, either push it to one side and make a go of it, or terminate the idea of a relationship so you can both move on."

"Okay, Marjorie Proops, what's brought this on?"

"I made such a mess of my marriage that I want other people to at least start off on the right track."

"I hear you."

Lennox blew through his teeth as he pulled up outside the block of flats.

"My dad's not here. He's at work," Gavin said through the intercom.

"It's you we've come to see," replied Lennox.

There was a pause before he released the door for them to enter. By the time they reached his floor, he was waiting at the front door with his arms folded squarely across his chest.

"I've already said all I know," he said, remaining in the doorway.

"It's rather a private matter which would be best discussed inside," Lennox said, aware of a neighbour taking her time putting her keys in her front door.

Gavin begrudgingly stood back and let them in, slamming the door behind them. The lounge was still a mess and felt overcrowded with them all standing around.

"Get down, Gus," he commanded, as the dog leapt up at Lennox.

Wednesday asked if they could sit; he acquiesced with a shrug.

"How are you holding up?" she began.

"Dunno really."

"Are you missing your mum?"

"Not particularly, she wasn't always there for me when she was alive. Besides, there's less to worry about now that I'm not wondering when her next stay in hospital, or suicide attempt will be."

Wednesday nodded. "How's your dad doing?"

Another non-committal shrug.

"Do you think he'll find someone else?"

"Maybe."

"How would you feel about that?"

"Wouldn't want to watch him mooning over some bird. I'll be in London again soon anyway." He picked up a car magazine and began leafing through it.

"Buying a car?" Lennox asked.

"Dad said I can get one when the money comes through."

"Anything in mind?"

"Not really." He continued leafing through the pages, head bowed low.

"Where were you, again, the night your mum died?" Wednesday asked.

"As I already said, I was here with Dad."

"Do you come up often?"

"Only when she's in hospital. I try and be supportive when I can."

"Did your father go out that evening?"

He looked up, folding the magazine in half. "He may have at one point. I went out to buy a few beers from the local shop."

"You didn't mention that before. How long were you gone?"

"Dunno, maybe half an hour or so. I stood outside the shop to have a fag. Dad doesn't know I smoke."

"Why did you omit this from your original statement?"

"'Coz I forgot, all right? Anyway, he was here when I got back. You lot think he did it for the money, he told me that."

"We have to explore everyone close to the victim. They often know their killer."

"She was on a unit with a load of fucking mad people. One of them did it. They're like animals; killing's an instinct for them, the mad bastards." Spittle bubbled in the corners of his mouth.

He was highly animated, and clearly knew nothing about his father's affair. But they had new information, so it was not a wasted journey.

Leaving the building, Wednesday inhaled deep breath replacing the rank dog-air in her lungs. "Let's go to the local shop and check out the CCTV, I want to check out his story before challenging Barry."

Lennox drove around the block until they found the only shop. Inside, Wednesday flashed her card at the shop owner, who obliged them by showing the relevant film. The substandard, grainy, black and white images showed Gavin duly buying beer then standing outside with his back against the window smoking.

"Well that changes Barry's statement somewhat. We'll need to challenge him about this. He might take it more seriously if we speak with him at the station," she said, watching Lennox remove a cigarette from the crumpled packet, place it between his lips, and light it. She found herself involuntarily inhaling as he did.

"How are things with Archie?" she asked, tearing her eyes away from the trailing smoke.

"He's still angry, and so is Lucy. I've asked to see Alfie this Saturday, but I'm still waiting to hear from her."

"She can't stop you seeing him."

"She can if she gets Alfie to refuse to see me."

"That's not likely to happen, surely."

"Who knows? He's quite taken to his new family unit."

"You worry too much. Let things happen slowly; you'll still have your sons at the end of the day."

"Says the childless, single woman. Or are you not single now?"

"No comment."

Entering the car, Wednesday called Barry Roche and asked him to come to the station after work.

"Let's see what he has to say for himself."

Chapter 17

Barry Roche arrived at the police station with perspiration dotted over his face. His clothes were crumpled, and the rim of his shirt collar was smeared with a black scum.

"Have you got them?" he panted.

"No. Let's go to the interview room," replied Wednesday.

Barry's face dropped as he followed the pair into the room. Wednesday pointed to the seat opposite them.

"It's come to our attention that Gavin left you in the flat alone for around forty minutes, whilst he went to buy some beer. This was omitted from both of your original statements."

"And? When you came to see me I'd just lost my wife, for God's sake. I couldn't remember every detail of that night. So what I was alone for a while?"

"It gave you time and opportunity to commit the crime."

Roche hid his face behind his hands, rocking back and forth in his chair. "I can't believe what I'm hearing. I knew this would happen if you knew I was alone."

"So you freely remember worrying about that fact, hence you decided to hide it with the aid of your son."

"No . . . No, it's just that I knew if you found out about Karen and my time alone, you'd put it all together to make me look guilty. I'm right, aren't I?"

"We have to wonder what else you've been lying about."

"Do you also suspect Gavin of this crime? He was also alone for some time?"

"He's been questioned, and has a solid alibi. You're not being charged with this crime, but we strongly advise you to stick to the truth and cooperate with us from now on. Understood?"

Barry nodded, but the fire in his eyes betrayed his resentment. "If that's all, I'd like to get home for tea unless you want me to tell you exactly what I'm going to eat first?"

Wednesday dug her nails into the palm of her hand. "We may have further questions so please remain local."

"I've just buried my wife. I'm hardly in the mood for a round-the-world trip."

"I'll get an officer to see you out," Lennox offered, seeing Wednesday's pinched mouth.

"Well that was painful and pointless," she said as Lennox entered her office. "There's something about that man that rubs me up the wrong way. He doesn't seem to be able to address a woman with civility."

"I noticed, but perhaps this case is getting to you more because of the location."

She looked up, sighing. "You're probably right, but I must leave my personal life at the door, as we all have to do."

"Well if it's any consolation, the unit's been quiet and uneventful since the murder. Susan may well have been a deliberately targeted victim, not a random act of violence."

"I agree, and the psychiatrist believes the other patients aren't at risk. But we're short on motives, apart from the husband having an affair and being in debt, which is hardly startling."

"Agreed, but don't forget the son."

"But what's his motive?"

"The promise of an expensive car."

Wednesday rocked her head from side to side. "A couple of things are bothering me. Dave Hyde is clearly violent towards women. He blamed Susan for stealing his cigarettes and now he's blaming Joan for things going missing. He needs watching closely and we need the psychiatrist to take that seriously. There are no other beds available to move Mum to."

She paused, taking a sip of coffee which was now cold. She wrinkled up her nose and shuddered. "We need to interview Eddie Brass's brother, Sam, and Melvyn Rollins's best friend, Chris White. I also want to see Olivia Manning again. Set them up, will you?" she asked before subconsciously rubbing the nicotine patch on her left arm.

"Why the hell did you tell the police you went to buy beer?" Barry barked at his son.

"They'd have found out sooner or later. Anyway, what have you got to fear?"

"Nothing, but I don't trust them. They could concoct something to connect me to her death."

"We'll have to wait and see, won't we?" he smiled.

"Is there somewhere we can talk?" Lennox asked, flashing his ID card.

"I'm on my own. My boss has gone to pick up some more CDs. We can talk here unless a customer comes in," replied Chris White.

Lennox looked around the music shop, seeing motes of dust floating in the dingy light, and suspecting a customer was not imminent. He and Wednesday followed Chris up to the counter.

He sported a dyed red Mohican, with four piercings in each ear lobe, a nose ring, and a pierced eyebrow.

"We understand you're Melvyn Rollins's friend, and you visit him at The Raven Unit," said Lennox.

"It might be fair to say I'm his *only* friend."

"Where did you two meet?"

"At secondary school. We were both misfits; I was a music and gadget geek, and Melvyn was just odd. We were both crap at sport, at communicating with girls, and at infiltrating any gangs. We've stayed in touch over the years."

"You're aware of the murder on the unit, I suppose."

"Yeah, freaky eh? And I was on the unit just that evening."

"That's what we want to talk about. Do you remember anything strange on the unit? Any unfamiliar faces? Any arguments?"

Chris rubbed the acne scars on his cheek with the back of his fingers. "Not really. Melvyn was in a weird mood, telling me that some of the other patients were out to get him. I didn't stay long."

"What did he say exactly?" Wednesday asked.

"I can't remember his exact words, but it was something about getting them before they got him. He didn't say who, and to be honest when he's like that, there's no talking to, or understanding him."

"What did you do after leaving the unit?" Lennox continued.

"I went to The Nag's Head pub on Lucas Street. Met with a couple of friends."

"So you have friends now."

"Yeah, they're into gaming and music like me."

"Just to back-up your story, can you give me their names." Lennox had his notebook ready.

"Sure, but is that really necessary?"

"If you want to be excluded from the list of possible suspects, then yes, it's necessary."

Chris gave the details to Lennox before a lone customer sauntered in. He went to deal with the man as they left.

"Doesn't seem the murdering type," quipped Lennox.

"You should know there's never a type, otherwise policing would be a darn sight easier."

Lennox smiled, shaking his head in a mock gesture as she unlocked the car.

"Give those names to Jones to check out. Who are we seeing now?"

"Olivia Manning."

Chapter 18

Olivia walked with the grace and fragility of a tulip bending in the wind as she ushered them into the ochre and cream lounge. The smell of fresh coffee infused the air from the pot sitting on the low table in front of the cream sofa.

Without asking, she poured three cups of coffee and instructed them to add sugar and milk if desired.

"Have you caught the murderer?" she asked in a velvet-soft voice.

"Not yet, we're still making enquiries." Wednesday paused to sip the steaming liquid. "How's your husband been since the murder? It must have been a shock."

"It was. The unit's his baby, so anything that hurts the unit, hurts him."

"Does your husband have any enemies?"

"Not that I know of. Why?"

"I was wondering whether someone wanted to damage the unit's or his reputation."

Olivia's face blanched. "Do you think someone will hurt him?"

"I don't know. We're exploring all avenues to see where the motive comes from."

"He's a well-respected psychiatrist."

"He can still make enemies from former patients and relatives, or even colleagues."

"You'll have to ask him that. He doesn't talk to me much about his work."

"If you think of something else, here's my card," Wednesday said, passing it across to her, before finishing her coffee, savouring the last drop.

"Where to next?" Wednesday asked, slipping into the car.

"Eddie Brass's brother, Sam. We're seeing him at the bank where he works."

The bank smelt of new carpet. It was as hushed as a library as a queue of people snaked along the cordoned path.

Lennox walked up to a woman putting leaflets into a stand, and asked for Sam Brass. She pointed out a man behind the counter dressed in a navy blue polyester suit with an orange tie. Looking up he saw them, and signalled he would be out.

"There's a room available for us to sit in," he said, leading the way to an airless box where the smell of carpet glue was augmented to an almost intolerable level.

"You said you wanted to talk about my brother."

"And the evening of the murder," replied Wednesday, dusting crumbs off the chair before sitting down.

"You think Eddie did it?"

"No, we're just piecing together who can remember what, and where people were around the time of the murder."

"What can I tell you? I don't even remember the woman who died."

"Did you hear or see anything strange that evening?"

"Not that I can think of."

"How has Eddie been since the murder?"

"He's so depressed I'm not sure he's noticed."

"You were visiting that evening. Where did you go after?"

"Home. And yes I live with my brother, so I was alone. I'm hardly likely to kill a woman I don't know."

"Has Eddie been ill all his life?"

"Since his twenties. It's been all about him ever since."

"You mean with your parents?"

"Of course. It's made him the precious one."

"I imagine that's been hard for you?"

"I know life's hard for Eddie, but I'd like to be noticed just once in a while. Still, I'm there for Eddie more than they are."

"If you think of anything else, do give me a call," she concluded, handing over a card.

The house was quiet when Wednesday arrived home. She gathered up the pile of post and junk mail lying on the doormat, and slung it on the console table.

Pouring herself a glass of bourbon, she sat in the carver chair and opened her handbag. Her hand closed around a pristine cigarette packet and a lighter.

She stared at the packet, charged by conflicting emotions. She removed the cellophane slowly, recognising the sound that triggered heightened anticipation. The smell of them was foul, yet the urge to smoke was overpowering. She pulled one out then moved to the back door, opening it wide before lighting it.

The first puff tasted disgusting and she was close to throwing it on the floor. But, the second puff sent a rush to her brain, rendering her helpless to the dizziness. It made her feel light-headed, the kind of lightness that took her away from her worries.

For a brief moment, worries about her mother and her own mental health vaporised. The third puff prolonged the spinning, but after the fourth, it had become habitual.

She swirled the bourbon around in the glass, watching the light catch the amber liquid. Disconnected thoughts about the case swam before her eyes. Then thoughts of Scarlett dropped into her mind. She was someone else to worry about.

Chapter 19

Barry Roche froze when the buzzer rang late in the evening. Visitors were rare.

Pressing the intercom, he demanded who was there. When Karen Reilly answered, he gulped a mouthful of air.

"It's chilly out here. Aren't you going to let me in?"

He pressed the buzzer before looking around the flat. He knew she would not appreciate the mess, but perhaps that was a good thing.

The night air had given her cheeks a rosy hue, and her blue eyes sparkled like dew drops in the morning sun. She pulled off her bobble hat and ruffled her hair.

"Aren't you pleased to see me?" she asked huskily.

"I'm surprised, I never expected you to come 'round here."

"Well I can now, can't I?"

He watched her entering the lounge, taking in the chaos. She surveyed the room like someone considering buying the place, before moving a pile of magazines from the sofa onto the floor.

Gus appeared from the kitchen and bounded over to her, pushing into her legs to be stroked.

"I've heard all about you, Gus," she smiled, vigorously rubbing him under his chin.

"What brings you here?" Barry asked.

"To see you of course. It's been a bit tense on the unit recently, and I've missed your strong arms."

"You could have warned me. Gavin could have been here."

"He'll need to know about us one day. We don't have to hide anymore. Susan's gone and the police know about us. We have nothing to fear."

"I can't be seen committing to you so soon, people would talk."

"People will always talk, gossip's what keeps a community together."

"I don't want to upset Gavin. He's not as hard as he looks."

"I could help him through the transition. I'm a nurse, remember."

Barry sat next to her on the sofa, allowing her to take his hand, and move it onto her lap. "I want you," she purred.

"I can't . . . Gavin could come in."

"He's a big boy, he knows people have sex."

He pulled his hand away. "It doesn't feel right, not yet."

She sat back and pouted. "I was hoping to move on to the next stage in our relationship. With Susan gone I thought we could be open about our liaison before moving in together."

Barry's heartbeat throbbed in his ears. "The flat's too small for you to move in. It was always a crush with three people."

"No, you'd move in with me, silly. This place is a dump. I have a house that's plenty big enough."

Barry sunk back into the sofa. "That's a lovely thought. Let's hold on to that until the time's right."

Karen wanted to say more but recognised he had switched off, so she shuffled over and picked up his arm before placing it around her. Nestling into his chest, she closed her eyes to the clutter. She could see he needed a woman, and that made her heart melt. He would be hers soon enough.

Wednesday looked up at the knock on her office door, and saw Alex.

"I found a dog hair on Susan Roche's jumper."

"Is it a black one?"

"How did you guess?"

"Because they own a black Labrador."

"And there was me thinking I'd made a breakthrough. Fancy going to The Crazy Duck after work?"

"I'll see how today goes. Hunter's not happy with the pace of investigation."

"I'll remain hopeful."

"'Hopeful' about what?" Lennox said from behind them.

"About meeting Eva after work."

"And there was me thinking you were hopeful of making a scientific breakthrough. Are you close to that yet?"

"I'm afraid not. I found black dog hair on the victim's clothing."

"So the dog did it?"

Alex gave a dry laugh.

"Well hadn't you better go underground and dig around some more?"

"On my way." Alex winked at Wednesday before squeezing past Lennox, avoiding eye contact.

"You don't have to be so rough on him," Wednesday sniped.

"Look at you, being all protective."

"You may be in a grumpy mood, but there's no need to inflict it on everyone."

Lennox moved further into her office and sat down, running his hand over the top of his head.

"Do you want time off to deal with Alfie?" she asked.

"No need. He's not responding to my letters and requests to see him again."

"I'm sorry. If there's anything I can do."

Lennox raised his hand and gave her a half smile, before standing up and leaving.

Wednesday was woken from a fitful sleep by the persistent sound of her doorbell ringing. Turning towards the clock, she saw it was only one in the morning. Climbing out of bed she shuffled to the window and peered from behind the curtains. The outside security light was on, but they were not visible.

"Who is it?" she said hoarsely, through the open window.

Scarlett appeared in view, waving up to her. "Just me, sis."

Wednesday's shoulders rolled inwards as she shoved her feet into her slippers whilst shrugging on her dressing gown. Each step she took resonated with anger at being woken up by her inconsiderate and hedonistic half-sister.

She opened the front door and dragged Scarlett in before chastising her. "What the hell do you think you're doing?"

"I couldn't sleep so I thought I'd pop 'round and see my favourite sis. I thought I'd ring rather than enter with my key and frighten you."

"It's one in the morning. Bloody hell, you push my patience."

"I wanted to let you know how happy I am; I'm back with Jacob." Scarlett skipped to the kitchen.

"That news could have waited, I've got work in the morning, haven't you?"

"I've not been able to sleep properly for days. I've been running on coffee and cigarettes. Talking of which, have you got any wine to go with my smoke?"

"Not at this time of night I haven't. Besides, you're driving."

"Couldn't I stay the night? I sleep better here," she said, retrieving a cigarette from the packet.

Wednesday opened the back door before sliding the kettle onto the hob. The smell of cigarette swirled around the kitchen, making her want to cough, yet smoke all at the same time. She wanted to keep her periodic smoking a secret, so the last person she should tell was Scarlett.

"You know Jacob's got a lot on his plate at the moment. A serious relationship is probably the last thing he needs right now," she said, pouring hot water into the teapot.

"Still harbouring feelings for him?"

"I won't quantify that with a response."

"You always had a problem with my ability to attract men over you."

"Maybe you're right, but I'm really not in the mood for that conversation. We really should be discussing *our* mum." She poured the tea and handed Scarlett a mug.

"Nothing's changed with her. I can't imagine what you want to talk about."

"The fact that her depression is currently severe. And the fact that there was a murder on the unit. Aren't you worried?"

"I know she's safe, you're investigating it."

"Then you know how busy I am. I don't have much time to visit her; so could you please?"

"I'd have more time to visit if you gave me some insider info on the crime. Come on, sis, I'll be discreet."

"You know Hunter watches me like a hawk. This is non-negotiable."

"Pity. Maybe I will visit her to see if I can get gossip."

"Don't drag her into any article." She drained the last dregs of tea before heading for bed, leaving Scarlett at the table.

"We've got Gavin Roche in the cells, Boss," Arlow informed Wednesday as she entered the station. "He's been sleeping off the alcohol. Should be sober now."

"What's he in for?"

"Affray outside a pub and GBH. He broke a man's jaw."

She hunted out Lennox before heading to the cells.

"I hope he has a hangover from hell," said Lennox.

Chapter 20

The grinding noise of metal on metal pierced Wednesday's eardrum as the cell door opened. Inside, Gavin Roche was sitting on the edge of the bed, cradling his head in his hands.

"Rough morning," Lennox said, more loudly than usual.

"Fuck, what do you want?" he rasped.

"Just a little matter of you losing your temper last night."

"Alcohol induced anger. I'm not like that normally. Ask anyone."

"We will."

"So what caused you to get so angry in the first place?" Wednesday asked.

"Some idiot said Dad killed Mum so he could be with his floozy."

"Which part of that made you angry?"

"Both parts of course. He didn't kill her and he hasn't got another woman. It's the unit's fault she's dead."

"How come?"

"They were supposed to keep all the patients safe. They failed in their duty." He groaned, rubbing his temples. "Any chance of a coffee?"

"Sure, in a minute. With a temper like yours, I wonder what you'd do if your father did find another woman?"

"I doubt he will. He's had a hard life with Mum and her illness. Probably put him off women for life."

"Life must have been hard for you too, growing up with a mentally ill mum," Wednesday said quietly.

"It was and it wasn't. I had school to escape to. I liked studying and I could escape into books. That's why I like uni."

"Then why aren't you there now, if it's your source of escapism?"

"Supporting Dad and mourning Mum, in my own way."

"I suggest you stay away from alcohol for a while. Is your dad coming to collect you later?"

"Yep, and he'll be bloody pissed off with me too."

"Well that's for you two to sort out. I'll get that coffee brought to you."

They left the cell and returned to her office.

"Do you relate to Gavin Roche's childhood, if you don't mind me asking," Lennox said tentatively.

"In parts yes."

Lennox shoved his hands in his trouser pockets and paced around. "I won't tell Hunter, I know you don't let it cloud your judgement."

Wednesday nodded her head slowly. "I appreciate your loyalty."

Voices rose above the hubbub in the Incident Room. Hunter appeared from his office and Wednesday and Lennox followed suit. A red-faced officer appeared, telling them Barry Roche was in reception, demanding to see his son.

"Deal with him," Hunter snapped in Wednesday and Lennox's direction, before returning to his office.

"Mr Roche, how may we help?" Wednesday asked, arriving in reception.

"Not only have I lost my wife, but you've arrested my son. Have you a vendetta against my family?"

"Let's go and talk in the interview room; it'll be more private."

"I don't want to talk, I want my son, and take him home."

"I understand, but there's still some paperwork to sort out. Let's get you a cup of tea."

Lennox went off in search of some tea, whilst Wednesday escorted Barry to an interview room.

"Will he be charged?" he asked.

"I'm not dealing with his case, but he did break the other man's jaw."

"It's been a tough time for him. For both of us."

"I understand, and I suspect his circumstances will be taken into consideration."

Lennox entered with a cup of milky sweet tea.

"I'm going to put the flat on the market, and move away from here. I need a fresh start."

"Where would you move to?"

"Possibly closer to London so Gavin can live with me and finish his degree. If he doesn't want that, I'll go to Nottingham where I grew up."

"Keep us informed of your situation."

Barry nodded before taking a sip of tea then pushing the cup to one side. Lennox took him back to the reception area to await Gavin.

"The angel of death moves amongst us," whispered Fiona Campbell in Joan's ear, as they sat in the TV lounge.

"I don't know what you're talking about," Joan said slowly.

"Society can't cope with us, so the angel of death comes to spirit us away."

"Who are they coming for next?"

"It's a surprise. We won't find out until he's been."

"I thought angels were women."

Fiona reflected for a few seconds. "They can be both I think, but I like to think of them as men."

Joan looked around the empty room before fixing her eyes on Fiona. "How do I know who the angel is? It could be you, for all I know."

Fiona rolled her eyes. "Angels have wings and can move around unseen. You only see the angel when they're coming for you."

"Perhaps we should speak to my daughter; she's a detective, you know."

"The police can't stop an angel, nothing can. We just have to wait and see who goes next."

"I don't care if it's me; I'm tired of life."

"Maybe the angel heard you. You may get what you want." Fiona got up and moved seats, to dispense her angel of death story to others.

"I don't like what you're saying," said Melvyn Rollins, wringing his hands. "You're making it up."

"Am not. I know about these things. You don't have to worry though; Joan's said she'd like to go next."

"Who will it be after her?"

"I don't know, the angel isn't talking to me."

Melvyn began breathing rapidly, rocking back and forth in his chair. A loud, long moan stemmed from his open mouth. The pitch grew higher and louder, alerting the staff.

Eric entered the room, followed by the student nurse, Sara. She walked up to Melvyn and asked what was wrong.

"She says there's a . . . an angel of death here . . . waiting to kill us all," he stammered.

"That's not true, Melvyn. Angels of death don't exist," Sara replied, looking Eric in the eye.

Eric took Fiona Campbell out of the room, and Sara followed quickly behind.

"Give them both a glass of milk and a brownie. It never fails to calm them down," he ordered.

Chapter 21

Wednesday tapped on Lennox's open office door.

"I've just had a bizarre call from Mum about an angel of death prowling the ward. She wants to see me and I'd like you to come too."

Once in his car, she noticed him drumming his fingers on the steering wheel. "Something playing on your mind?"

"Archie and his demonic behaviour, if you must know."

"That's rather harsh."

"Harsh words for harsh times. I wonder how low he's going to go."

"Maybe he's just rebelling in his new environment."

"The YOI doesn't tolerate bad behaviour. He's lost his privileges for TV and computer."

"Are Lucy and Alfie visiting often?"

"She won't allow Alfie to go; she thinks the place will traumatise him. She may be right, of course."

"Maybe. Are you going to attempt to see Archie again soon?"

"I desperately want to, but he wants to see Lucy each visit, and of course she doesn't want me there too."

"I'm sorry, I don't know what to say."

Wednesday willed her heartbeat to slow down as they entered the unit. As they headed towards the nurses' station, the staff stood to attention. When she said she was just visiting Joan, they visibly relaxed.

"Hello, Mum."

Joan sat quietly in her chair facing the garden.

"It's my turn soon, but I don't mind. Only I'm scared when night falls. He could be in the shadows."

Wednesday moved closer to Joan, perching on the bed. She indicated with her eyes for Lennox to take the chair on the other side.

"Who told you about the angel of death?" Wednesday asked.

"I can't remember. She said we can't see them unless it's our turn."

Wednesday cradled Joan's hand in hers, gently rubbing the thinning skin with her thumb.

"Did she say whether one of the nurses is the angel?"

Joan turned to her. "I don't know, but they say nurses are angels, don't they?"

"It's okay, Mum, we'll sort it out."

Wednesday turned to Lennox, shrugging helplessly. For once her organic way of working had been obliterated like an ant hill dusted with poisonous powder.

"It was a woman who told you this, right?" he asked Joan.

She nodded.

"Was she young or older?"

"Young. She keeps twisting the ring around her finger as though she's not used to it yet."

"Fiona. I think it's her illness talking, Joan. But we'll have a word with her; see what the matter is. All right?"

Joan nodded cautiously before averting her eyes.

"Let's go," Wednesday said quickly, standing up. "We'll pop back and see you before we go." Bending down, she kissed Joan's forehead.

"We'll have to see the nurses before we see Fiona," Wednesday said, striding down the corridor.

Wednesday recognised Joshua from a distance, thanks to his height, and ponytail.

"My mother's upset. Fiona Campbell's convinced her there's an angel of death on the unit."

"Mrs Campbell suffers with delusions. It'll be nothing," Joshua mumbled.

"All the same, we'd like to talk to her to see where this came from."

"Are you implying that one of us is the angel of death?" Eric said, appearing from his office.

"Not at all," Lennox intervened, "but we have to check in case she really did see someone prowling around that night."

Eric said nothing, waving his hand in the direction of the TV lounge.

Fiona was dressed in brightly coloured clothes, with garish make-up on her face. Wednesday recognised signs of the manic phase.

They gently broached the subject with her to try and deduce what she saw.

"I didn't actually see him. You only see him when it's your turn."

"Why do you refer to the angel as 'him'?" Wednesday asked.

"I like to think of them as men. I want a male angel to take me away, not a female one." She eyed Lennox.

"You know the night Susan Roche died? Did you see anyone who shouldn't have been here?"

Fiona jiggled her head from side to side as she rummaged through her memories. "No, I don't think so. You can stay now if you want, and help me look," she said directly to Lennox, twirling the wedding band around her finger.

"If you do remember anything, please let us know." Wednesday did not hold out much hope. Fiona was an unreliable witness, with shadows of delusional visions in her mind.

"Are they treating you well in here?" Wednesday asked quietly.

"I don't like it when they make me eat my meals. I don't want to get fat."

"I'm sure you won't."

Lennox witnessed Wednesday's visceral attachment to the young woman, sensing a touch too much empathy on her behalf. He did not want to see, lest he felt obliged to pass it on, and he despised Hunter for putting him in that situation.

"I'll need to sleep soon to keep myself beautiful for my husband. I have one, you know," she said as she began peeling off her cardigan.

They left her quietly.

"I want to say bye to Mum. Do you mind if I pop in alone?"

"I'm sure I'll manage in the company of Nurse Angela who's just materialised," he said, jerking his head in the direction of the nurses' station.

"Be good."

The words were still leaving her mouth, as he was striding away.

"The angel of death isn't real, Mum. Fiona's mind plays tricks on her. Remember you're all ill in here."

Joan puffed out her cheeks. "I don't like it when you talk like that. You're making out we're different."

"You know I don't think of you like that."

"Where's Scarlett? Is she in here yet? I shouldn't have had children."

"Scarlett's not in here, she's busy with work. And you're a wonderful mum, by the way."

"You're just being kind. What happens if one of you or both end up like me?"

"We'll handle the situation if and when it arises. Just concentrate on getting better."

"Or just dying," she whispered.

Wednesday kissed Joan on the top of her head before walking back to the nurses' station to voice her concerns. She saw Angela touching her hair involuntarily and smiling as Lennox spoke. She had seen it all before.

"Recent events have really got to my mum."

"We are aware, *Miss* Wednesday. Just as you know how to go about solving crimes, we know how to nurse the mentally ill," replied Eric, from the chair behind the desk.

"I'm allowed to voice my concerns as a daughter," Wednesday responded with a curt nod of her head, before dragging Lennox away.

"He bothers me," Wednesday said, walking to the car.

"Is that as a DI or a daughter?" Lennox replied.

She threw him a heated glance.

Chapter 22

Gavin had still not returned to university. Much to the relief of Barry, however, he had left to run an errand, leaving Barry in peaceful solitude. When the buzzer rang, he assumed Gavin had forgotten something, so pressed the button and left the front door open for him.

"Expecting me were you?" Karen Reilly said as she stood in the doorway.

"Hell no," Barry replied without thinking.

"Nice to see you too."

"Sorry, you surprised me that's all. Gavin's just popped out, he won't be long. What can I do for you?"

"I'm thinking I've spoilt your surprise."

"Surprise?"

"Well, I can see your flat's for sale, so I assume you were going to tell me you're moving in with me." Stepping forward, she held his head between her hands and kissed him hard.

Barry pulled away, looking over her shoulder. "You'd better come in."

There was semblance of order blossoming in the flat. A couple of brown boxes stuffed with books and knick-knacks were pushed up against one wall, clearing some of the shelves, leaving only a layer of dappled dust on display.

"I want to move away from the area, maybe with Gavin, give us both a fresh start."

Tiny red dots splattered along the bridge of her nose, splaying out over her cheeks. "And when were you going to tell me this?"

"It's only just gone on the market. I haven't had the time to tell you."

"But you've had the time to start packing."

"The agent said it wouldn't sell in this state."

"So where are you thinking of moving to?"

"Maybe closer to London if Gavin wants to finish his degree. I'd have to rent, can't afford London prices. If not I could buy a place further north."

Karen walked beside the dining table, running her finger along the surface, gathering dust along the way. Looking at her fingertip, she blew the clump into the air and watched it zigzag down towards the carpet.

"Both of those options would make it difficult for us to see one another, unless you stayed at mine each weekend, or expect me to move with you?"

The closer she got to him the further he surreptitiously shuffled away. On feeling the window ledge in his lower back, he decided to speak.

"Let's just see how it goes and keep in touch."

"I sense you're blowing me off, and I don't like it."

The sound of the front door opening halted Barry's response. He held his hands up in surrender as Gavin appeared.

"Nurse Rhodes has just called to see how we're doing," he said to his son, willing his voice to remain calm.

"At home?" Gavin said incredulously, letting Gus off the lead.

"Your father's not being quite truthful," Karen began, turning towards Gavin. "He asked me over for a cup of tea, as we got on well on the ward, and . . . well, you can guess the rest." A saccharin smile crept over her face.

"Dad?" Walking around her, he marched up to Barry. "You're thinking of dating already?"

"No, son, Karen and I are just friends."

"Oh, you'd given me quite another impression," Karen piped up.

Barry looked from one to the other; beads of perspiration forming on his rippled brow.

"Only kidding. But I'd have loved being your step mum," she purred, smiling at Gavin.

She walked over to Barry, and on the pretence of a peck on the cheek, whispered, "You'd better watch out," whilst pinching the skin on the inside of his upper arm. Nodding to Gavin, she sashayed out the door.

Wednesday's phone rang on her desk.

"I've got some results. Shall I come up, or do you want to come down?"

"I'll come down." She waved at Lennox, indicating for him to follow her.

The wide smile on Alex's face diminished when Lennox also entered his laboratory.

"What have you got?" she asked.

"I've just received the test results on the dressing gown rope belt. They found epithelial skin cells belonging to Barry Roche."

"That's a step in the right direction."

"Except that he could have helped tie the belt around her waist at any time. We can't prove when the cells got there," added Lennox.

"Maybe you should try and find out," Alex chipped in.

"We're not miracle workers."

Wednesday felt irritation prickle up her spine. "So no other skin cells were found. The killer could have worn latex gloves, though. There's an endless and convenient supply on the unit."

"Roche doesn't know what we know. Maybe find out from him how much personal care he provided for her," Alex offered pointedly towards Lennox.

"Thanks, Alex. Let's hope something more conclusive turns up for one of us, sooner or later," Wednesday said quickly before guiding Lennox to the door.

"I'm stopping off at the courtyard. Fancy joining me for a virtual smoke?" he asked her on the way up.

"Think I will. I could do with decompressing my mind."

Wednesday turned her collar up against the chill in the air and watched Lennox light his cigarette. Since smoking one at home, her cravings had become fierce.

"Perhaps I could take one of the female nurses out for a drink and glean insider info on the staff?" he offered, smoke trailing from his mouth.

"That's a thinly veiled disguise of your eagerness to date Angela Rhodes."

"I thought you knew me better than that."

"It's precisely because I know you I say it. Your reputation followed you up from London. I see women fawning over you daily."

"I don't seem to have that affect you."

"I'm your boss and far too astute to be beguiled by your charm."

"I thought it was because I'd dated your sister."

"Half-sister as well you know. Now give me a couple of puffs on your cigarette and keep quiet about it. That's an order."

"Can I see you in my office for a minute, Angela?" Harvey Manning said, walking up to the nurses' station.

On entering his office, he closed the door before pushing her up against the wall and closing his mouth over hers. After a few seconds, he pulled away, catching his breath.

"So have you got that policeman to ask you out yet?"

Angela straightened her blouse. "Not had much opportunity, that other detective doesn't leave him alone for long."

"You'll have to try harder. Next time they're here I'll occupy her whilst you work your magic on him." He lowered his head and kissed her. "I'm counting on you."

Chapter 23

It was eight in the evening by the time Lennox left the station. He rummaged around in his coat pocket for his cigarettes whilst walking to his car.

"You took your time, Jacob," Scarlett said dulcetly, leaning against the bonnet of his car.

He paused. "I didn't know we were meeting up."

"I like surprising you, it keeps our relationship fresh."

Unlocking his car, he slid into the driver's seat as she opened the passenger door and stooped down. "Where are you taking me?"

"I'll take you for a drink if you stop calling this a relationship."

"You drive a hard bargain," she smiled, climbing in. Pulling a lipstick from her handbag she coated her pout slowly and purposefully.

Lennox knew he was in for a long night as he drove to a pub on the outskirts of Cambridge. He did not want to risk bumping into anyone he knew.

"How's the case going?"

"You know I can't answer that."

"I'm only making innocent conversation."

"That word doesn't belong in your mouth."

"I've never let you or Eva down, have I?"

"That's because we don't give you much to go on. Are we going to talk shop all night?"

"Not at all. I thought we'd go back to mine after a drink, and I'd cook something for dinner."

Lennox smiled, pulling into a pub car park.

Wednesday slammed the driver's car door, craving a cigarette and close to asking Lennox for one. Sensing her tension he spoke.

"Do you want a cigarette?"

"I do, but I won't. I've not touched the packet I have at home since my weakness. But thanks." She popped a mint into her mouth and offered him one. "I need to call in at the unit, drop something off for Mum, all right?"

"Sure."

The sun reverberated off the wet road into her eyes as she drove the twisting lanes. On arriving at the unit, she parked before swiftly leaving the car, without saying a word.

Lennox stood next to the car and threw a cigarette between his lips as he watched her disappear inside.

"I've brought you some clean pyjamas, Mum. Oliver said he'll be late tonight as he has a pottery order he needs to finish."

"Or is he seeing his lover."

"He doesn't have one, he loves you to pieces."

A scream suddenly perforated the air, making Joan jump. Wednesday rushed from the room and into the corridor. Seeing Joshua and Angela run, she followed them.

Wednesday stood outside the door and listened to them trying to calm Fiona Campbell down. She was screeching that someone was in her room.

Wednesday knocked on the door. "Is there anything I can help you with?"

Joshua told her they were okay, and Angela gave her a cutting look. She got the message.

She hovered outside trying to decipher the whispers coming from the room. Fiona was agitated and shouting about someone in her room wearing a scary mask.

Lennox entered the unit, having heard the racket, and asked Wednesday what was going on.

"Not sure if Fiona Campbell is suffering from visual hallucinations or there really was someone in her room."

"Have you spoken to her?"

"The nurses are with her; Joshua and Angela." She gave him a sideways glance.

All was quiet as the nurses retreated from the room. Not looking, Angela bumped straight into Lennox.

"I didn't know you were here," she smiled.

"Just passing through."

Wednesday moved away and followed Joshua to the nurses' station.

"How is Mrs Campbell?"

"Quiet now that we've sedated her."

"How can you be sure there wasn't someone in her room?"

"Because we haven't let anyone on here except for you two. Everyone's been strung out since the murder."

"Staff included?"

"We've all been rather unsettled. We'll be happier when you arrest the person."

"Who do you think did it? Someone on the unit or from the outside?"

"I've no idea; I thought that was your job."

"Everyone likes to play detective. Don't tell me you haven't discussed it."

"We think someone from outside the unit."

"Why would someone want Susan Roche dead?"

"Who knows? I've got to do the drug round now, sorry." He turned around to unlock the drug trolley from the wall before pushing it down the corridor, where Lennox was still talking to Angela Rhodes.

Wednesday signalled to him they were leaving.

"Learn anything interesting?" she asked.

"That I have a date this evening."

"With Angela Rhodes?" A pinched expression scarred her face.

Lennox nodded, waiting for the lecture, but all he got was silence.

"Just be careful," she said, trying not to sound too censorious.

"I always am."

"Don't risk pillow talk in the pursuit of sexual gratification. You're worth more than that."

Chapter 24

Angela was already sitting at a table when Lennox walked into the bar. The soft music and low lighting gave the bar an insalubrious feel, suiting his mood.

Angela was so engrossed in swirling the red wine in the bulbous glass, she was unaware of him until he coughed politely.

"You look lost in thought," he said, tossing his coat over a chair.

"Sorry, the death on the unit has really got to me."

"How about another drink?"

"I'm okay with this one thanks, I'm driving."

Lennox wandered over to the bar and ordered a half before returning to the table.

"Don't you get counselling at work when something like this happens?" he asked.

"Yes, but it doesn't take away the fear, or the residual images. How do you cope with seeing so many awful things?"

"It's part of the job, although it never fails to surprise me what humans are capable of doing to one another."

"You must be a brave and clever man, too."

"I don't know about that."

"Working out the crimes must take a lot of thought, I mean, how do you go about working out what happened to Susan Roche?"

"It's a team effort, lots of interviews and legwork."

"It's so intriguing. Oh do tell me a bit about how you're getting on. I promise I won't tell anyone."

"There's not much to say so far. We're investigating every angle."

"But you must surely have a suspect in mind. The husband perhaps? It's often the spouse isn't it?"

"It frequently is, but I can't give you those kinds of details for this case."

"Boring. I thought you'd be more scintillating company."

"I'm sorry to disappoint you."

"There are other ways you can make it up to me," she smiled hopefully.

"Maybe one day when the case is over."

"Well don't take too long," she said huskily before finishing her wine then reaching around for her coat. "I look forward to a more successful rendezvous in the near future."

Lennox raised his glass to her and nodded. He watched her calves as she moved slowly to the exit, cursing Wednesday's voice in his head.

Wednesday and Lennox were back on The Raven Unit to interview Rene Blower and her husband, Howard, in the empty lounge.

"Thank you for meeting with us," Wednesday began. "We're aware that the night of the murder you were unwell, and may not have been aware of what was happening around you."

"She was having a psychotic episode, so clearly had nothing to do with the murder," Howard snapped, pacing around in front of the window.

"We're not accusing either of you of being involved in the murder, sir. We're wondering whether either of you noticed anything strange earlier in the day or previous days."

Rene sat impassively in the chair, gazing at the wall.

"Has your wife said anything since that evening?" Wednesday asked carefully.

"She's been catatonic since then. You'll not get much out of her, I certainly haven't."

"I'm sorry. Have you had to take time off work to be here?"

"I work shifts, I'm a fireman, so no."

"It must be hard having a stressful job and a wife who's ill."

"It is."

"Did you notice anything strange that day? Different people on the unit or hanging around outside?"

"I didn't visit that day, I was on duty at the fire station."

"Perhaps on the previous?"

"I was resting at home. We'd been tackling a fire all through the night. I was knackered."

Howard's muscles flexed under his thin sweatshirt, and the protruding veins in his neck throbbed. "What are you interested in exactly?"

"We're trying to piece together events around the murder."

"Sounds more like you're being nosy about my relationship with Rene."

"Your private life is your own."

"Not when you have a mentally ill wife it's not. Everyone needs to know everything, from what we eat for dinner to how often we have sex."

"You sound upset."

"Upset? That's an understatement. I'm fucking pissed off with this life. I mean, look at her. I raise my voice but she doesn't even flinch. What's the point of these people, eh?"

"Do you get emotional support from somewhere?"

He let out a dry laugh. "My family didn't want me to marry her in the first place. Who knew they were right?" He paused to cough. "Anyway, I'm not going to stay married to her much longer, and I don't care how bad that makes me look. My marriage is shambolic."

"You're planning on leaving her?"

"I've started divorce proceedings. I call in to see her occasionally to see whether she's able to talk or listen coherently. Seems I'm still not in luck. Can I go now?"

"Certainly, thanks for your time."

Howard turned to look at Rene then left without saying another word.

"I'm surprised it doesn't happen more often," Wednesday said, picking up her bag.

As they walked down the corridor, Melvyn Rollins appeared from the TV room and stood in front of them, bobbing up and down on his toes.

"Have you got the killer yet?" he whispered.

"Not yet, but you'll all be informed when we do," Lennox replied.

"Oh God, who will it be next? I can't sleep at night. Fiona said someone was in her room. We're all going to die." His voice rose to a shrill pitch, alerting the nurses.

Sara arrived, and wrapped one arm around his waist and put the other on his hand before quietly leading him back to his room.

Eric sauntered up from his office, looking at the detectives coldly before entering Rollins's room, and closing the door.

"Doesn't look like we'll get much more here today," said Lennox.

"Let's go and see Barry Roche, see exactly how much personal care he gave to Susan."

Chapter 25

"What do you want now?" Barry demanded through the intercom. "Just a few more questions," Wednesday replied.

"Can't you just phone me?"

"We're here now."

There was a pause before the door latch buzzed.

Arriving at his flat, the door was wide open. The dog gave them a warmer greeting than his owner who was nowhere to be seen.

"We were wondering whether you had any outside help come in to help with Susan's personal care, or whether you did it all yourself?" asked Wednesday, locating him in the kitchen.

"I did it all myself, but only when she was really bad, otherwise she took care of herself."

"The belt from her dressing gown came back from forensic showing your skin cells and Susan's on it."

"And that displays my guilt does it?"

"It places you at the scene and doesn't help us find someone else."

"I know I touched the dressing gown before she went there, and maybe during her stay. Besides, the murderer may have worn gloves."

Wednesday nodded briefly. "Are you sure your wife didn't have any problems with anyone, in or out of the unit? Neighbours?"

"No."

"Where's Gavin?" Lennox asked.

"Out. I don't know where. He's not a child I don't keep tabs on him."

"Has he decided to go back to university?"

"I don't know."

"Have you found somewhere else to live?"

"There's a two-bed terrace house in East Ham I could afford to rent. And with all the re-generation around there, I'm bound to find some business."

"You seem to have thought things through."

"I have to move on, and so does Gavin."

"Do keep us up to date with your progress."

"I'm sure you'll know as soon as I do."

They walked away from the oppressive atmosphere, enriched with nothing except dog hairs clinging to their clothes.

"Can I see you in my office for a minute?" Hunter asked Wednesday as they arrived back at the station.

She followed him in, closing the door behind her.

"Any progress on the case?" he asked.

"Not really, Guv. Forensic evidence places Barry Roche on the belt used to hang her, but he used to tie the belt for her anyway. My gut tells me there's something not quite right on the unit, but I can't place what it is."

"Is that over-anxiety because your mother's there?"

"Not at all. Whether she was there or not, my gut would still tell me the same thing." She cursed inwardly, sensing a red-speckled rash creeping up her neck.

"What's the gossip out there?" he indicated through the window into the Incident Room.

"Gossip?"

"Come on Eva, you can be honest with me. What are they saying about me?"

"There are rumours about your marriage, but I've been too busy to speculate." Her cheeks were now on fire.

He indicated for her to sit, which she reluctantly did.

"And what are your thoughts?"

"I don't have any. I like to keep my personal life private, so I treat others in the same manner."

"Very noble of you," he smiled wryly. "I am in fact separated from my wife and she's pushing for a divorce. I want you to know as I might be . . . distracted."

"Sorry," she whispered.

"Okay, I think I've said everything." He paused as though expecting a further response. "Aren't you curious as to why I'm getting a divorce?"

Wednesday clasped her hands tightly together until the extremities turned white. "Private life, Guv, remember?"

"Quite right."

A knock at his door broke the uneasy atmosphere. Maria Jones walked in with some papers for him to sign, so Wednesday took the opportunity to leave without the need to search for parting words.

Walking back to her office she saw Lennox watching her. He raised his hands in the gesture of surrender, smiling broadly.

The house felt empty when Wednesday returned home. She made cheese on toast before searching fruitlessly for something to watch on TV. Inevitably, she returned to the kitchen table to ruminate over the case.

Opening a notepad, she began scrawling down the names of those close to the victim. It was feasible that a patient had committed the crime, but by thinking that, she had to consider her mother as a suspect. Unthinkable.

The members of staff could also be culprits; having lost their patience with Susan, they strangled her then hanged her to cover their crime. Plausible.

How about an intruder? Perhaps someone in Susan's personal life they had yet to discover? The problem was that Barry was reticent to disclose much about Susan's or his life. Without his assistance they were going to struggle to find someone in their periphery who had a grudge against either of them. She was at an impasse, seeing lots of threads but nothing to substantiate a rope. Did Susan have a rejected lover lurking in the background?

The sound of the doorbell made her jump.

Opening the door, she found Alex standing there with two bottles of beer in his hands.

"Thought you could do with one of these."

Wednesday smiled and let him in, noticing how youth still glowed after a hard day.

"How do you know I've had a bad day?"

"Just because I'm in the basement doesn't mean I don't get to hear what goes on upstairs. Anyway, I'm not here to rehash the day, but to chill you out."

"I don't think I'll be great company. I'm trying to view the case with a helicopter mind, but it all looks so messy and shrouded in secrecy."

"That's work talk."

"I told you I'd be boring."

"Perhaps sitting next to me on the sofa will distract you."

Wednesday opened the beers and took him through to the lounge, knowing full well that nothing was going to distract her, not even him.

Sam Brass entered The Raven Unit and made a detour before visiting his brother.

He tapped on Eric's office door, walking in without waiting. Eric was on the phone and held up his hand to stall him. He ended the call quickly.

"What can I do for you?"

"It's the thirteenth of the month. Friday the thirteenth, lucky for some, eh? The usual?"

Eric nodded, handing Sam a brown envelope, and receiving a bag in return. Sam smiled and left to visit his brother.

Chapter 26

After Alex left, she did indeed feel more relaxed. He had provided the cushion against the world she required. When they were away from society he felt right, but she disliked being with him in a world of younger women.

She contemplated visiting her mother, but could not abide stepping foot in the unit when off-duty.

As though summoned by the desperate vibes of loneliness, Scarlett arrived at the house and instantly raided the fridge for something alcoholic.

"The editor's hassling me to get more news on the Raven murder. Can't you, for once, give me a snippet of insider info? Is there a murderer on the unit? A madman with a noose?"

Wednesday frowned. "You'll have to dig your own field; I can't let you trample on mine. Is that all you've come 'round for?"

"I was wondering if you knew what Jacob was up to. He's not answering my texts or calls."

"It's Friday night and our weekend off. I've no jurisdiction over what he does in his spare time."

"I know, it's just that I hate not being able to contact him, and you see him daily. It's not fair."

"Life never is. Have you only just noticed?"

"You sound bitter."

"Instead of pestering me, you should be visiting Mum. And don't give me that crap about hating hospitals."

Scarlett downed half a glass of wine before pouring another glass.

"I suppose you're staying the night," Wednesday said with a sigh.

"Cheers."

It took several seconds for the sound of the phone to interrupt Wednesday's Saturday morning lie-in.

"It's Oliver, sorry to wake you, but I'm really anxious about Joan."

Wednesday sat up on her elbow, cradling the receiver in the crook of her neck. "What's wrong?"

"She's, well . . . not improving; in fact I think she's sinking further into her own personal hell. Last night she kept seeing things in her room. People wearing scary masks."

"Did you speak to the staff?"

"They said they'd check on her. What with her low mood and these hallucinations, I'm worried about her."

Wednesday shuffled into an upright position. "I'll call in to see her later, and talk to the staff if necessary. Try not to worry, Oliver, she always pulls through."

Now awake, Wednesday padded downstairs and slid the kettle onto the Aga. The packet of cigarettes in her handbag gnawed away at her willpower, and with Scarlett still asleep upstairs, there was nothing to stop her.

With a mug of coffee in one hand, she walked into the garden and brushed leftover brown, crispy leaves from the bench. Removing a cigarette from the packet, she put it in between her lips and lit it. She closed her eyes and inhaled.

Smoking had always aided her to reflect on the case in hand, and now was no exception. Oliver's concerns rumbled around her mind, along with the odd things she heard on the unit. She drew deeply on the cigarette whilst a plan burgeoned in her mind, like the green tips of crocuses and snow drops, forging through the soil in clumps near her feet.

Scarlett arrived in the kitchen as Wednesday was rinsing out her mug.

"God I need some coffee," she said wearily.

"There's a pot already made. Help yourself."

Scarlett sauntered over to the pot and poured herself one.

"I'm going to see Mum today and I want you to come with me," Wednesday said.

"Are you going to let me sit in on some interviews?" she asked, opening the back door.

"No, we're going to sit with Mum and chat to her like the daughters we are. She must be bored in there."

"I imagine the meds take the edge off that," Scarlett said before lighting a cigarette. "Besides, I thought she was so depressed she couldn't hold a conversation." She blew smoke into the air, watching it swirl around above her head. "I can smell smoke on you, by the way, sis," she grinned.

Joan was sitting in the TV lounge when they arrived. Her eyes remained fixed on the screen when they greeted her from the doorway.

"I told you it was pointless coming," hissed Scarlett.

Wednesday dug her elbow into Scarlett's ribs before walking in.

"Mum," Wednesday said, kneeling in front of her. "I've brought Scarlett to see you."

Joan's eyes flickered before continuing to gaze blankly straight ahead. Dark shadows lurked beneath her eyes, and her lips were dry and cracked. Wednesday offered her a plastic beaker containing tepid water, but Joan remained impassive to the gesture.

Wednesday stood up again and gazed around the room. In the far corner sat an expressionless Rene Blower, whilst Melvyn Rollins sat by the window biting his nails and humming quietly.

Scarlett was still standing in the doorway, fearful of inhaling the entrails of madness.

"Come and sit next to her," commanded Wednesday with a forceful flick of her arm.

"She doesn't want to," Joan whispered. "She's afraid of me."

"Don't be silly, Mum. Of course she wants to see you, don't you," she replied, glaring at Scarlett.

Scarlett shuffled forward, sitting gingerly on the edge of the chair, whilst Wednesday sat the other side.

"I see terrible things at night," Joan said quietly.

"Probably just nightmares," Wednesday replied

"No, I'm awake when I see them."

"Do they say anything to you?"

Joan shook her head. "You don't believe me, do you?"

Scarlett was about to speak, but Wednesday stepped in. "You're unwell at the moment, that's why you're in here. It's just a phase." She placed her hand on Joan's.

Wednesday looked at the other two patients and wondered whether they were having a similar experience. She stopped herself from going over to them. Today she was just a daughter.

That evening, Wednesday found herself alone at home, ruminating over the day and Scarlett's attitude to visiting their mum. Negativity swamped her as an eddy of tears ran down her cheeks, leaving her no option but to go to bed and read.

She was still reading at one in the morning when the doorbell rang. Startled, she moved to the bedroom window and peered from behind the curtain, and there, parked behind her car, was Lennox's.

Concerned, she grabbed her dressing gown from behind the bedroom door and ran downstairs.

"What's wrong?" she asked breathlessly.

"What's right? I mean how much can one man take?"

She pulled him inside so as not to disturb her neighbours.

"What the hell are you on about?"

"Archie's in isolation for attacking another boy with a homemade weapon. I mean, what's happened to the little boy he once was?" He pulled a bottle of bourbon from his coat pocket. "I need a friend to drink this with . . . Please."

She wanted to refuse, but seeing the depths of darkness in his eyes, she took him to the kitchen and got out two glasses.

"Did you get to see him today?"

"No, boring Brian called me to let me know. Lucy and I only communicate via him now."

"When will you see him next?"

"He's lost all his privileges, but says he doesn't want to see me or

Lucy; who's going fucking nuts, again." He emptied the glass in one gulp before filling it again. "Perhaps none of this would have happened had I been a better father, and stayed with Lucy?"

"You can't keep blaming yourself."

"Yes I can. I'm a failure as a father and as a husband. It wouldn't surprise me if you thought I was a shit detective too."

"You're meticulous and ordered which I admire. I need you to balance me out."

Lennox finished his second glass and poured a third. "At least somebody needs me."

"All the women at the station swoon over you. I'm envied by them."

He shrugged, dropping his chin onto his chest. "I'm no catch, just ask Lucy. Besides, I'd rather be idolised by my sons than a bevy of women."

"I've never seen you so low, Jacob. I'm not sure what to say."

"Don't say anything, just drink with me."

"You'd better stay the night. Santé."

Chapter 27

"Yes?" Barry said drowsily through the intercom.

"It's me, Karen."

"Karen? Have you any idea what time it is?"

"Clearly, but I couldn't shift you from my mind. I just had to come and see you."

"I'm barely awake; I couldn't hold a sensible conversation at this hour."

"I don't want to talk."

"Please go, Karen. Come back tomorrow evening at a more civilised hour. Gavin's here."

"I've risked a lot for you. You owe me."

"Not now, *please*." And with that he disconnected their communication channel before dragging himself back to bed.

Wednesday found the crime scene report of Susan Roche's room on her desk. They found the fingerprints of the victim, her husband, her son, and the members of staff on the unit. It did not offer her the breakthrough she was hoping for.

"There's a Jordan Campbell here to see you, Boss," said Maria Jones as she stuck her head around Wednesday's office door.

Wednesday thanked her before summoning Lennox to follow her to the interview room.

"Mr Campbell, what may we do for you?" she asked.

"You're probably going to think I'm being an idiot, but I'm worried about Fiona."

"In what way?"

"I know she was ill when she was admitted to the unit, but I feel her mental health is declining. She's afraid she'll be killed."

"Have you discussed this with the staff?"

"They tell me she's doing fine, and she hasn't voiced her fears to them. I said you'd find me foolish."

"We're not denying your feelings, or hers, but I'm not sure what you want us to do about it?"

"All I'm saying is that something isn't right on that unit, and I'm worried for my wife. Shouldn't you be worried too?"

"And why is that?"

"Fiona overheard the staff saying that your mother's a patient on there."

"Whether she is or isn't, is not the point. We're taking the murder on the unit very seriously . . ."

"I don't doubt that," he interjected, "but I want to be assured that nothing like that is going to happen again."

"We have our eye on the place, sir," Lennox said.

He let out a long sigh. "I just want this nightmare to be over. I will blame you if anything happens to her."

Lennox got an officer to show Jordan Campbell out before turning to Wednesday. "Are you all right?"

"Are police officers not allowed to have family members who are mentally ill? Because it feels that way to me."

"Of course not, it's okay," he blushed furiously.

Wednesday laughed quietly, "You're so easy to wind-up at times. Now, let's go and interview the relatives of the other patients, to see if they all feel the same way as Jordan Campbell."

"It's good of you to see us, Mr White," Lennox began. "We know you're Melvyn's best friend, and in the absence of family members, could you tell us how you're finding Melvyn's health these days?"

"Still as anxious as when he went in."

"The same, no worse?"

"I couldn't really say. Why?"

"Does he complain about feeling unsafe on the unit?"

"Yes, but I took that as part of his anxiety. Why all the questions? Is something wrong?"

"We're just making enquiries."

"Well you're worrying me."

"If you have concerns further down the line, please call us," Lennox concluded, handing him a card.

Their next visit was to Howard Blower, who answered the door still wearing his fireman uniform, black bags bulging under his eyes.

"We were wondering how Rene was doing?" Lennox asked.

"I haven't been for a few days. Why?"

"When you did see her, did you notice any improvement?"

"She's festering in there, as far as I can see. I'm sorry but I've just come home from a night shift, I'm too tired for this." He shut the door quietly without waiting for a response.

"Where to next?" Lennox said, fumbling with a packet of cigarettes in his pocket.

"Let's call in on Oliver. At least we can smoke there in peace," Wednesday replied.

"He knows you're smoking again?"

"Scarlett sussed me out, so they'll all know, and right now I don't care."

"Fair enough," Lennox said with a spring in his step.

They found Oliver in his studio at the back of the house, hands shaping a teapot out of clay. Residue of turmeric-coloured clay plastered down the hairs on his forearms, up to his elbows. He barely looked up as they entered, bringing a cool draft in with them.

"Is this a bad time?" Wednesday enquired.

"I'm just thinking how the clay's malleability is rather like the mind of someone with a mental illness; it's sometimes too malleable, allowing irrational thoughts to roam free."

"It's not like you to be maudlin. Is Mum okay?" Wednesday asked, perching on an old milking stool, trying to lock eyes with him.

"I thought her depression was lifting at one point, then hallucinations kicked in and now she's convinced someone's out to get her, like they did that other poor woman."

Wednesday looked across at Lennox, who took his cue.

"Have you spoken to the staff about her?"

"I have, but they said they thought she was doing well. Should I be worried about Joan?"

"We're keeping an eye on the place, but you keep an eye on her too. We'll get to the bottom of this soon."

They watched Oliver smooth the teapot with a wet sponge before slicing it off the wheel with wire and setting it to one side to dry. "She's not been this ill for a while. It's upsetting."

Wednesday rose from the stool and moved towards him, reaching out with her arm. "I'm truly sorry, Oliver. If you want me to come 'round later to talk or listen, just let me know."

"That's kind of you, but don't worry about me, just find the culprit. Doing that may relieve her, and me, of some worry." He pecked her on the cheek, leaving a powdery residue behind.

"Next stop, Eddie Brass's brother," she said, heading for the car.

Chapter 28

The bank informed the detectives that Sam Brass had the day off. Undeterred, they headed for his home.

After a couple of rings of the doorbell, he answered wearing a grubby t-shirt and ripped jeans. His face coated in a glistening sheen.

"This isn't really a good time for me."

"We won't keep you long," Lennox stated, taking a step forward.

Sam sighed, letting them in.

Wednesday unbuttoned her coat. The grubby net curtains poorly masked the condensation coating the windows in the lounge-diner.

"We want to talk to you about your brother, Eddie," Wednesday said, looking around for somewhere to sit.

Following her gaze, Sam removed some papers from a chair, dumping them on the floor.

"I don't know what more I can tell you."

"Actually, we wanted to know how you've found him of late. Do you think his mental health has improved?"

Sam paused for a few seconds. "I suppose so. I don't really think about it."

"But you do visit him."

"Of course, he's my brother."

"Well is he conversing with you better, sleeping better and eating more?"

"Yeah, I suppose he is. What's this about? Shouldn't you be speaking to his doctor?"

"We like to take family perspectives into consideration too. So you don't feel he's regressed?"

Sam looked at her blankly.

"He's worse," Lennox clarified, much to Wednesday's annoyance.

"I don't think so. You said you wouldn't be long, only I've got things to do."

"That's all, thanks."

The detectives returned outside; the cooler air refreshing them.

"He almost chased us out," remarked Lennox.

"Haven't you got used to being unpopular by now?"

He was about to comment until he noticed the smirk on her face.

"Let's drop in on Barry Roche, see if he can tell us how Susan was prior to her death," she said.

Checking that they had gone, Sam sprinted to the landing and reached for the hatch in the ceiling with a long pole, before pulling down a ladder.

Once up there, he parted the heavy polythene curtains hanging from the rafters and walked into the brightly lit space. The breeze from an oscillating fan caught the curls framing his face as he strolled around the hydroponic growing system.

He marvelled at green growth swaying in the artificial breeze, savouring the thought of the money it signified.

After ringing the intercom, the detectives heard Gavin Roche's voice.

"Dad's not here," he said idly.

"Perhaps we could come in and speak with you then," Lennox replied.

"Whatever."

The door buzzed allowing them in. The entrance had been cleared of all the junk making it feel more spacious, although it still smelt fusty.

Gavin had left the front door open with only Gus standing there panting to greet them. Wednesday squeezed passed him, ruffling him on the head.

"We wanted to know how your mother was prior to her death," Wednesday asked.

"Depressed," he answered, rolling his eyes.

"What I meant was, was she getting worse during her stay?"

"I don't know, I didn't visit that often, I was at uni. You'd have to ask my dad."

"Is he at work?"

"Nope."

Wednesday sighed quietly.

"Perhaps you could tell us where to find him," Lennox said firmly.

"I don't actually know where he is. I woke up this morning and he was gone."

"Gone? Where to?"

"Dad never goes anywhere that costs money. We never had proper family holidays when I was growing up."

"That must have been hard," Wednesday said.

"Not really. I didn't want to be cooped up in a caravan with my mum in one of her moods."

"I see. May we take a look in his bedroom?"

"What for?"

"See if his belongings are missing."

Gavin waved his hand before flopping down on the sofa.

The bedroom was soulless, in need of repainting and modernizing. The bed was unmade and the curtains were partially drawn, giving a sinister feel to the room.

Walking over to the wardrobe, Wednesday opened the doors to find a dozen empty coat hangers. Lennox pulled out a drawer in the dresser and found that too was empty.

"Looks like he's done a runner," stated Lennox, taking a look under the bed, only to find a pair of web-covered beige slippers.

He stood up, brushing the dust from his trousers, and followed Wednesday back to the lounge.

"It would appear your father has taken most of his clothes with him. Who would he go to? Friends? Family?" Wednesday demanded.

Gavin remained slouched on the sofa. "He doesn't have any friends thanks to Mum's madness. We're not close to any family either."

"What about a favourite destination? Perhaps somewhere he went with your mother when she was well?"

Gavin shifted around in his seat. "I've no idea. Why's it so important anyway . . . Oh, I've got it, you think he killed Mum and now he's disappeared." A wide grin turned his mouth into a grimace.

"We're in an ongoing investigation about his wife's death. We need to keep in touch with family members whilst it's taking place."

"Have you tried his mobile?" Lennox asked.

"Nope, do you want me to?"

Lennox stared at him until he moved to retrieve his phone from the sideboard. He pressed some keys then listen for a few seconds. "He must have it switched off."

"Is this normal behaviour for him?" Wednesday asked.

"Not that I know of, but I don't live here normally. Who knows what he's like when I'm away?"

Wednesday hesitated before asking the next question. "Perhaps your father has another woman. It's not unusual where the wife is mentally ill."

Gavin shrugged. "That nurse, Karen something, was 'round the other night, but I doubt she'd shag him?" Incredulity seeped from his eyes.

"Karen Reilly? It's possible."

"No way, she could do better than him."

They left the flat, sauntering downstairs in silence.

"Do you ever wonder about Oliver doing that?" Lennox asked as he climbed into the car.

"It's crossed my mind. However, if he's not in his pottery studio, he's with Mum wherever she may be. He's totally dedicated to her."

Gavin shut the front door, after checking that they had truly gone. Retrieving his mobile from his back pocket, he pressed speed dial.

"The police have been here asking about Mum's mental health. They wanted to know if she was worse before dying. I just wanted to let you know."

Harvey Manning was in his office on the unit when Wednesday and Lennox arrived.

"What may I do for you?" he asked calmly, closing his laptop.

"We wanted to talk about your patients in general," Wednesday began, sitting down opposite him.

"Would that include your mother?"

"It's a general query about them all, including Joan Willow," she replied coolly.

"Fire away."

"We've interviewed close family members or friends of each patient, and they all say the same thing. They believe their mental health has deteriorated since being here. What do you say to that?"

"I refute their allegations. This is a small unit that has the time and the staff ratio to manage the patients' individual needs. I have noted no such problems, and I dislike the propensity to scourge the unit."

"That's not our intention, but we do have to follow every lead. Someone somewhere may have something against the unit and is intentionally causing trouble."

"I think the NHS enquiry would have found something wrong on the unit by now?"

"Maybe, but it's still ongoing."

"The problem doesn't lie with us. I think the problem lies with Susan Roche. Cast your net wider around her would be my advice."

"Do you know something we don't?"

"Not at all, I just know the problem isn't here."

"Thank you for your time," Wednesday said, standing up. "We won't take up any more of it."

She could feel herself bristling with irritation as she and Lennox walked away. She paused outside Joan's room.

"You can go in if you wish," Lennox said.

"And have you report back to Hunter? I don't think so."

"You know me better than that. I've had nothing but praise for your conduct. I know it must be hard having her here with all this going on."

Wednesday shrugged as she watched a woman pushing a trolley laden with a large pot of tea and a mountain of chocolate brownies. She smiled inwardly knowing what a sweet tooth her mother had.

Fiona Campbell watched the detectives through the TV lounge window before phoning her husband.

Chapter 29

Sara Morris left the NHS interview in tears. As she rushed to the staff toilets, Eric Knight spotted her and quickly followed. He entered the room to find her locked in a cubicle.

"What's wrong? What happen in there?" he asked.

Sara's sobbing halted at the sound of his voice.

"I'm finding all of this . . . really stressful."

"What did you say to them?"

Sara paused to blow her nose. "They asked me to account for my every movement. How many times I visited which rooms." Another sob and a blow of her nose.

"Did you tell her about our smoking breaks?"

"I had to; they could tell I was leaving something out. I looked guilty of something and rather than of murder, I decided to tell the truth."

"So you've dumped me in it too."

"I tried not to, but they didn't believe a student nurse would act in such a way alone."

"Great, just great."

"I did say it was my fault. If I hadn't needed to speak to my boy-friend, you'd have never left the door open unattended. I'm sorry . . ."

"Fat lot of good that does. I was in charge that night. This could be really bad for me."

His heels squeaked sharply on the vinyl floor as he left the room. Sara decided to keep out of his way for the remainder of her shift.

Karen Reilly pitched up at the station requesting to see Wednesday and Lennox. She was taken to an interview room to await them.

The elephant-grey walls felt claustrophobic as she sat alone, picking at her chipped nail polish.

The detectives entered the room.

"I think I may be wasting your time," she said before they even sat down.

"We'll be the judge of that," Lennox replied, pulling out a chair.

She sighed, resigned to her situation. "I've been trying to contact Mr Roche, but he's not replying, which is most odd."

"Do you need him urgently," replied Wednesday, watching her every move.

"I think it can wait," she replied, clasping her hands together under the table. She paused to take a deep breath. "Oh well, as long as you think he's okay. I'll be going now." She moved to stand but Wednesday put out her hand and indicated for her to stay.

"Do you offer this after-care to all your patient's families?"

"Mr Roche is alone; men always struggle alone."

"He has his son."

"He doesn't live there permanently. He'll be returning to uni soon."

"Or maybe not."

She looked at them both. "Do you know something I don't?"

"In an investigation, we often know a lot more than the people involved."

Karen's cheeks blushed a watercolour-hue of crimson as she gazed into her lap. "I'm glad everything's all right with him. Sorry to have wasted your time."

They allowed her to leave before heading for the courtyard.

"So what do you make of that?" Wednesday asked, pulling a packet from her pocket and offering Lennox one.

"Seemed rather concerned; too concerned in fact." He lit his cigarette and inhaled deeply.

"Perhaps Barry's not reciprocating her feelings?"

"Maybe he's running away from her?"

"Would she be strong enough to haul the body up?"

"Easy, I reckon."

They stood in the enclosed space, drawing on their cigarettes and reflecting on what they just witnessed.

"We need to find Barry Roche," Wednesday said finally. "Have there been any sightings of his car?"

"Nothing as yet, but the search is still on." He paused and took an intake of breath then faltered.

"What do you want to say?" she asked.

"I just wondered whether you thought about having kids one day?"

"God no, I'm far too selfish. They seem to leach every ounce of energy, patience, money, and happiness from their parents."

"Perhaps that's true. Archie's caused me so much pain, I barely like the boy, even though I still love him. Alfie is a different boy altogether. Dare I say it; he's the kind of son I want."

"And Archie is the one you hoped you'd never get, eh?"

"Does that look bad?"

"Not to me. I can't imagine what it's like for you. But you can't blame yourself. He's made his own decisions and choices. He's old enough to know right from wrong, you taught him that."

"I still wonder whether he acts this way because I'm in the force. What better way to get back at the dad you hate?"

"You're thinking about it too deeply. Come on, let's go inside and move this case along."

They stubbed their cigarettes out, leaving their feelings of anxiety about their own lives in the ashtray.

Chapter 30

"Who was that on the phone?" Olivia asked.

"Nothing for you to be concerned about," Harvey replied, pouring himself a whiskey.

"You're not involved with another woman again, are you?"

He took a large swig of drink, staring at her over the rim of the glass.

"No, I learnt my lesson last time. What are we having for dinner?"

"Braised lamb livers with spring greens and new potatoes. Are you hungry?"

"Not really. I might retire to my study."

Olivia went to speak but thought better of it. Returning to the kitchen, she turned off the oven before making her way to bed with a bottle of sherry.

Three sherries down, Olivia heard the front door open then close. She heard the car start before disappearing into the distance. Alone again, she sighed.

Lennox was already at the station when Wednesday arrived. Walking into the Incident Room, she found him surrounded by female officers laughing at his witty repartee. Seeing her, he winked conspiratorially. Rolling her eyes she turned away, bumping into Hunter.

"May I have a word?"

She opened her office door and waved him through, wishing she had bought a fresh coffee on her journey in.

"I think I may have given you the wrong impression the other day," he began as he sat down. "I wasn't implying that *you* gossiped about me, nor was I hinting that I needed a shoulder to cry on."

"Actually, I didn't think either of those things. I imagine you're going through a tough time and I'm glad you feel you can talk to me."

His silence hung cloying in the air. Wednesday moved her hand slowly to switch on her computer, as though any sudden movement would snap him in two like a dead branch in a hurricane.

"Any updates on the case?" he asked finally.

"Only that all the patients have apparently regressed since being on the unit."

"Isn't that exactly why they're in there. Didn't I read something about a phenomenon called extinction burst?"

Wednesday raised her eyebrows. "I think that's more to do with behaviour modification, Guv." She knew he was a well-read individual, but even so, he still managed to confuse issues at times.

"I thought they could be raging against the medical restraints, so they got worse before getting better."

"I hadn't considered that. Maybe there's some truth in what you say, although I've never really noticed it before with my mum."

"Does this new unit follow different rules and guidelines, perhaps?"

"They have a higher ratio of staff to patients, so individuals get more intense intervention."

"Which is why it's bemusing how Roche's death happened at all? I don't believe everyone was where they said they were. It's a case of catching the perpetrator out. Everyone lies, remember."

His words saddled her with the weight of needing resolution.

That evening, a storm whisked the clouds and darkness together to form an oppressive mantle over Cambridgeshire. People rushed along pavements as cars swept through the rain, casting a fountain of spray onto unfortunate pedestrians.

Lennox opened the door to his bedsit and slung his wet coat over a chair. His kitchen cupboards revealed a paltry array of food stuffs. The only constant supply of liquid sustenance were bottles of beer and a bottle of whisky.

His mood was lifted when he found a packet of peanuts to accompany his beer. Kicking off his shoes, he put his feet on the coffee table and switched on the TV, flicking through several channels before settling on the news, and ripping open the packet.

Tossing handfuls of salted nuts into his mouth, he sank further down into the sofa, getting as comfortable as possible, so when the intercom buzzed he was tempted to ignore it. However, whoever it was, was not ready to retreat, so on the third sound, he heaved himself out of his comfort-space and snarled into the intercom.

"It's me, Angela Rhodes. The nurse from the unit."

Lennox almost choked on a peanut as he brushed particles of salt from around his mouth.

"How do you know where I live?"

"I checked your medical data."

"That's illegal."

"You wouldn't go after a desperate woman?"

"Why are you desperate?"

"I'd rather have this conversation face-to-face."

Lennox cast a swift eye over the space and decided he looked the desperate one. He buzzed her in and opened his front door.

She was wearing a beige trench coat cinched at the waist, knee high black leather boots, and a silk scarf tied around her swan-like neck.

"Sorry to drop in like this, but you can't blame a woman for trying." She reeked of expensive perfume, which lingered in the air as she moved around.

"What's the problem?" he asked, remaining standing.

"Aren't you going to offer me a drink?"

"Last time we had a drink together, I seem to remember you rushing off."

"Sorry, that was very rude of me. I'd like to make it up to you, if you'll let me." She gazed around the bedsit and held her breath at the sight. "How about we go for a meal; my treat."

The logical part of his brain told him to throw her out and drink more beer, but another part reminded him that he was both hungry and lonely.

"Okay, I'll agree to a drink first before deciding what to do next."

Angela sat down as he moved to the fridge. "I've only got beer or whiskey to offer."

"Let's start with the beer and save the harder stuff for later."

"You're rather sure of yourself."

She smiled sweetly, accepting a bottle of beer with the cap removed. "So are you closer to catching the bad guy? I'd feel safer on the unit if I knew he was in custody."

"There's no evidence to say they'd attack a member of staff."

"But they could start. I've a stretch of night shifts coming up. Perhaps you could pop in and visit occasionally to check all is okay?"

"I'm sure that won't be necessary, but I could ask for a patrol car to drive pass-by occasionally for reassurance."

"I'd rather it was you."

Lennox smiled before tipping some beer into his mouth.

Wednesday sat with Joan and Oliver in the family room on the unit. The couple seemed to have aged, which heightened her sense of mortality.

"How's the pottery coming along?" she asked.

"I got that large order out to that fancy shop in Cambridge, but it's been quiet since."

"Hopefully the advent of the wedding season will bring in some special orders."

"If not, I've a long wait until Christmas."

They had been talking that way for forty minutes, whilst Joan sat staring into the middle distance. Both had tried to coax some semblance of conversation out of her, but to no avail. The whole experience was draining, so as Wednesday rose to leave, Joan chose that moment to speak.

"There's lots of whispering and shadows moving about in the night."

"Who's whispering?" Wednesday asked, noticing Oliver shaking his head slightly.

"The whispers are real, not in my head," she replied pointedly in his direction.

"We believe you, Mum. Can you hear what they're saying?"

"No, but I know it's a man and a woman, or sometimes two men."

"Do you recognise them?"

Joan shook her head, clasping her hands tightly together.

"Do you know what time of night you hear them?"

Again, Joan shook her head, only more vigorously.

Wednesday put her hands on Joan's. "Don't worry, Mum. I'll look into it."

"Don't tell them I told you, will you?"

"I won't." She kissed her on the forehead and smiled at Oliver before leaving the room.

She sensed the staff at the nurses' station watching her as she left.

Joshua and Sara looked at one another before commencing the drugs round.

Chapter 31

Wednesday knocked on Hunter's door and waited for him to wave her in. On entering, the smell of bacon danced around the room, triggering her regret of dusty muesli for breakfast.

"Sorry," he said with a mouthful of bacon sandwich, "no time for breakfast, hence the canteen sandwich." He wiped a slick of grease from his chin with a serviette.

"I was wondering if we could step-up monitoring the unit, as I suspect something nefarious is happening at night."

"And how have you deduced this? It wouldn't be info from your mother would it?"

"If I said yes, would you deny me my request?"

"I might."

"Then it's from my own deductions after interviewing *all* of the patients."

Hunter placed the half-eaten sandwich on the brown paper bag, wiping his fingers on the now translucent serviette.

"Tell me more about your deductions," he said, pointing to the chair.

As she sat she became aware of her shaky legs and clammy palms.

"Not only do most of the relatives report slow progression or a decline in the patients, but at least three patients have seen someone lurking around, or shadows in their rooms. There seems to be a lot of activity at night."

"Are they not the symptoms of mental health issues? How do you know that the patients don't hear and see these things normally?"

"Not all mental illnesses have such symptoms. Besides, they all talk about hearing and seeing similar things. That's too much of a coincidence."

Interlocking his fingers behind his head, he tipped back in the chair. "What are you proposing?"

"A night stakeout of the unit. Lennox and I would do it and see what happens around the place."

"It would take more than one night to get a full picture. I'm not sure, leave it with me."

She left his office feeling bereft. Her one hunch requiring action had been quashed by him for the time being, and it did not feel good. She dashed into her office for her bag then indicated to Lennox to follow her to the courtyard.

He watched her light her cigarette and inhale deeply before speaking.

"A few minutes with Hunter and you're desperate for a smoke. What happened in there?"

"Nothing, absolutely nothing, and that's what hurts."

Lennox quizzed her with his eyes.

"He believes my hypothesis about the unit is because of something my mother said. He's dismissing my views, and I'm angry, that's all."

"I see. So what do you want to do now?"

"Bide my time to see if he changes his mind; he did say he wanted to think about it. But—"

"But?"

"How do I know you're on my side? I mean, you have orders to keep an eye on me."

"I thought I'd cleared that up."

"That was prior to me thinking I may have to go against his wishes."

Lennox pursed his lips. "You're my direct boss, so I'd do as you ordered."

"And then tell Hunter?"

Lennox looked her directly in the eyes. "Do I really need to answer that?"

She smiled, stubbing out her barely smoked cigarette before moving inside.

The recent stillness of the Incident Room had been replaced by a rumble of activity. Hunter clapped his hands just as they arrived.

"Barry Roche's car has been spotted in Blackpool. The force there is searching all B-and-Bs, which as you can imagine is a daunting task in a holiday resort. A photo has been e-mailed over."

"Anything we can do here, Guv?" asked Damlish.

"DI Wednesday and DS Lennox will interview him when he arrives here. The rest of you, continue to dig into the background of the patients and their families." He paused to look at Wednesday. "With the exception of Joan Willow. Now get to it."

Wednesday's face was on fire as she paced quickly to her office. Why did the team always need reminding of her mother's illness?

It was midnight by the time Barry Roche arrived at the Cambridge police station. He was disgruntled about being forcibly relocated.

"You're treating me like I'm guilty of something," he moaned, before sipping the tea he had just been given by an officer.

"Running off does make you look that way, plus your mobile's been switched off constantly. Even your son had no idea where you were."

He took bird sips of the scolding drink. "You're right," he began, "I am running away, but from someone, not a crime I committed."

Wednesday leant towards him. "Who?"

Roche's head lolled back as he closed his eyes. "Karen Reilly. We began having an affair not long after Susan was admitted to the unit. It began with mild flirtation." He took another sip. "But it soon became apparent, after Susan's death, that she wants more of a commitment than I'm willing to give."

Lennox stifled a yawn, as Wednesday urged him to continue.

"She kept dropping 'round, and I was worried Gavin would find out. He'd go nuts, and he's all I've got left." He put the drink down and rested his head on the table, savouring a moment's peace.

"So you'd have us believe that your wife's death had nothing to do with you, right?" said Lennox.

He nodded vigorously.

"So who would want your wife dead?"

Roche shrugged. "I can't imagine anyone wanting that. She wasn't a sociable person, she didn't have friends to offend."

"Perhaps Karen would have preferred her out of the way?" Wednesday queried.

His face blanched.

"Did she ever say it would be easier for you both with Susan out of the picture? Perhaps seeing you with Susan on the unit angered her?"

He shook his head. "She's not like that, she's a caring person. She's a nurse, for God's sake."

"They're not immune from committing crime. I suggest you tell us anything she said regarding Susan, or you could be considered an accessory."

Barry pressed the flat of his hand against his forehead, screwing his eyes shut. Beads of sweat clustered around his nose, and gathered along his top lip.

"I'm telling you, it couldn't be her. She never once mentioned getting rid of Susan."

"So how was she to attain commitment from you?"

"I was going to play it cool and see what happened with Susan. I mean, see if she got better or whether she'd stay the same." He paused and looked at them both. "I don't know what I was planning really. I just wanted some physical attention. Susan's been out of bounds for over a year." His face shone, illuminating tiny threads of broken veins on his cheeks.

"Karen's been trying to contact you, so you might want to think about what you're going to say the next time you meet," Lennox said with a touch of relish in his voice.

Barry returned home, hoping Gavin would be there to shield him from whatever Karen had in store.

Chapter 32

Eric Knight threw the official letter from the health authority onto the kitchen table before lighting a cigarette. He let the smoke furl from his nostrils whilst pressing speed dial on his mobile.

"I'm officially off the unit until the NHS complete their investigation, so we need a new place for the drop-off."

"What about your place?"

"No chance, the police are hanging about."

"Well what do you suggest?"

"How about a pub somewhere between us."

"That would be The Horse and Hound in Chester Street. What time?"

"Nine thirty tonight. Dress low-key, I don't want you looking like a rent-boy." Eric hung up and moved toward the fridge to grab a beer.

He switched on the TV to catch the local news, finding the murder on the unit had dropped down the running order, much to his relief. But being suspended angered him, and alcohol was a convenient remedy, for the time being.

A shower of rain peppered the ground as Wednesday darted into the station, her head jumbled with concern about her mother.

Walking with her head bent down she walked straight into Lennox, heading in the opposite direction.

"Geez, Boss, not like you," he said, preventing her from toppling over by grabbing her shoulders.

"Sorry," she muttered.

"I'm off to buy a cappuccino, fancy one?"

The corner of her mouth lifted slightly, but he was gone before she had time to give him some money.

Lennox took a large swig, leaving white froth clinging to the burgeoning shoots of a moustache, which curved around his mouth, culminating on his chin. He placed hers on her desk.

"Are you growing a goatee?" she asked, hiding her smile behind her cup.

"I fancied a change," he replied, stroking the bristles. "Have you thought more about when you want us to watch the unit?" he said in a hushed voice.

"I'm biding my time for when it feels right. Go too soon and we could scare whoever away."

Perching on the edge of her desk, he looked thoughtfully into the cup. "What are you expecting to find?"

"I've no idea, which is why Hunter won't go with it. He wants concrete facts; up high are breathing down his neck."

"Would you like me to mention the idea to him?"

Wednesday buried her face in the cup so he could not see the rage on her face. She counted to ten before resurfacing.

"What makes you think he'll listen to *you*?"

Sensing his faux pas he tried back-peddling, but she was stuck on his comment, unable to move forward.

"That's a back-handed way of telling him what I plan to do?"

"Not at all." He drained his cup before throwing it in the bin. "I wished he'd never set me this task."

"Or maybe that I hadn't guessed."

"You're a smart woman. I would have told you anyway."

She watched him for a moment, letting him squirm uncomfortably, until he broke the silence first.

"The offer remains; I'll go with whatever you choose to do."

"I will take the flack if we get caught," she said before draining the cup, launching it towards the bin, and missing.

Eric Knight sauntered across the pub car park, weaving his way through the random smokers outside the entrance.

Inside, the low beams and poor lighting made him duck and squint around for Sam Brass, whom he eventually found sitting in an alcove, next to an empty fireplace, with a half-drunk pint in front of him.

"Do you want another one?" Eric asked, nodding towards the glass.

"Nope, I'm not staying. Have you got it?"

"I have," he replied, patting his deep coat pocket.

"This isn't going to work long term, you know."

Eric nodded before moving to the bar to order a whisky on the rocks. He returned to find Sam texting on his mobile.

"I've got to be somewhere soon, so let's get on with it," he said.

"I'm trying to make this look natural. Let's finish our drinks and talk for a while."

Sam clenched his jaw, "I've got fuck all to talk to you about. In fact, I want this to be the last transaction until the police have cleared off."

"You can't do that. Your brother would never cope."

"I'll make sure Eddie's okay."

Eric's arm shot across the table, grabbing Sam's wrist tightly.

"You listen to me you little shit," he hissed, "you do exactly as I say, or you'll have more than the police to worry about."

"Are you threatening me, old man?"

Eric tightened his grip before wrenching the mobile from Sam's clutch, and encasing it in his other hand.

"Taking my phone isn't going to frighten me."

"It's not meant to; I just want your attention for a few seconds to check that you really understand. You will continue to supply me. I know people who could break a few bones for starters."

Sam stared at him, trying to free his arm, twisting so it nipped his skin. "All right," he finally conceded. "But if the police sniff around, you keep my bloody name out of it."

Eric downed his drink, jerking his head in the direction of the door. As he lit his cigarette outside, Sam sidled up to him and borrowed his lighter, before slipping him a package in return. Eric returned the favour before they parted ways.

Chapter 33

"I've thought of another way to look at what's going on in the unit," Wednesday said to Lennox, over her messy desk. "We talk to Olivia Manning about her husband; his work, hobbies, etcetera."

"Perhaps we should take her out of her comfort zone and ask her to come to the station."

She smiled. "Organise it."

"Was it necessary to make me come here? Couldn't you have come to my house?" Olivia complained, taking a seat in the interview room.

"We thought it might be easier for you to talk away from your husband," Wednesday replied quietly.

"He's at work, won't be home for hours." She twisted her leather gloves between her hands. "What do you want to know?"

"Does he have many bad days at work?"

"He had quite a few when the unit opened. He said he'd been sent the worse cases as though the authority wanted the unit to fail."

"Why would they want that?"

"The unit is his project but it's expensive. They've given him two years to make it viable otherwise it gets closed down."

"I see. That must be a great worry to him."

"As I said, things seem to have calmed down, except for the murder. Now that's a major issue for him. It's bad publicity."

"Indeed. So I imagine he'd want to work with us to get the matter closed."

"Isn't he?" she looked up, perplexed.

"He doesn't always make himself available. He seems reticent at times to share information about the unit."

"Maybe he's just very busy. It's a very important job with lots of responsibility."

Wednesday nodded, tapping her pen on the table, letting the tension mount in the room.

"How are things at home with all this stress going on?"

Olivia watched the tapping pen for a few seconds before looking Wednesday in the eye. "Fine. If he's stressed he spends a lot of time in his study."

"Does he go out a lot in the evenings without you?"

"What are you implying?"

"I'm not implying anything, I just know some men like to hide in the pub."

"Well my husband doesn't. If he goes out in the evening it's usually to the unit on an emergency."

"Was he at home the night of the murder?"

"I'm not sure . . . I mean I don't keep track of the days when he is or isn't home. Why don't you just ask him?"

"We're just corroborating accounts."

"If he said he was, then he was. I'll be glad when this is all over one way or another."

"Meaning?"

She shifted around in her chair. "I suppose, if I'm honest, the unit has brought much stress upon my marriage."

Wednesday watched her until she saw she would say no more. They rose and Olivia followed suit.

Watching her disappear out of view, Wednesday turned to Lennox. "Let's hope she goes home and tells him all about this meeting."

Lennox smiled before shaking a packet of cigarettes at her.

Harvey Manning finished writing up his notes before closing down the computer. Just as he was slipping on his coat, a knock came at the door, and Eric Knight entered the room.

"What are you doing here?"

"We need to talk."

"I'm about to go home. Phone me tomorrow." He snapped his brief-case shut.

"Not if you want this unit to continue being successful. Now, we need to straighten out our stories."

"I have nothing to straighten out. I was with my wife the night of the murder."

"I'm not talking about the murder . . ."

Angela Rhodes burst into the room, dressed in a denim mini skirt and a figure-hugging black leather biker jacket.

"God, sorry, I thought you were alone," she said, slowly backing out of the door.

"It's all right, Eric was just leaving."

Eric looked between the pair for several seconds, hoping that one of them would acknowledge his presence as more than merely a nuisance. He was disappointed, but undeterred.

"We will have this conversation, *Doctor*. If not today, then tomorrow." He walked to the door almost knocking over Angela in the process.

"What's wrong with him?" she asked.

"Hacked-off at being suspended from the unit. Nothing important."

"So we've no need to worry then?"

"All you're required to do is to worship me and make me happy," he replied, grabbing her by the back of her neck and kissing her hard on her mouth.

Pulling up in the unit's car park, Wednesday's heart plummeted at the thought of entering the building and being swamped by air soiled by mental illness. She had changed into jeans and a cashmere jumper to mark her out as a visitor and not a detective.

Joshua Plough was doing his rounds. Doris Smith sat at the nurses' station, the overhead light shining off her pure silver hair.

"Hello, Miss Wednesday, how are you?"

"Not bad. How's my mother?"

"Last time I saw her she was asleep in front of the TV."

"That's not like her."

"I'm sure she'll wake up for you."

Wednesday smiled wanly before moving to the lounge. Joan was indeed asleep, and Melvyn Rollins was sitting in the corner watching a quiz show anxiously.

"He'll lose all his money if he gets this question wrong," he said breathlessly, his left knee bouncing up and down rapidly.

Wednesday shrugged, giving him a half smile as she sat in the chair next to Joan.

"Mum" she whispered, putting her hand on Joan's arm and shaking it gently. "Mum, it's Eva."

Joan's eyelids formed a crescent moon shape as they gradually opened. Her eyes took moments to focus; her pupils were dilated and dark like the eclipse of the sun. Wednesday had never noticed that before.

"How are you feeling?"

"Fine . . . Calm . . ."

"Have they increased your medication?"

"Not that I know of, dear daughter."

Wednesday smiled. It had been a while since she had heard that phrase.

"Hello," Oliver said from the doorway. "Hope I'm not interrupting mother-daughter time."

"Not at all."

Oliver walked over to them both, kissing Joan on her forehead, rousing her briefly.

"Have you noticed her dilated pupils, before today?" Wednesday asked, as he sat on the other side of Joan.

"Can't say I have, why?"

"Perhaps I'm being overly precious about her. I'm developing a warped view of this place."

"Are you? Apart from the murder, I'm pretty pleased with the place. Joan loves having her own room and ensuite." He looked across at her. "You look tired."

Wednesday nodded. "I am. Work's busy, I'm worried about Mum, and I miss my occasional evening chats with Scarlett. We don't catch-up as often as we used to."

"I know she misses you too," he smiled.

Harvey Manning entered his home, placing his briefcase on the console table before picking up the post. He shuffled mindlessly through the envelopes, before seeking a glass of wine.

Anticipating his need, Olivia had poured a glass of Chablis, handing it to him as he entered the kitchen.

"Good day?"

"Busy," he replied dryly.

"I had a busy day too. I had to go to the police station."

Chapter 34

For the first time since arriving home, Harvey looked at his wife. "Whatever for?"

"They wanted to know about your work and how the murder has affected you."

"They've already asked me," he snapped.

"I thought they must have."

"So what did you tell them?"

His tone of voice made her jump. Placing her hand across heart, she took a step back.

"What did you say to them?" he demanded, placing his glass on the table.

"I . . . I just said you were worried the murder would be bad publicity for the unit as you only have funding for two years."

His jaw muscles twitched. "And?"

"I can't remember what else I said. I did say you don't talk to me about your work so I couldn't tell them much."

"Next time they pay you a visit, refuse to talk without me present, understand?"

Olivia nodded rapidly before turning her attention to the beef roasting in the oven.

Alex Green knocked on Wednesday's office door.

"The dog hair came back from the specialist. It's from a black Labrador. Your victim has such a dog, but the DNA doesn't match. The hair has come from another dog."

She nodded.

"Are you okay? I haven't seen much of you lately. Have I done something wrong?"

She gave him a faded smile. "I'm fine."

"You always use the word *fine* when you either can't or won't divulge your true emotions."

"You can deduce from that what you will." She returned to the computer screen. "Oh and Alex, it's not you."

He smiled and tilted his head. "Good to know."

Lennox tapped on the open office door. "Sorry to intrude, but something's going on at the unit. I thought we should get down there."

"Fill me in on the way. I'll drive," she replied, grabbing her bag.

The alarm was blaring as they got out of the car. The unit was on lockdown so it took several minutes for someone to respond to the door buzzer.

"I can't let you in right now," Angela Rhodes said through the intercom.

"We were alerted by a member of your staff that an incident has occurred, so I suggest you let us in rather than cause an obstruction."

Inside, the sound of the alarm was magnified, making conversing virtually impossible. Wednesday resisted the urge to run to her mother's room.

Striding to the nurses' station, the alarm ceased, leaving a ringing tone in everyone's ears. Angela stood before them, arms folded across her chest.

"Who called you, exactly?"

"The person didn't give a name," replied Lennox.

"You must know if they were male or female."

"The message was passed on to us."

She rolled her eyes.

"So what's this all about?" Lennox asked.

"I thought your source would have told you," she smiled.

"We're not here to play games," snapped Wednesday. "What's happening?"

"One of our patients attacked a member of staff. Granted it's quite serious, but we can handle it."

Wednesday knew she had deliberately left out the names so she was ignorant of her mother's situation. Crushing her nails into the palms of her hands, she resolutely remained silent.

A flurry of activity was coming from Dave Hyde's room; voices talking in hushed tones. Wednesday attempted to step around Angela, but she blocked her way.

"We were called to the unit therefore we have to investigate the situation," she said as Lennox moved next to her.

They walked up to Dave Hyde's room and stood in the doorway, trying to see beyond the two staff in there. Wednesday knocked on the open door, attempting to grab their attention. Harvey Manning turned around and grimaced.

"This is bad timing, detectives."

"What's going on?" Wednesday asked.

"Mr Hyde's just had an episode, but he's calmer now."

Wednesday was about to speak when the student nurse, Sara Morris, turned around, displaying a burgeoning bruise across her right cheek bone and eye socket. She quickly turned away again.

"Were you assaulted?" Wednesday said, stepping into the room.

"It was my fault. I'd been warned he was displaying florid paranoid tendencies today. I shouldn't have come in alone," Sara replied.

"She's not pressing charges," Harvey butted in. "It's part and parcel of being a psychiatric nurse. She has to learn."

Wednesday held her breath for a moment before heading for her mother's room. Lennox followed behind, quietly. They found Joan listening to the radio, seemingly lost in her world.

"Hello Mum."

Joan turned, straightening her back and smoothing down her skirt. "You've brought your boyfriend, that's nice dear."

Wednesday opened her mouth to speak but Lennox put his hand on her arm.

"Nice to see you, Joan. How are you feeling today?" He perched on the chair next to her.

"Better for seeing you." She looked across at her daughter. "I hope you're treating him right."

Wednesday rolled her eyes. "There's been a lot of commotion on here, hasn't there?"

"Sounded like a fight in the corridor; lots of running about. Will they come after me too?"

"Who exactly?"

"It was a man's voice. Has he killed again?"

"No one's died, Mum. Which man?"

"Not sure, all the men sound the same, apart from Oliver. Where is he?"

"I'm sure he'll be here later."

"These drugs make me so forgetful. Are you ashamed of me?" Her head dropped forward, as though waiting for the axe to fall.

"Of course not." Wednesday smiled, patting her hand. "Now tell me what you heard?"

Joan shook her head. "I kept dropping off to sleep. I was woken by the shouting."

"What was being said? Please try and remember."

Joan just shook her head.

"Did you call the police station to let us know?" Wednesday whispered in her ear.

"No, dear. Should I have?"

"Not to worry. Has the doctor been in to see you today?"

"No, but I'm here now," Harvey said, tapping on the door at the same time. "Just come to check on you, Mrs Willow." He moved closer to the bed, making Wednesday's skin crawl.

"My daughter's a detective, Doctor. She'll find the bad person who's causing you trouble."

"I don't doubt she will," he replied, looking at Wednesday from under his arched eyebrows. "Let's hope they don't strike again before she does."

Chapter 35

"You don't like Harvey Manning much, do you?" Lennox asked, dragon-like smoke trailing from his mouth.

"He's a bully-boy misogynist. There's not much to like about him." Wednesday coughed on the smoke scratching her throat.

"He certainly doesn't like women with power."

"I wonder whether he'd have taken the murder more seriously had the victim been a male patient."

Lennox blew smoke rings into the air; something he had been perfecting in the privacy of his own home. "Have you seen Scarlett lately?"

"No, why?" She peered at him through the pall of smoke.

"She called 'round last night, looking for a shoulder to cry on."

"What about?"

"She'd been on a first date with a woman she met at an art gallery. They were having a meal in an up-market restaurant when Scarlett mentioned she was bi-sexual. The woman was deeply offended—clearly a man-hater by the sound of it—and after an altercation she stormed out of the place, leaving Scarlett to pay for the bill and get a taxi home . . . Well to my place."

"Oh God, you didn't—"

"No, I made her a cup of tea then drove her home." He took a last drag before crushing the tab end underfoot. "I get the feeling she wants to move back in with you."

Wednesday put her tab end in the ashtray. "I'm not sure how I feel about that. Did she ask you to mention it?"

"No, that's totally my doing. I just thought I'd give you a heads up."

Howard Blower finished his shift at the fire station and made his way to a nearby pub, where he was royally greeted by Kelly, the barmaid.

"How was work, honey?" she asked, pulling him a pint of Guinness.

"Took the engine to a primary school and let the kids sit in it."

"Bet they loved that," she smiled.

He took his drink and swallowed a couple of large mouthfuls. "I'm off to see Rene to see if I can get her to sign the divorce papers."

She looked at him, trying to study the thoughts behind his hazel eyes. "How do you think she'll react?"

"Not well, undoubtedly. But this has to happen; I have to be rid of her one way or another."

"Knowing you, I'm sure you'll have a few plans in mind."

He smiled. "Perhaps this so-called angel of death will do me a favour and take her out of the equation."

"What would you do with your new-found freedom?"

"Show you a good time, for starters, if you fancied."

She leant over the bar, pushing her breasts together. "I thought you'd never ask," she smiled, offering him a wink before serving another customer.

"I've thought of nothing else, of late," he muttered under his breath, downing his drink before heading off to the unit to persuade Rene to finally set him free.

Chapter 36

Rene pushed her plate of untouched food away and picked up the plastic beaker of water. She took bird sips of the liquid, watching her fellow diners over the rim of the beaker.

A few people were talking about the evening's television schedule, whilst other people sat in dreary silence, much as she was doing.

"Not enjoying your meal?" Angela Rhodes asked.

Rene shook her head; words stuck in her throat like a large boiled sweet.

"You really should try and eat more. You need to aid your recovery so you can get back to your gorgeous husband."

"Do you fancy him, then?" she whispered.

"That's not what I meant. I just thought you'd be desperate to get back to him, a big hunky fireman like that."

"He *is* gorgeous. And he's all mine. I'm a very lucky woman." A brief flicker of happiness flashed across her face before the dark shadow of jealousy engulfed it.

She watched the nurse move to another table to dispense pleasantries and throw saccharine blankets around needy shoulders. She wondered whether the sentiments were genuine or bolstered by the fact that she received a wage at the end of the month.

A change in the nurse's demeanour piqued Rene's curiosity. Following her gaze she saw Howard leaning against the door frame. He was dressed in a fitted t-shirt, which accentuated every nuance of his strapping figure.

She caught her breath as she watched his eyes panning the room, finally resting on her. All she saw was revulsion in his otherwise dead eyes. Her head began spinning out of control.

"Can we go and talk in your room?" he asked, approaching her.

She held out her frail arm, desperate to be protected by his strength, but he simply pulled her to her feet before letting go. There was, after all, no fire.

"How are you feeling?" he asked flatly.

"Better now that you're here. I really need a hug."

"I bet one of the other patients in here would oblige."

"What do you mean?"

"I'm sick of pretending, of feeling like I have to play the dutiful husband."

Rene perched on the edge of her bed hoping he would sit next to her. "I'm confused."

"I don't believe you are. It's simple, I married a vivacious blonde who couldn't get enough sex. Remember when we did it on the sofa at that party? You were wild."

"I still can be."

"No, that person left years ago, and truth be told, I should have too."

She stiffened, gripping a pillow in her hands. "But you stayed because you loved me."

"I was fooling myself and everyone around us. I felt compelled to stay, to ensure your recovery out of duty. Now I know I have no effect on that."

"But without you, life would be . . . I won't survive."

"I don't really care whether you do or not. You're already dead to me." He pulled out the envelope from his inside coat pocket, retrieving the papers from within. "Sign these and you'll finally make me happy."

Rene struggled to read the papers; the words danced around like snakes writhing in a pit. As the words halted in certain places she managed to read *divorce*.

"Is this what you really want?"

"Absolutely."

"What if I refuse?"

"I'll be free of you, one way or another."

"How did you get Hunter to approve this stakeout?" Lennox asked, opening a packet of crisps.

"We're running short of options. This is a new angle he can tell his boss about."

"You really expect us to get a new lead from this?"

"I don't rightly know, but I feel better giving it a go."

They waited for their eyes to adjust to the gloom that had descended; the air scented with cheese and onion crisps and mints. Wednesday battled with somnolent waves, when suddenly something caught her eye. She nudged Lennox, indicating towards the trees by the unit. Someone was moving around in the shadows. Lennox threw the packet in the footwell before picking up the night-vision camera.

"Who is it?" Wednesday hissed.

"Can't see, they've covered their head."

"Keep your eyes on them, they may slip up."

A couple of seconds later, Lennox groaned. "They're inside, what do you want us to do?"

"Go inside and see who shouldn't be there. Let's go."

They closed the car doors quietly, before sprinting to the unit. Wednesday pressed the buzzer tapping her foot rapidly. When a voice finally responded through the intercom Wednesday demanded immediate access.

Pushing their way through the door, they marched straight up to the nurses' station to find the startled student nurse, Sara Morris. Fading marks still visible around her eye socket.

"Who are you on duty with?" Wednesday asked, pulling the rota sheet towards her.

"Er . . . Josh and Doris," she stammered.

"Where are they?"

"In Rene Blower's room. She's been upset all evening."

Lennox hurried to the room and peered in. He raised his thumb to Wednesday to confirm the fact.

"We saw someone creeping onto the unit," Wednesday whispered to Sara.

She drew a sharp intake of breath as Lennox reappeared at the nurses' station.

"I need you to put all the lights on," instructed Wednesday. "Erase the shadows."

Sara flicked on the corridor lights, then, accompanied by Lennox, she entered each bedroom and did the same. Most patients remained asleep thanks to their medication.

Wednesday entered the TV and family lounges. Nothing was out of place.

They all converged at the nurses' station, including a perplexed Joshua and Doris. Wednesday filled them in and suggested they watch the corridors to make sure no one entered the bedrooms. She and Lennox would check out the other rooms.

"Let's check the laundry room first," she commanded.

Lennox opened the door quietly before flicking on the light. Only the humming noise of the tumble dryer broke the silence. Nothing looked disturbed.

They proceeded along the corridor, entering the staff kitchen to find it also empty and undisturbed.

Voices emanated from several bedrooms as some patients were finally disturbed by people creeping around their rooms. Wednesday and Lennox gravitated towards the voices, and found Joan Willow to be one of them.

"Are you all right, Mum?" Wednesday asked, forgetting her role for a minute.

"I'm tired."

"Detectives, I found something strange in Rene Blower's room," Joshua said from the doorway.

Wednesday squeezed Joan's hand before following him.

"I was about to give her a drink of water from the jug by her bed, when I smelt this." He held the cup under Wednesday's nose.

"Bleach."

"Thank God it was strong enough for me to smell it. Imagine if she'd poured it herself whilst semi asleep."

"Indeed," replied Wednesday. "It's probably a long shot but I'd like to take the jug back to the forensic lab, see what prints they can find."

Joshua nodded solemnly.

"Who visited her today?" Lennox asked.

"Just her husband. He didn't stay for long though."

"I'll also need to see the staff rota. Who filled the jugs?"

"The healthcare assistant, Doris Smith. She wouldn't do anything like this."

"All the same, I'd like you to check all the water jugs, and I'd like to see Doris in Eric Knight's office now please."

They were perplexed as to how someone entered the unit, with no forced entry visible. Yet another missing piece of the puzzle.

Chapter 37

Doris Smith tapped feebly on the open office door. Deep ridges on her face dragged down towards her turkey-like neck, as she hovered in the doorway, wringing her hands rapidly.

"You wanted to see me."

"Come in, sit down. I'd like you to tell me the routine for filling the patients' water jugs," Wednesday requested.

"I collect all the jugs on the trolley, wheel them to the kitchen, fill them up and distribute them to each patient."

"Are the jugs numbered or named?"

"No, I give them out randomly. It's only water after all."

"Where's the bleach kept on the unit?"

"Locked up in the cleaner's cupboard. The key hangs in the kitchen, so anyone could take it. Why would I want to do this awful thing?" her shrill voice pierced the air.

"We're not accusing you, just gathering facts."

Joshua knocked on the door. "All the other jugs seem fine."

"Good. I've requested uniform to patrol the perimeter, and an officer to place themselves on the unit. We'll get back to the station," she said. "We'll need your fingerprints for elimination purposes," she told Doris, who looked ready to burst into tears.

They left the unit and walked to the car.

"We definitely saw someone. How could they get onto the ward, put bleach into the jug, and disappear before we could catch them?" Wednesday said, bemused.

"Someone who knows their way around, I guess."

"Well as soon as the day lifts we'll visit Howard Blower and see what he has to say for himself."

Howard Blower rubbed sleep from his bleary eyes as he opened his front door.

"What's happened?" he asked.

"We'd like to ask you about your visit to the unit last evening," replied Wednesday.

"What on earth for?" He woke up at the question. "I went to see Rene, like I sometimes do when not on duty."

"It wasn't a normal visit according to witnesses."

"Meaning?"

"Apparently the interaction between you both was tense, and Rene's been quite upset."

"You'd better come in," he said, waving them through.

The lounge looked un-lived in, like a Victorian parlour.

"I don't know what business it is of yours how my visit went, but if you must know, I took divorce papers for her to sign, but she refused."

"So what do you plan to do now?" Wednesday pressed.

"There's some law stating if you don't live together for two years you can just get divorced, even if the other party disagrees."

"So you're moving out then."

"Not bloody likely. I pay for this house. Rene can move in with her parents. She doesn't cope well alone."

"Or perhaps a simpler option is to get rid of her, then all your worries are over."

He frowned, deepening the lines between his thick eyebrows.

"A large amount of bleach was found in your wife's water jug in the early hours of the morning. Where were you at that time?"

"My shift finished at six then I came straight home." He walked over to the window and looked up at the brightening sky.

"You haven't asked if she's okay."

"You'd have told me straight away if she'd been hurt, rather than quiz me about my visit."

"Fortunately, a nurse smelt the bleach before she had the chance to drink it."

"Thank goodness. I don't love the woman, but that would have been nasty. I wouldn't wish that on her."

"That may be, but someone obviously does. What about family feuds or a spurned lover?"

His head rocked back with laughter. "She's incapable of finding someone else to love her. I often wished she would find some poor sod to take my place."

"I meant a lover spurned *by you*."

Composing himself, he crossed his arms, and clamped his lips together.

"We'll obviously check your rota, and you'll need to come to the station to have your fingerprints taken. In the meantime, if you think of anything else, give us a call."

Walking away, Wednesday wondered if the bleach issue was the same perpetrator, or a completely different person. They needed to find a common denominator between the women, beyond the unit.

Slamming down the receiver, Harvey Manning paced around his study before wrenching the door open.

"Olivia. Olivia where are you?" he bellowed.

She was in the kitchen making a cake. She quickly wiped her floury hands on her apron and sprinted to the hallway.

"Whatever's the matter?"

"There's been another bloody incident on the unit."

He blurted out the story Lennox had just told him on the phone.

"I'm worried about you," she exclaimed. "What if someone tries to harm you? I couldn't bare the idea of being without you."

"Don't be ridiculous; no one's going to harm me. The patients are the targets."

"All the same, can't you ask the police to protect you?"

"They don't have the man-power to do that."

She leant against the wall. "Can you think of anyone who doesn't want the unit to succeed?"

"I can't think of anyone. This is not a personal attack on me or the unit. This has something to do with those women."

Olivia closed her eyes, willing the tears to be reabsorbed.

"Don't be silly," he said, "I'll be fine. I'd worry more if I had a family member on the unit. I bet that detective's anxious."

"I forgot you told me her mother's a patient."

"Well, I'm not going to let someone ruin my unit's reputation. I'll go there now and make sure everything's running smoothly," he said, putting on his cashmere jacket.

"Do you have to go? I'd feel more relaxed if you worked from home today."

"My unit needs protecting. I'll see you later, don't bother about dinner."

She watched helplessly as he left the house. Returning to the kitchen, she threw the cake mixture into the bin.

Harvey arrived at the unit in time for staff change-over, where he caught sight of Angela Rhodes. As if sensing his regard, she looked up but he offered no smile in response to hers.

Watching him enter his office, she wondered what she had done wrong.

Flicking through his address book, he found what he wanted, then left the unit without saying a word.

Chapter 38

Eric Knight opened his front door to find Harvey standing there.

"Let me in, you fool," he snapped, towering above Eric.

Eric pressed himself against the wall to let him pass. The smell of baking caressed the air; Harvey followed the smell to the kitchen.

"I'm astounded at you," he mocked.

"Your unit wouldn't survive without me, so I suggest you stop ridiculing me."

The smile briefly left Harvey's lips, before a grimace replaced it and his hand shot out, grabbing Eric by the throat.

"Don't threaten me you snivelling little rat. I could crush you with a bad report, and have you struck off."

Eric's eyes bulged from their sockets, tears glazing his vision temporarily. Harvey unclenched his grip before throwing him against the wall.

"What the fuck do you think you're doing?" Eric spat.

"I'll tell you what's pissed me off shall I? The unit's my prize possession, my path to excellence, and the murder risks spoiling everything. I've not received a new referral since." He paused. "I thought things would blow over when the police solved the crime. But not only are they taking their own sweet time, this bleach incident seems to point to someone targeting the unit."

"And I'm to blame for this?"

"I put you in charge of the unit. You were meant to keep things running smoothly, but you've failed miserably."

"I've not committed these crimes and I don't know who has."

Slamming the palm of his hand against Eric's shoulder, Harvey leant into his face. "That's not good enough. You step up to the mark, or I'll find someone else who will."

"You forget I'm currently suspended. And for the record, who the hell could you trust to take my place?"

Harvey rubbed the top of his head, breathing out hard down his nose.

"All right, I'll make a case to the NHS investigating team about you returning to the unit. In the meantime, keep an eye on things as best you can."

Eric grinned sourly as he left.

"The Raven Unit is the common denominator in these crimes, but I can't make out why," Wednesday uttered, massaging her temples.

"Would that place the esteemed psychiatrist at the top of our suspect list?" replied Lennox.

"He'd have more to lose than gain by doing that, but I'd sure like to press his buttons to see what he'd say."

"Let's call him in to the station for an interview."

"Under what guise? We've no evidence pointing in his direction to warrant such a move."

"The unit being central to our case should be enough."

She looked towards Hunter's office. "Okay, but let's call in on him at the unit instead."

"I'd like to drive, I need to think," Lennox stated before grabbing his jacket from his office.

They arrived at the unit to find Harvey in his office with officials from the NHS investigation team. Karen Reilly said they had been in there for over forty minutes.

"We'll wait," Wednesday said, unbuttoning her jacket.

Karen shrugged, turning to answer the phone.

"Why don't you pop in and see Joan?" Lennox suggested.

"I'd rather not, I want to stay focused on the case."

Lennox opened his mouth to speak but thought better of it.

After another twenty minutes, Wednesday contemplated returning, when the office door opened and two navy-suited men strode into the corridor. Both carried bulging briefcases, avoiding all eye contact.

The detectives walked up to the open door and knocked. Harvey looked up and grimaced.

"Solved the crimes?" he sneered.

"We'd like to learn more about the concept of this unit, Doctor

Manning," Wednesday replied, stepping into the room.

"I don't see what that has to do with the murder."

"And the bleach incident. The common denominator is this unit."

He sat back in his chair and indicated for them to sit.

"I'd always had an interest in severe and enduring mental illness. My dream was to have a small unit with a high staff-to-patient ratio, where I could really study the effects of mental illness on individuals."

"Doesn't that exist already?" Wednesday queried.

"I thought you'd know the answer to that question."

Wednesday clenched her fists in her lap, arching an eyebrow.

"Anyway, I secured backing from a drug company before approaching the local health authority, and this is the baby of my creation." A wide grin brushed across his face.

"So this is primarily a research unit?" Wednesday questioned.

"I see it as going hand-in-hand with the care of the patients. Mental illness cannot be cured but can be managed to minimise the demolition of a person's life, and that of their family."

"So that's your philosophy. How long do you have this place?"

He frowned.

"Your wife told us you have two years to make it work, otherwise you lose your funding."

"If you knew, why bother to ask?"

"I was checking that your wife's correct."

"Has this helped with your investigation?"

"Are you sure you can't think of any disgruntled patients or family members?"

"Absolutely not. This has more to do with the women involved rather than me or the unit."

"We have to look at all possible angles, especially when we have very little to go on."

"In my experience, mental illness can desecrate a marriage; even the strongest ones. Therefore, I'd scrutinise the relationships of the women involved."

"Thanks for the insightful suggestion," Lennox said sarcastically.

Wednesday stood up. "We won't take up more of your time." She smiled briefly.

Leaving the office, she glanced in the direction of the communal rooms.

"Want to say hello now?" he asked.

"I'll just pop my head around the door, check if she's okay. Come with me."

The TV room was empty so they moved to the family room, where they found Fiona Campbell and her husband, Jordan, whispering in one corner of the room. Melvyn Rollins was sitting by the window, rocking slowly and wringing his hands.

"Looking for your mother?" Sara Morris asked, walking up behind them.

"Yes, where is she?"

"She's strolling in the garden with her husband."

Wednesday's shoulders relaxed. "I won't disturb them."

The locksmith handed Howard Blower a set of new keys and took the cash in return, before returning to his van. Stepping inside, Howard locked the door before pouring a drink and toasting the air.

Chapter 39

"Any fingerprints on the water jug?" Wednesday asked Alex Green.

"Only of the nurse, Joshua Plough, and healthcare assistant, Doris Smith. But they're to be expected. The perpetrator may have worn gloves, or not touched it at all. Sorry."

"Don't apologise, I wasn't expecting a breakthrough."

"Glad to note my services are appreciated."

Rolling her eyes, she left the lab, feeling like she had just had a lover's tiff.

In the Incident Room, Lennox was stroking his goatee whilst looking at the photo of Susan Roche on the white board.

"Any thoughts?" Wednesday asked, walking up behind him.

"Susan is what, seven years older than her husband? She's no great beauty and he's not bad looking. I wonder what drew them together."

"Love doesn't rely on looks alone. Perhaps she hooked him with her personality."

"Really?

"Women with mental illness can still be alluring, fun, and sexy."

"I can't see that . . . oh sorry . . ."

"Just remembered my mother? The stigma attached to mental illness pervades society, please don't contribute to its ongoing strength."

Lennox nodded. "I can be an insensitive bastard at times."

"Moving on, what are your thoughts about Susan and Barry Roche?"

"We know he was having an affair, and his marriage to Susan was in tatters. I'm still convinced he had a hand in her murder, with maybe his son."

"Gavin?"

"He was embarrassed about Susan's condition. Perhaps he wanted rid of her."

"He didn't live with her anymore."

"He was promised a car, and God knows what else."

"Go on."

"Their fingerprints on the scene wouldn't cause alarm."

"But what about the bleach incident? Where does that fit in?"

"Gavin's not stupid, maybe he wants us to think there's a serial killer targeting the unit."

"Sounds plausible."

"Exactly. Shall we have an informal chat with him?"

"Let's go with your lead, Lennox. He may feel ready to talk."

Gavin's dove-grey eyes clouded over on opening the door to the detectives.

"I don't suppose you've found Mum's killer."

"We'd like to have a word with you actually. Is your father home?" asked Lennox.

"Nope, does he need to be?"

"Not at all. Can we come in?"

"I'd rather you didn't, but I don't think I have a choice in the matter, do I?"

The dog lay apathetically in front of the gas fire until he saw Wednesday. He padded up to her and pushed against her leg.

"How have you been feeling lately?" she asked, bending down to stroke Gus.

"Fine why?"

"A death in a family has repercussions we sometimes don't expect. We sometimes see changes in other people."

"Like what, for example?"

"Perhaps you've noticed a positive change in your father since the death of your mother. Perhaps you didn't realise how unhappy he was, or perhaps you already knew."

"I see what you're implying. You suspect my father or me of killing her to have a better life."

"People have murdered for less."

"My life's been all right."

"I'm pleased to hear it. Does the same go for your father?"

"Are you asking whether I suspect he did it? He hasn't got the guts."

"So you've considered that scenario?"

"He would have done it years ago if he'd had the gall. I mean, she blighted most of his life. He loved her, but the woman he married had gone."

"How do you know this, exactly?"

"When she was in hospital, he'd sometimes drink too much and blurt stuff out."

"Perhaps you wanted to help your old man," interjected Lennox.

"Not fucking likely; I don't love him that much. I wouldn't waste my life in prison to free him from his."

Gavin's increased animation disturbed Gus. Stretching his legs, he sauntered over to him to rest his head on his knee.

"What was your relationship like with your mother?" Lennox asked.

"Average when she was sane, and virtually non-existent when she was barmy." He half-smiled at Lennox whilst stroking the dog's velvety ears.

"So you don't blame the unit for her death?"

"I don't know who to blame, as it happens. And clearly you police don't know either."

Wednesday curled her toes in her shoes, looking briefly at Lennox to check his face for signs of lacking in patience. His tolerance for young people was at an all-time low.

"Thank you for your time, Gavin, we'll see ourselves out," Wednesday said, signalling to Lennox with a nod of her head.

"What is it about young people that makes them think they're wiser than anyone else?" he grumbled, as they left.

"Youth and a sense of invincibility."

"Well it hacks me off."

Back at the station, there were rumblings around the Incident Room about Hunter's dire mood. Through his office window, he was seen pacing around, talking frantically on his mobile.

"You'd think he'd pull the blinds down so we couldn't see him," Maria Jones whispered to Wednesday as she arrived.

"Perhaps it's to do with the case."

"I doubt it, it's his personal mobile. More to do with his marriage I would guess."

Wednesday pressed her nails into the palms of her hands. "Perhaps we should all focus on the case, and less on Hunter's life," she said firmly.

"DI Wednesday, may I see you in my office," he called from his office doorway; frown lines zigzagging across his forehead.

Wednesday spun around, and with a quickening heart, walked towards him.

"Yes Guv."

"Close the door and take a seat," he instructed.

He sat down opposite her, clasping his hands in a prayer-like position on his desk. "How do you cope with having a fraught personal life and the demands of the job?"

Wednesday shifted uncomfortably in the chair. "I let my personal life look after itself when I'm at work. Then when I'm home, I try not to let work seep into my mind."

"Sounds easy enough."

"Not always." She allowed a smile to fleetingly grace her lips. "It's good to have someone to talk to, who won't judge you or betray your confidence. Keeping things bottled up can do a lot of damage."

"Not that easy to find, in my position." He inhaled deeply before letting a stream of air blast through his flaring nostrils. "I'll try and find someone like you clearly have." He held his breath for a few seconds before giving her a valedictory wave.

Reaching the door, she turned around. "You might want to pull your blinds down when the personal stuff can't wait."

She walked back to her office and closed her door, thinking about what had just happened. Was he reaching out to her as a confidant? What would she do if he started flirting with her out of a desperate need to feel loved again? Memories of a road once travelled pricked her mind.

Chapter 40

"Let's hope you don't have nightmares again tonight, Mrs Willows," Karen Reilly said as she brought Joan her medication. "You look tired," she continued, bending down to pick up Joan's legs to swing them onto the bed.

"Now, I'll get you some hot milk and a brownie to help you sleep."

Joan watched her disappear into the gloomy corridor, afraid but unsure why. She wanted to go home.

In the morning, all the patients sat in the TV lounge half-watching the news.

Joan leant in towards Fiona Campbell and whispered in her ear. "I saw people in masks again, last night. Did you see anything strange?"

Fiona pulled away. "Stop trying to put thoughts in my head. I won't have it."

Her response shocked Joan, leaving her feeling vulnerable and alone.

"What's eating her?" Melvyn Rollins asked, cocking his head in Fiona's direction and rubbing his hands together.

Turning to him, Joan repeated what she saw last night.

"I saw monsters," he whispered, his top lip quivering. "I know it must be my mind playing tricks, but they're so frightening."

"They must be real if we're both seeing them. Should we tell the staff?"

"No, it could be them playing silly buggers with us, you know, to alleviate their boredom and laugh at us. You should tell your daughter, she'll sort it out won't she?"

"She won't solve a fucking thing," piped up Dave Hyde who had appeared asleep next to Melvyn. "Women detectives are like non-alcoholic beer; shite."

Joan was about to retort when Melvyn put a shaky hand on her arm; fear burning in his gaze. She closed her eyes and prayed for a speedy return home.

"I don't know what you are on about, but I've got more troubles than you lot put together," Rene announced.

"What makes you think that? We're all fucking loony in here, you mad bitch." Dave sat up, eyeing everyone in the room, daring them to speak.

"I was talking about my husband wanting a divorce, actually."

Dave laughed in a staccato fashion. "That's not fucking surprising, just look at yourself. I bet having sex with you is like bouncing on top of a jelly fish. Squish, squish." He roared with laughter whilst the rest of the room averted their eyes, staring at the floor or out the window.

Rene puffed out her crimson cheeks. "What would you know? I bet you only get any if you pay for it." She slapped her hand across her mouth as soon as the last word spilled out.

Dave rose to his feet, trembling with rage, staggering towards her like a wind-up toy. He was within striking distance of her, when Eric appeared in the doorway.

"What's this racket? Is this how you behave in my absence?"

Dave froze, his arm hanging mid-air.

"Do some of you need extra medication?"

"You're back," exclaimed Melvyn, rubbing his hands together.

"Indeed I am, much to your nervous delight I see," he laughed. "As it was murder and not suicide, I'm not culpable, so they had to let me back." His smile looked like a grease slick on water. "So I expect order to be restored to the unit. Sit down, Hyde, and stop throwing your weight around."

Dave slunk back to his seat, but not before throwing Rene a steely glance. She puffed out her chest, secure in the knowledge that Eric was scarier than a dozen Daves.

Wednesday sat at her desk mulling over the scraps of paper cast about. Her eyes were continually drawn to the one on which Joan's name was scrawled. It was obvious to her that Joan was innocent, but for the sake of impartiality she had to include her, so why was her eye drawn to her?

She could not deny she feared for her safety, yet Joan's own doctor said it was the best possible place for her, and said a move could be detrimental to her mental stability. And a move to where? Her hands were tied.

A tap at her door drew her eyes to Edmond Carter. She beckoned him in with a smile.

"How's the case going?" he asked.

"Numerous suspects with the added complication of mental illness being the trigger factor," she sighed.

"Your expertise in the field will stop you getting carried away. Trust yourself."

She shrugged. "It's just everyone thinks I should get to the bottom of this quickly, and as each day goes by, I'm sure I'm disappointing Hunter."

"You've a good track-record, stop beating yourself up."

"I'm sure you didn't come up here to give me a pep-talk. What can I do for you?"

"A test result has just come back. A chemical analysis shows evidence of Tetrahydrocannabinol in Susan Roche's body."

"That's found in cannabis, right?"

"Indeed, THC. Due to her being not so young, the drug stayed in her system longer."

"There was no mention of her being a user. I wonder whether it was a one-off or an ongoing habit?"

"I've just sent off a strand of her hair for drug analysis, which will tell us more. But it may add another dimension to the case."

"In what way?"

"Did her dealer visit the ward demanding the money she owes him? She couldn't pay so he killed her."

"Nice theory, but all that does is add another person to the equation. At least the other suspects are already known, but a dealer?"

Lennox's head appeared over Edmond's, catching the tail-end of the conversation.

"I'm sure I don't need to give you much of a rundown on cannabis," Edmond said as Lennox moved to stand next to him. "Suffice to say, there are more potent strengths of the stuff around compare to the weed in our day."

"Skunk," interjected Lennox.

"That has a higher strength of THC, so exacerbates the hallucinogenic effect. It can produce elation, uncontrollable laughter, nervousness, anxiety, and mild paranoia. Not something for someone on antipsychotics to be dabbling with."

"Those are also symptoms of mental illness. How would we differentiate between the two?" she queried.

"An experienced psychiatrist most likely could."

"Perhaps we should discuss this with the eminent Harvey Manning," scoffed Lennox.

"I'd like to keep our findings under wraps for now. I already have misgivings about the man."

"What you two do with this info is up to you," Edmond stated before walking away.

"Perhaps we could visit Joan and see if she's seen or smelt any drug evidence," Lennox suggested, pulling his car keys from his pocket.

"Discreetly remember, I don't want any potential repercussions for her."

"Understood, Boss."

Chapter 41

"I didn't have a nightmare last night," Joan announced casually.

"That's great. How are you feeling?" Wednesday asked.

"I'm fine, so much so, Doctor Manning's told me I'll be going home soon."

"Really?"

"He says I've improved dramatically."

Wednesday eyed Lennox.

"So you feel brighter and less hopeless about the future?" she queried.

"I suppose I do. He tells me I'll feel much better at home with Oliver. He says you'll also feel more relaxed with me at home rather than here, which is too close to your case."

"Did he now? What else did he say?"

"That you've got it wrong about the killer being on the unit. He firmly believes it was someone in Susan's life who did it."

"Interesting," Wednesday muttered. "Have you ever seen someone smoking a joint on the ward or in the garden?" she whispered.

"Not that I'd noticed. Most people smoke roll-ups anyway."

"It does have a distinctive smell."

"I know what cannabis smells like, but I can't say I've noticed it. But it wouldn't be a surprise if someone was; no one here has a totally happy life."

"No one anywhere does," Wednesday said bitterly.

"Stop blaming me for your failings. You're doing a good enough job all by yourself."

Wednesday inhaled deeply, but was cut short by Lennox's voice.

"Has anyone ever offered you illegal drugs in here?" he asked.

"That would be stupid seeing as everyone knows Eva's my daughter."

"Fair point."

"Ah, just the person I wanted to see," Harvey Manning said from the doorway.

Wednesday turned around, feeling the hairs on the back of her neck ripple. "What's the problem?"

"No problem, just the opposite. I want to book a discharge planning meeting for your mother, she's ready to go home."

"So she tells me."

"She'll complete her progress there; home is the best place for her now. I'll see her as an outpatient. I'll get my secretary to send you the date." And with that he walked away.

Wednesday gave Lennox a wry smile and inclined her head towards the door.

"Got to go. I'll see you very soon," she said, bending down to kiss Joan on top of her head.

"And you look after my daughter," Joan demanded of Lennox.

He smiled, patting the back of her hand before following Wednesday, who was shaking her head slowly, out the door.

Entering the unit, Sam walked straight to his brother's bedroom.

"I can't believe you're still in bed, Eddie. Get up and come for a walk in the garden, I want a smoke."

Eddie turned slowly towards his brother, easing his eyelids open. "I don't want to. Smoke in here."

"You know that's not allowed. What's up with you?"

"I think it has something to do with my mental illness," he replied sourly.

Sam rolled his eyes. "If you're not in the mood to see me, I might as well go home."

Eddie rolled over, pulling the sheet over his head.

"When are we going to challenge Manning about the dope in Susan Roche's system?" Lennox asked Wednesday as they made a coffee.

"He'll most likely say it has nothing to do with his precious unit, which of course, it may not. She could have had a family member bring it in for all we know. Let's go and talk to her husband."

Barry Roche was coming out of his building as Wednesday and Lennox pulled up. Pretending not to see them, he hurried towards his van, his keys at the ready.

"Mr Roche," Lennox called out. "We need a word." He drew level with him at the van. "You're in a hurry."

"I'm going to do a quote for a job. I can't afford to miss it."

"This won't take long; we just want to know whether Susan took any illegal drugs?"

He let out a guttural laugh. "You have to be kidding. Susan was straight-laced, there's no way she'd touch that stuff."

"What about your son?" chipped in Wednesday. "Perhaps he's partial, and thought his mother would benefit."

"I don't like what you're saying. My son may be a student, but he's no druggie."

"We're not trying to upset you, but trace elements of cannabis were found in your wife's system. We're trying to ascertain whether she was a long-term user."

"You've done nothing but smear me and my family since she was killed. Unless you've come to arrest me, I'll be off."

"That went well," said Lennox as they watched the van roar off.

"Nurse Plough, come and see me now," barked Eric Knight.

Joshua licked his parched lips on entering the office.

"I can smell alcohol on your breath. What the fuck is going on?" demanded Eric.

"It's the stuff going on here, it's getting to me."

"The NHS have exonerated us; she was murdered. What have you got to worry about?"

"There's a rumour going around saying the unit's going to be closed following the bad publicity. And we'll be blacklisted so no one will employ us."

"What utter crap. The unit's functioning well. Our beds are full and I bet there's a waiting list building up for the next available bed."

"So why has no one taken Susan Roche's bed?"

"Because Doctor Manning wants us to wait out of courtesy to the family. Now you'd better clean up your act before someone else notices. I should report you, but we've had enough of that. Get a strong coffee." He dismissed him with a wave of his hand, like ridding his fingers of a clinging, soiled tissue.

Chapter 42

Harvey Manning was still in a meeting when Olivia arrived at the unit. Undeterred, she entered the kitchen to make a large pot of hot sweet tea, to dole out with her sympathetic prose.

"Hell, sorry, I didn't see you arrive," Joshua gasped, entering the kitchen, empty coffee mug in hand.

"I thought I'd offer the patients a listening ear to unburden them of the worries caused by recent events."

"Good idea," he replied, loading his mug with coffee granules and sugar. "Um . . . Has Doctor Manning mentioned anything about the unit risking being closed?" The colour of his cheeks betrayed his emotions.

Olivia stopped stirring the tea. "No, why, has someone told you that?"

"Just rumours. It's just that I love it here, and well, I wouldn't want anything to happen to spoil it."

"I'm sure you've nothing to fear. Harvey would fight tooth and nail to keep this place going. He would have told me if something like that was in the offing."

His shoulders relaxed. He took a large mouthful of coffee, burning his tongue in the process. "Okay, thanks," he mumbled before hurrying out.

Most of the patients were sitting in the TV lounge, watching a nature programme. Olivia wandered around to each of them, handing them a cup of tea regardless of whether they wanted one. She stopped at Joan Willow and took the seat next to her.

"How's your daughter getting on with the case," she asked quietly so as not to disturb the others.

Joan looked at her and frowned. "Do I know you?"

"We've met before. I'm Olivia, Doctor Manning's wife."

Joan stared at her face more closely. "Oh yes, I remember you. I don't really know, Eva doesn't discuss work with me."

"I'm worried about my husband, you see. I'm worried he could be in danger, or the stress of it all will make him ill. I so want this to be over."

"Don't worry," Joan said, putting her hand on Olivia's. "My daughter's wonderful; she always gets them in the end."

Olivia smiled feebly before moving next to Melvyn Rollins.

"How are you feeling today?" she asked.

"As well as can be expected when one lies awake at night, terrified the angel of death is coming for them."

"You're not still afraid of that old story. You have staff watching over you day and night; no harm will come to you."

"Try telling that to Susan."

"I still think that had something to do with her husband," she whispered.

That aroused his attention. "I'd heard rumours, but just took them to be the babblings of the mad."

She leant in closer. "She often talked to me of his compassion fatigue, short temper, and his wandering eye."

"Did she? But why would he kill her?" he whispered back, leaving his cup of tea untouched on the table next to him.

"I don't know, perhaps he just wanted her out of his life because she was ill."

"So why haven't the police arrested him?"

"Perhaps they need more evidence, or they're waiting for him to make a wrong move."

"If you're right, then I've nothing to fear." He sat back in his chair and sighed, before launching his torso forward again. "But what about the bleach in the jug? Why would he do that?"

"I can't understand that, but I bet it was just an accident."

Melvyn visibly relaxed once more, soaking up her words like a proverbial sponge. He closed his eyes for a moment, relishing the emotion. When he opened them, she had moved on to someone else.

Arriving ten minutes early for the discharge planning meeting, Wednesday took the opportunity to smoke a cigarette in the car. As expected, Scarlett had found some lame excuse not to attend, so Wednesday let her frustrations seep out of the open car window along with the smoke.

She watched Harvey arrive in his ostentatious sports car, pulling up at speed outside the unit. She took one last, deep drag on her cigarette before jettisoning the butt.

Joan was sitting in the family lounge along with Oliver. They both smiled as she entered.

"Everyone here? Good, follow me," Eric Knight ordered.

Joan poked her tongue out at him behind his back, making Wednesday smile.

The office was infused with Harvey's aromatic aftershave. He nodded courteously as they all took a seat.

"I'm very pleased with Joan's progress. Her paranoia has subsided, as have her depressive lows. I'll continue seeing her as an outpatient, to monitor things. How does everyone feel about that?"

A loaded silence dominated the room, until Wednesday spoke.

"It's always a time of high anxiety when Mum comes home. We're on high alert in case she stops taking her meds again."

"I'm afraid our service is rather like a revolving door. We do our best to prolong the time people spend in their own homes, but the pressures of life sometimes lead them straight back to us." Clasping his hands together, he rested them on his desk.

"I feel I've heard every analogy for mental illness over the years. However, I firmly believe she's not always well monitored in the community. Of course we want her home, but she invariably gets forgotten about until she's propelled back to you."

"I hear what you're saying, however I can assure you that she won't be forgotten by anyone here. The community mental health team have been notified of her return tomorrow, if that's okay with you, Mr Willow."

Oliver nodded, squeezing Joan's hand. "No problem at all," he smiled.

Harvey rolled up his jacket collar as he walked to his car. The day had been a long one.

Reaching his car he pulled the keys from his pocket, only to have them swiped from his hand.

"What the hell?" he gasped as a fist met the right side of his face.

The blow knocked him to the ground. Dried leaves snapping like crisps, clung to his cheek. He tried to ram his briefcase against the assailant's shins, but found it kicked from his hand before he had the chance.

He scrabbled along the ground, caring not his cashmere jacket was soaking-up mud and debris. He tried to shout, but a well-placed boot to his ribs stopped him. He was beaten.

A kick in the face split his nose; blood eddied down his left cheek as he lay in a foetal position; pain searing across his face.

"Take what you want," he gurgled through the blood.

But instead of having his pockets rummaged through, or his briefcase or car taken, he received another kick before the assailant ran off into the shadows.

He lay there groaning, suddenly aware of the cold, hard ground under his aching body. Pulling a handkerchief from his pocket, he placed it gingerly over his nose before shifting closer to the car so he could sit up with his back against the door.

The only moisture in his mouth was blood from his nose and split lip. His hand trembled as he retrieved his mobile and dialled.

"The Raven Unit," announced Eric.

"I'm in the car park, I need help," Harvey said hoarsely.

Eric stared blankly down the phone before venturing outside, where he found the area darker than usual.

"Over here," Harvey called out as he saw the light through the open door.

Eric rushed over and bent down to inspect him.

"Shit, are you hurt?"

"I think my nose is broken, and I've fractured a rib. Get me inside without the patients seeing."

Crouching down, Eric wrapped Harvey's arm around his shoulders before lifting him to his feet. Harvey groaned as his racked body was pulled unceremoniously to an upright position. The pair shuffled to the door Eric had left open, then he concealed Harvey in his office.

"You should go to the emergency department with that cut; it needs stitches," Eric said, peering at his nose.

"I can't manage to walk over there on my own. Call Olivia and get her here. Now." He paused to cough, spraying crimson droplets over his soiled jacket.

"Did you see who it was?"

"Of course I bloody didn't, I had his boot in my face half the time."

Eric listened to the ringing tone, tapping his foot rapidly on the floor. Finally Olivia answered, and Eric imparted the news.

"Is he all right?" she squealed.

"A trip to the emergency department should sort him out. He wants you here now."

"On my way," she said before disconnecting the call.

When she arrived, she was ushered in discreetly.

"I said I was worried about you. The police have got to protect you now," she said, crouching down to see the full extent of the damage to his face.

"Just get me over to the hospital, we'll worry about the police later."

"No, as soon as we return home I'm calling them, they need to know."

She and Eric stood either side of him, easing him gently to his feet. Groaning, he hobbled slowly to the door, leaning on his wife.

As Eric watched the pair move away, he took his mobile from his pocket and pressed speed dial.

Harvey rested his head in the passenger seat as Olivia drove them home. His nose was covered by a fresh, white dressing, and his ribs were only bruised, but nonetheless sore.

"When we get in, take yourself to bed and I'll bring you up a cup of tea after I've phoned the police," she said quietly, gripping the steering wheel hard as she focused on the road.

The following morning, Wednesday and Lennox drove to the Manning's home.

"How many assailants were there?" asked Wednesday as she settled on the sofa.

"Only the one I think. It all happened so fast."

"I've been worried about my husband's safety ever since the murder on the unit; and now it transpires I was right to be. What are you going to do about it now?"

"We're trying to ascertain whether this is to do with the murder or a totally different agenda altogether. Do you have any thoughts on that Doctor Manning?" Wednesday asked.

"I've got no bloody idea."

"Did you hear their voice?"

Harvey shook his head gingerly.

"I think this may be a good time to bring up the subject of illegal drug use on the unit," said Lennox.

Harvey looked up quickly, his eyes watering and wide. "What on earth are you talking about? Is this another smear campaign to add to my currents woes?"

"Nothing of the kind. A result came back for Susan Roche showing levels of THC in her system, and we were wondering how that could happen on your unit?"

"How should I know? I don't prescribe cannabis; it doesn't mix well with anti-psychotics."

"I'm aware of that, but it does make me wonder whether a dealer was in the vicinity and you were there at the wrong time."

"This is all unsubstantiated, malicious slander. Concentrate on the murder, and leave me out of all this. I told Olivia not to call you," he spat, glaring at his wife.

"We would have found out, and for all we know, your attack could be linked to the murder. We keep all channels of thought open."

Harvey sighed loudly, rubbing his temples with his middle fingers. Olivia took her cue.

"These past weeks have been very disturbing, and you can see the strain it's put on my husband. All I ask is for you keep an eye on the unit; I'm worried about his safety." Olivia reached over, touching his knee tenderly.

"That may not be possible. I suggest you get a member of staff to accompany you to and from the car, and vary your routine until we investigate further." Wednesday shuffled forward on the seat in preparation to leave.

"That won't be enough if someone comes back to finish the job." Olivia's voice sounded reedy and weak.

"I suggest your husband think carefully about his acquaintances then," began Lennox, "as this wasn't a robbery gone wrong. Nothing was taken, not even a blank prescription pad. The motive's a mystery."

"I've a headache. I'm going to bed." Harvey eased himself up before leaving, without glancing back.

Olivia smiled weakly at the pair. "You have to forgive him; he's still in shock. He pretends he's not upset, but I can see he is."

"No worries," replied Wednesday, "he may actually remember more about the attack in a few days. Get him to call us if he does."

Olivia led them to the front door and watched them leave before tiptoeing upstairs to check on him.

"You seem rather distracted," Wednesday said, slamming the car door.

"There's a meeting at the YOI about Archie, and I really want to go. His caseworker wants both parents to be involved."

"Then go, it's not up to anyone else."

"Lucy objects, saying she finds being in the same room as me intolerable. Brian's going, of course."

Wednesday glanced at him, seeing his furrowed brow. "What's Archie's view?"

"He's ambivalent, which is an improvement I suppose."

"An alternative could be to send a letter to be read out, you know, giving your point of view."

"That's why you're a DI and I'm a DS," he smiled.

Wednesday pulled into the station and parked up, before telling him she needed to see Hunter, alone.

Chapter 43

"The light in the unit's car park had been tampered with, most likely making the attack on the doctor calculated," Damlish said as Wednesday entered the Incident Room.

"Any fingerprints or such-like discovered at the scene?"

"No, the bulb was removed. The assailant was very careful."

Wednesday carried on walking to Hunter's door, tapping on it lightly. He waved her in whilst finishing a call.

"Sit," he said, putting down the receiver. "How's the case going?"

"Slowly, Guv. The attack on Manning has shaken him but his bravado masks the truth. It looks like the attack was planned and he was the true target. The unit attracts problems and I don't know why."

"Have you spread the net wide enough?"

"We've looked at the patients, families, and staff."

"You're obviously missing something, maybe you should re-interview everyone, see if their stories change." A text message distracted him momentarily. "Was there anything else?"

Wednesday chewed the inside of her cheek. "My mother's coming out tomorrow, and I wondered if I could have the morning off to collect her and settle her back home?"

Hunter's cornflower-blue eyes bore into her, as she felt a red rash dappling her skin. She shifted in her seat.

"I've scrutinized how mentally ill people feel and are treated, and it's upset me. I haven't always been a good enough daughter; I've shirked my responsibilities at times."

"I see," he said, rubbing his chin. "Well then, take the time you need. I need you to be focused on your work whilst here."

He made his grant of leave sound like a chastisement, making her feel uncomfortable. She rose to leave then paused.

"Does having mental illness in my family make me a less viable DI, Guv?"

"I'm not sure how to answer that. It hasn't been a problem thus far. Do you see it becoming an issue?"

"That's not quite want I meant. Do you personally worry about my sanity?"

He looked at her, shaking his head slightly. "Should I be? Sort out your mother tomorrow then come back and crack on with this case." He picked up his mobile and checked for more messages.

With her head held high, Wednesday strode to her office, her heart pounding in her chest. Lennox watched candidly from his office, whilst mindlessly doodling on a piece of paper.

Wednesday's stomach churned as she entered the unit. Taking a deep breath, she breezed up to the nurses' station and enquired if Joan was ready.

"She's all packed up and keen to leave," replied Eric.

Wednesday did not hang around for small-talk, preferring to gather Joan and her belongings and whisk her away back to Oliver.

Joan looked expectantly at the door as Wednesday entered.

"Ready to go, Mum?"

"Indeed, I could do with a cup of tea brewed in a china teapot, not the great big stainless steel ones they use here."

Wednesday smiled, picking up her suitcase and vanity case, the same ones she had used for as long as Wednesday could remember.

On their way out, Eric handed her a green plastic bag containing Joan's medication and told her an outpatient appointment would be sent through the post. She knew the routine well enough.

The journey to her parents' house was conducted in a shared need of silence, reminiscing over what had been and what was to come; each wondering how long she would manage to stay out of hospital this time.

Oliver greeted his wife at the door like she was a new-born. He had a pot of tea brewing.

"Oh that's so good," Joan said, holding the china cup with both her hands.

"Would you like me to come by after work and cook you a meal?" offered Wednesday, dutifully.

"No thanks love, I've already made a shepherd's pie to pop in the oven later," Oliver smiled. He had become an old-hand at coping with Joan's return.

Wednesday felt surplus to requirement as she watched the pair melt together. She wondered whether she would ever find what they had.

The Incident Room was buzzing by the time she returned.

"I didn't want to text you whilst you were with your family, but we've got an incident," Lennox started, as he followed her to her office. "Rene Blower's managed to get out of the unit and return home in a taxi, only to discover her husband's changed the locks. She's smashed a window and got the neighbours ten-year-old son to climb through and open the door. She's now holding the child hostage, demanding her husband take her back."

"God, I was only at the unit earlier."

"I know. Hunter wants us to go to Rene now; he thinks your mental health experience may help encourage her to free the child."

"You can drive," she said, grabbing her bag.

A distraught woman stood on the pavement outside the Blowers' house, with a fresh-faced constable hovering nearby.

Lennox parked as close as possible before they both got out and strode over to the constable.

"What's the latest?" Wednesday asked her.

"The husband's on his way back from work. Rene is refusing to communicate with anyone except him. The boy seems to be taking things in his stride, but I can't say the same for his mum," she replied, nodding her head in the direction of the woman.

Just then, a blue Ford screeched to a halt behind them, and out jumped Howard Blower.

"What's the stupid cow done now?" he asked through gritted teeth.

Wednesday turned to face him. "She's in a fragile state, and the only person she'll talk to is you. May I suggest you be more sympathetic, at least for the sake of the child?"

He looked down at her, clenching his jaw. "All right, what do you want me to do?"

"Talk to her via the landline, we can't risk you also being held hostage. Listen to what she has to say, and try to persuade her to release the boy."

"Not sure it'll do any good. I don't want her back and she knows it."

"Humour her until the situation is over."

He took the mobile from Wednesday's hand and dialled his home number. It rang five times before Rene picked up.

"It's me, Howard. What's this all about?"

"You've changed the locks. Am I shut out of your life for good?"

Howard puffed out his cheeks. "I thought someone had tampered with the lock, so I changed it for security reasons."

"You didn't tell me, or give me a new key."

"I wasn't expecting you to come home without me." He looked towards Wednesday and shrugged.

"Ask her to release the boy then you two can talk face to face, through an open window," Wednesday whispered.

Wednesday listened to him before a long pause ensued. A knot twisted in her stomach, sending a bubble of acid zipping up her throat.

"She's agreed, but she wants a swap, him for me. She wants to talk inside."

"That worries me, I'm not sure about that?"

"I'm stronger than her, she can't harm me. Let's do it."

Before she had time for further discussion, Howard strode up to the front door and knocked. Outlines of two people could be seen approaching the door through the bubbled glass. The child's frantic mother bounced around like an agitated horse waiting for the start of a race.

The door opened just enough to let Blower in and the boy out. As soon as he was free, he pelted to his mother's open arms. She sobbed tears into his hair as he stood wide-eyed, staring at the police and the blue flashing lights.

The young constable took mother and son to an awaiting ambulance, leaving Wednesday free to focus on the situation in the house.

"We'll give them a couple of minutes before I phone through."

"How about I go 'round the back, and you cover the front," Lennox suggested.

"Take a constable with you. We won't barge in lest it spook her. I don't want her harming herself or him."

Lennox crept around the back with a female constable whilst Wednesday dialled the home number. Howard answered.

"We're still talking, but I must warn you, she's barricaded the back door. We're in the lounge and she's placed a pile of clothes, doused with white spirits all around us." He paused to moisten his lips loudly. "She's also doused the pair of us. We'll be alight before you reach us. She means this."

Wednesday screwed her eyes shut; she knew it was wrong to let him go in, her gut had told her so. "Remain calm and don't antagonise her. We'll get to you."

She radioed through to Lennox to update him.

"What's your plan?" he asked.

"I'm going to walk over to the open window and try and engage her in conversation. I want her to stand down peacefully. Get a fire engine here, no sirens."

She entered the front garden, calling out to Rene.

"Don't come any closer," she screamed. "I only want to talk with Howard."

"I was happy with that up until he told me you were both soaked in white spirits. Now I don't want to come in, but I do want to know what will make you come out."

"Only Howard can make that happen. He has to want me back in his life, and he has to kiss me passionately to prove it. I will tell if he doesn't mean it."

"I'm not sure this is the right way to go about things, Rene. You could have couples counselling, perhaps."

Rene shut the window, then Wednesday heard voices which she strained to hear.

Suddenly, Rene's shrill voice pierced the air. Howard's voice counterbalanced hers, sounding tense. Pressure mounted in Wednesday's mind as she picked up her radio.

"Go in by a window, now," she commanded Lennox, as she smashed the window with a garden ornament, and scrambled over the windowsill, dropping onto the lounge floor.

The stench of white spirits burnt her nostrils as she edged towards the couple. "It's time to stop this, Rene."

"What the hell are you doing?" hollered Howard, raising his hand.

The click of the lighter in Rene's hand sent the whoosh of the first flames filling the room. Several seconds later, screams ricocheted around the walls. Wednesday lunged towards the pair and tried to pull them out, but the flames frightened her.

To her relief, a couple of firemen barged in, dosing the flames with foam.

The pair crumpled to the floor before being hoisted up by the firemen and taken quickly outside into the fresh air. Wednesday and Lennox followed suit, their eyes and throats stinging with the chemical assault.

The Blowers were being treated by the ambulance crew.

"We need to take them to hospital," said the paramedic.

"How bad are they?" Lennox asked.

"Mainly superficial, but the woman has more severe burns to her hands. You two should get checked out for inhalation damage."

Lennox nodded, but knew Wednesday would be eager to interview Rene as soon as possible, rather than waste time being checked out.

They got into Lennox's car, staring straight ahead for a few moments. The smell of white spirits and smoke swirled around them, extinguishing the desire for a cigarette.

"To the hospital I presume," he said, switching on the engine.

Wednesday nodded, clasping her hands together tightly in her lap, blinking back salty tears.

Chapter 44

"I was wondering when you'd be brave enough to face me, rather than just spy on me," growled Sam Brass.

"You'd better let me in then," Gavin Roche replied, stepping through and pushing Sam aside.

"What do you want exactly?"

"I want a cut of your profit otherwise I'm going to the police."

Sam let out a forced laugh. "You think you can come here and get me to roll over just like that? I ain't handing anything over."

"Then we have a problem, don't we?"

"Nope, no problem. You can just piss off and crawl back to your sad family life."

"You know nothing about me," spat Gavin.

"I know your old man's in the frame for murdering your mad mum."

Lurching forward, Gavin pushed Sam to the floor, knocking over a plant pot perching on a table. Sam was quicker to his feet than Gavin anticipated, so he was not ready for the punch that caught him straight on his jaw. He faltered backwards, saved only by the closed kitchen door.

"Now don't be stupid," Sam said, pressing his forearm into Gavin's throat. "I may be older than you, but I'm not feeble of mind or body. Now, I don't quite know what you think you're doing, but you're playing with dangerous people. People well out of your league."

"I'd cope," gasped Gavin. "Perhaps I could be an asset."

Sam eased the pressure. "What you talking about?"

"I'm a student in London, surrounded by lots of students looking for the next high or chill. Get my drift?"

Dropping his arm, Sam took a small step back. For a second, his head spun with the thought of his enterprise hitting London. "What's in it for you?"

"Half the profit of everything sold in London, and I get to pick my own runners."

"You want to be the boss of the London branch."

"Exactly. You don't have a choice; it's a no-brainer." He watched Sam wipe the back of his hand over his glistening forehead.

"I'm not making a snap decision."

"I'll give you twenty-four hours. I'll see you tomorrow. No need to see me out," he said as he strode towards the door, brushing the creases from his coat sleeves.

Sam waited until Gavin closed the front gate and disappeared from view, before thumping the back of the sofa; a scream rumbling in his chest. But perhaps he could use Gavin, for now at least.

Lennox was in his personal heaven watching nurses scurrying around, tending to their patients.

"When can we interview Rene Blower?" Wednesday asked the doctor standing by the nurses' station.

"We've sedated her for the pain, so you won't be able to talk to her until tomorrow," he replied dryly.

Wednesday smiled briefly, giving him her card.

"Let's go back to mine for an omelette. Just when I think I've got a handle on things, something comes out of left-field," she said as they left the hospital.

"I thought that suited your organic method."

"Don't be so pedantic."

Lennox looked sheepish for a second then threw her one of his charming smiles. She had no trouble seeing why he was so sought after at the station, or by Scarlett, come to that. She phoned Maria Jones to let her know of their plans, ignoring the sigh she received in reply.

Harvey accepted a cup of tea from his wife before ushering her out of his study.

"You're not planning on doing anything foolish are you?" she asked.

"I'm not a fool, you should know that. But I don't trust the police to find out who did this to me. I thought I'd ask around myself."

"Who do you know to ask?"

"Never you mind. Shut the door behind you."

Olivia left and wandered to the kitchen. She fixed herself a gin and tonic, hoping he would reappear shortly in a better mood.

Harvey pulled out his mobile from his jacket pocket. "Eric, I demand you find out who was behind my attack."

"I've already asked around, but no one knows," Eric replied.

"So what do you suggest?"

"I think it's the same sicko who's targeting the patients."

"But why me as well?"

"Perhaps it's a case of mistaken identity."

"Don't be ridiculous, the patients don't wander around the car park at that time of night. Someone knew it was me. I'm the intended target. It's your job to find out who did it."

"How the hell am I supposed to do that?"

"That's for you to work out. You've got nefarious friends; don't disappoint me." He threw his mobile on his desk and pushed his cup of tea aside. Retrieving a bottle of brandy from the desk drawer, he poured a large measure into a cut-glass tumbler and swirled the amber liquid around, hoping a revelation would enter his mind.

Forty minutes later, and three glasses consumed, Harvey felt no nearer his goal. He knew he needed the incident wrapped up shortly, otherwise fear would erode his natural confidence. He wondered who he could turn to if Eric failed.

Placing his knife and fork together on his empty plate, Lennox pushed it to one side, before reaching for his packet of cigarettes.

"Why don't we forego a smoke, and move to the lounge with a coffee to discuss the case," Wednesday suggested.

He shrugged before following her and flopping into the armchair.

"I hesitate to say this, but I fear I've been blinded at times because of Mum."

"Is that why you wanted to meet here to discuss this; fear of the walls having ears?"

Wednesday pulled a cushion over her stomach. "Perhaps. Or maybe I can only see things clearly here, as it's entangled with my personal life."

"You sure you want to discuss this?"

"I'm showing that I trust you implicitly. I may have wobbled from time to time due to your dalliance with Scarlett, but work-wise I know you have my back." It amused her to see his cheeks flush.

"Hunter wants us to re-interview everyone, so let's make a plan," she said finally, pulling a dog-eared notepad from her bag.

Chapter 45

Wednesday spotted Chris White's red Mohican through the shop window, as he served a customer. A faint smile of acknowledgment flashed across his lips, as the shop bell announced their arrival.

The customer left, clutching a CD wrapped in a paper bag.

"What can I do for you two?" he asked from behind the counter.

"Have you visited Melvyn lately?" Wednesday replied.

"A couple of days ago, why?"

"How did you find him?"

"Still a bloody nervous wreck. Not sure what good that place is doing him."

Wednesday nodded.

"You're in the music business, right?" asked Lennox.

"And?"

"I was wondering about the drug scene that often goes with it. Would you know much about that?"

"Firstly, I sell music here, not drugs. People want Lady Gaga and The Rolling Stones, not crack and dope. And secondly, I play the bass in an indie band. We play in run-down pubs and social clubs. I don't have the time or money for drugs."

"We're not interested in your personal use. We're more interested in whether you know of local dealers."

"I've personally smoked dope recreationally in the past with Melvyn. It's probably what turned him in the end. I stopped to concentrate on my music, but he couldn't let go of the stuff. I don't know of any dealers currently."

"Does he still smoke it now?"

"I don't know, but I wouldn't be surprised."

"Well, thank you for your time. We'll get back to you if need be."

They left the shop, walking purposefully to the car before heading off to visit Sam Brass, who was not at work due to being ill, according to the bank.

The front door swung open sharply after Wednesday rang the doorbell. Sam's face blanched.

"The bank said you were at home, sick," stated Wednesday.

"So?"

"We'd like to ask you a few questions."

Brass coughed, stepping to one side to let them pass.

"How's Eddie doing?" Wednesday asked.

"Fine, but surely you haven't come to find that out."

"Of course not. We just wondered whether your brother smokes cannabis."

Brass's eyes widened. "Not anymore, as far as I'm aware of. Why do you ask?"

"We're making enquiries."

"What's it got to do with the murder?"

"Questions out of context may make little sense to you."

"Sounds like a wild-goose-chase to me. Someone got murdered; they didn't die of a drug overdose."

"Have you noticed strange people hanging around outside or on the unit?"

"I work in a bank. I don't know what a drug dealer looks like," he replied with a shrug and a throaty cough.

Holding her finger under her nose, Wednesday indicated to Lennox they were leaving.

"What did the police want earlier?" Gavin Roche asked as he stood on Sam's doorstep.

Sam searched the street, glancing left and right. Grabbing Gavin by the arm, he yanked him inside. "What the bloody hell do you think you're doing? We don't want to be seen together."

"Chill, we're just concerned family of patients on the unit. They'd never guess our other connection." Gavin launched himself at the sofa, sprawling across it with his gangly limbs.

"Well that's where you're wrong. They're already sniffing around a drug connection to the unit."

"Really? That woman doesn't look like she's got it in her."

"Don't underestimate her. There's more behind those cow-eyes than she makes out."

Gavin raised his eyebrows. "Got the hots for her, have you?"

"Don't be thick; I'd never shag a copper."

Gavin smiled wryly. "Where's your dad, by the way?"

"Never you fucking mind. Now are you here to discuss London, or not?"

"I don't see the need for discussion, I just need to know when I start as your partner; I'm heading back to uni soon."

Sam looked him up and down before rolling a cigarette. "How do you know you can hack it as a dealer?"

"It can't be that hard, the stuff sells itself in the student world."

"You mentioned your own runners, who do you have in mind?" Sam flicked the lighter, before inhaling deeply.

"There are a couple of guys who hang around me, who'd do anything I ask. I wouldn't have to pay them much; the kudos of working for me would be enough."

"You think a lot of yourself, don't you?" Sam blew a few smoke rings into the stale air. "I'm the boss around here, so don't think you can out-smart or out-rank me. I'll give you a trial period of two months. If I deem you to fail, you're out."

"No fear," he replied, cracking his knuckles. "I'll bring in big bucks, you wait and see." He pushed himself off the sofa with his hands. "I'll collect my first consignment in a couple of days."

Sam reached out, grabbing him by the upper arm and narrowing his eyes. "Bring two thousand with you and we're talking."

Gavin stared into his eyes before dropping his gaze and walking towards the door. He let it swing open as he left, a smirk hanging on his lips.

Wednesday and Lennox arrived at the Mannings' house at the agreed time. Olivia let them in, directing them to the lounge where her husband was convalescing.

"How are you feeling today, Doctor?" Wednesday asked, sitting down.

"A little sore now that the bruising's coming out, but I'll survive."

"Any more thoughts on your attacker or the motive?"

"Not the slightest idea."

"Your wife looked worried when she answered the door. Is she feeling unsafe here?"

"You'll have to ask her. But I wouldn't take her too seriously; she's a drama queen."

Wednesday stared at him, speechless, as Olivia entered with a tray of refreshments.

"They're wondering if you feel unsafe in the house," he said, nodding in their direction.

"I'm anxious about your wellbeing, that's all," she replied, handing out the cups and pointing to the milk and sugar on the tray.

"Still can't think of anyone who'd wish him harm?" Wednesday asked, noticing Olivia's reddening cheeks.

"Not a single person. Perhaps someone in the medical field is jealous of his success . . . I don't know really."

"You obviously think jealousy could be behind this, so you must have a few ideas on who would feel that way."

Olivia looked at her husband. "I don't actually know many of his colleagues. I don't socialise much in his world."

"It's not up to us to come up with a list of suspects; I'm the victim here," Harvey said hoarsely.

"And victims often know their assailants. Have you ever received any threatening letters, e-mails, or phone calls?"

"No, and I also haven't had an altercation with anyone. You being here only shows you've no idea who's behind this."

"And it's for that reason I'm really worried about him," Olivia chimed in.

"Perhaps you should go and stay with your mother if you're overly stressed about this," Harvey quipped.

"I want to stay near you; make sure you're okay."

"I forget you could karate chop anyone who approached me," he laughed.

Olivia rolled her eyes. "This isn't the time for joking around, this is a serious matter."

Harvey performed a mock salute, then promised he would think about any strained working relationships.

As the detectives left, Harvey shut himself in his study and retrieved a mobile from his desk drawer.

"I have to see you."

Chapter 46

Melvyn's face turned various shades of puce as Dave Hyde's hands tightened around his throat. Black dots floated before his eyes as he tried to look into his assailant's face.

Spittle formed at the corners of Dave's mouth as he bore down over his victim on the bed.

"Why?" rasped Melvyn.

"You're poisoning my fucking drinks, you bastard. You'll die before me."

Melvyn's head spun as his lungs attempted to gasp the smallest amount of oxygen. He sensed his body shutting down.

"You're the bloody murderer around here. With you gone, we'll all be safe." He pressed down with all his might and watched Rollins's eyes roll back and blank out.

Stillness hit the sweaty atmosphere, forcing Dave to sit back on his haunches to examine his handiwork. In the dim light, Melvyn's neck looked raw and slightly swollen. Dave salivated, prodding the lifeless body with his sausage-like finger. He glanced towards the closed door, fragmented thoughts racing through his mind.

Shoving his arms behind Melvyn's back, he hoisted him up the bed and rolled him onto his side so he was facing the window. He then pulled the quilt over him, just leaving his head exposed. He hovered over the body before creeping back to his bedroom. Fortunately, Karen and Sara were too engrossed in a trashy magazine to notice the shadow of his frame sweeping along the corridor wall.

Once in his room, his pounding heart took on a more restful pace, allowing him to slip under the covers and fall asleep.

Fifteen minutes later, the nurses floated around the unit checking on each patient by opening the doors and peering in. On opening Melvyn Rollins's door, they heard faint moaning and rasping noises emanating from the bed. Sara stepped further into the gloom, concerned at the sounds. She stood next to the bed and bent over slightly.

"Are you okay, Melvyn?" she whispered. When she got no response, she spoke louder. "Melvyn? Melvyn?"

She turned around to find that Karen had moved on to the next room. Turning on the bedside light, she inhaled sharply at the site of his swollen neck; hand and fingertip marks emblazoned around it. His breathing was laboured and shallow.

"Karen, Karen, come quick," she yelled, suddenly feeling inadequate with her student status.

Hastening footsteps echoed down the corridor until Karen's calm voice soothed the agitation. "You'll wake the others, what on earth's wrong?"

"I think he's been attacked, look at his neck, and he's struggling to breathe properly. *Look.*"

"Calm down, a nurse must remain cool-headed in challenging situations. Besides, you're probably wrong . . . oh, I see," she said as she took a closer look. "Help me lift him up the bed, and put extra pillows behind his back," she ordered, as Melvyn groaned further.

"Should I call Doctor Manning?" queried Sara.

"No need, this isn't a psychiatric emergency."

"What about the police?"

"Certainly not. We don't know what's gone on here. It might be self-inflicted for all we know. Pour him some water and get a straw so he can take small sips."

Sara disappeared, leaving Karen alone.

"Did you do this to yourself?" she whispered, inches from his face. "I said did you do this, because if you did, it's not very clever."

Melvyn peeled his eyes open slowly and parted his lips to speak, only to close his eyes and mouth once more.

"Has he said anything?" queried Sara, returning with the straw.

"Bugger all."

"Let's leave him and see him in ten, we need to finish the round. We'll call the GP in if he's still like this."

Sara glanced back at the bed before pulling the door to and scampering after Karen.

Some of the other patients had been disturbed by the goings-on in Melvyn's room. One of them was Dave Hyde.

"What's wrong out there?" he asked from his doorway.

"Nothing for you to worry about," answered Karen in a clipped manner.

"Is somebody dead?"

"What makes you say that?"

"The commotion in these dark hours."

"You should sleep and not concern yourself with others."

He returned inside, leaving his door ajar. He stood there trying to hear what was going on, but could only make out the odd muffled cry and mutterings of the mad. The muscles twitched in his jaw as he shuffled back to bed, only to lie awake staring at the ceiling.

Wednesday's mobile rang in her bag as she ascended the stairs to the station. The number registered as The Raven Unit. "Hello?"

"There was another attempted murder last night," said a clearly disguised husky voice.

"Who's this?"

"That doesn't matter. You need to get here and check it out before it happens again, but you can't say you got a tip-off otherwise they'll know who I am."

"Who's the victim?"

"Melvyn Rollins—" the line went dead before Wednesday hastened to the Incident Room. She beckoned to Lennox to join her.

"Boss?"

"We need to get to the unit, I'll explain on the way. You can drive."

Once they arrived they wasted no time in ringing the intercom. Angela Rhodes frowned as they approached the nurses' station.

"We're re-interviewing everyone. I'd like to start with Melvyn Rollins," Wednesday said.

"He's not that well currently. Why don't you start with someone else?" When she was met with silence, she scraped her chair back and headed for his room.

Melvyn was sitting in an upright position taking small sips of water through a straw. He physically jerked as they entered, sloshing water down his striped pyjama top. His hand shot to his neck, barely managing to hide all of the injuries.

"Has someone hurt you, Mr Rollins? I won't touch your neck, I only want to look," Wednesday said soothingly.

He slowly dropped his hand away from his throat, revealing the marks. Wednesday turned to Angela. "Has a doctor seen this?"

She shook her head. "Karen said there's no need. She suspected he's attention seeking."

"It shouldn't matter. You don't seem to be taking this seriously. Who did this to you?" she asked, turning to him.

"I didn't see," he whispered.

"Did they speak to you?"

He shook his head slowly.

Wednesday sighed. "If you know who it is and you're scared, we can take steps to protect you. If it's someone on this unit you're giving them the opportunity to do it again." She scrutinized his face closely, scouring the crevices between his eyebrows for any hint of doubt or imminent revelation. "I want a doctor's report on the injuries, and we'll be back later to chat with the other patients," Wednesday stated striding out of the unit.

Slamming the car door, she reached for the packet of cigarettes, before stopping herself. The car rocked as Lennox climbed in.

"You want a smoke?" he asked.

"I do but I won't. The lines around my mouth are getting deeper."

Wednesday twisted strands of hair around her finger as Lennox drove them back to the station.

"From recollection, I think the marks on Rollins's neck were larger than the ones on Roche's. What about you?" she asked.

"I agree, so what you're saying is this attacker isn't the same as our first one. Two separate crimes."

"Maybe. I took a photo on my phone and e-mailed it to Alex."

"How about visiting Eric Knight, see what he has to say about the unruly behaviour on his unit."

Chapter 47

Eric Knight was covered in sweat when he answered his front door.

"Can we come in?" Wednesday asked.

He patted his forehead with a grubby hand towel as they stepped inside. Slamming the door, he directed them to the kitchen throwing the towel on the floor.

"Have you heard about the recent incident on the unit," Wednesday asked, pulling out a kitchen chair to sit on.

"As you can see, it's my day off. Why, what's happened?"

His face remained impassive as Wednesday filled him in.

"I suppose you want to know where I was last night," he said.

"Seeing as you're offering," replied Lennox.

"I went to visit my mother and ended up staying for tea. Then I came home alone, watched TV, then went to bed, alone."

"Why the sweat?"

"I've got a gym in the spare bedroom; I work out once a day." He flexed his biceps, raising his eyebrows at Wednesday.

"Has Melvyn Rollins got any enemies within his family or friends?" pressed Lennox.

"He's an enemy to himself, never mind anyone else."

"What do you mean?"

"He allows his anxiety to get the better of him; he's a foolish man."

"Is there anyone on the unit with an intense dislike of him?"

"They all just about tolerate one another. I doubt there's enough animosity to kill him, though."

"He was attacked, viciously by the looks of things."

"We have a unit full of people capable of such deeds. You're looking for a fruit fly in an attic full of spider webs."

"You're avoiding answering the questions, so I'll say it again, Melvyn's enemies." Lennox's voice boomed around the room.

"Dave Hyde seemed pissed off with him yesterday morning, not sure why though."

"Didn't you try to find out?"

"He can't talk when he's pent-up; his emotions cloud his mind and judgement."

"So he could be capable of attacking Melvyn."

"As I've already said, any of them are capable, given the right mood."

Wednesday crushed her fingernails into the palm of her hand. "You have a dim view of your patients." She turned her back on him and walked towards the front door, closely followed by Lennox.

Jordan Campbell loaded his wife's suitcase into the boot of the car, before returning inside the unit to collect her.

"You'll be fine," encouraged Angela.

"I don't want to be a burden to my husband," she whispered back.

"Well, take your meds, attend your outpatient appointments, and concentrate on keeping well. Focus on your marriage, you've got a lovely husband."

Jordan sidled up to his wife and put his arm around her waist. He thanked Angela, before guiding Fiona to the car, placing her in the passenger seat.

"Let's hope you never have to stay in this place again," he said, switching on the engine and crunching the gears.

Fiona watched the unit draw further away through the window; tears welling in her eyes.

Wednesday put the phone down before walking over to Lennox's office.

"As we suspected, the marks on Melvyn Rollins's neck don't match Susan Roche's. Let's go and see if his memory's come back. I'll drive."

Drumming her fingers on the steering wheel, she waited for Lennox to climb in. Revving the engine, she narrowly missed a patrol car entering the car park. Sheepishly, she raised an apologetic hand before moving on.

"Time for a smoke?" asked Lennox.

"I haven't had one all morning and I'd like to keep that up. You'll have to wait."

Lennox nodded sagely, suddenly understanding her mood.

They found Melvyn in the lounge, rocking steadily back and forth.

"How are you feeling today?" Wednesday asked, approaching him.

"Fine, couldn't be better," he snapped.

"Can you remember any more details from yesterday?"

"No." His rocking increased, making the chair creak.

At that moment, Dave Hyde entered the room, taking a seat opposite Melvyn. Wednesday observed Melvyn's hands twisting frantically, and sweat gathering on his top lip. She glanced at Dave, catching him fixing his stare on Melvyn.

"Perhaps you have some thoughts on the attack," Wednesday said, directing her question at Dave.

"Heard nothing, saw nothing," he replied sharply.

"Seems to be the order of the day; strikes me as strange on such a small unit."

"No one heard that Susan woman die, so why would we hear Melvyn? He's a fucking mouse of a man."

Melvyn looked up from under his bushy eyebrows, contemplating his next move. Fear paralysed his cognition, and the vinyl floor undulated under his feet, until an overwhelming sense of self-preservation hit him.

"He did it," he whispered.

"Pardon?" Wednesday leant in closer, trying to catch his words.

He raised a shaking hand, pointing at Dave Hyde. "He thinks I'm poisoning his drinks, but I haven't. I haven't," he repeated loudly.

Dave shifted around in his seat before lunging forward towards Melvyn. Wednesday was quick to her feet, blocking Dave from reaching his target. His open, spade-like hands connected with Wednesday's face, pushing her backwards onto Melvyn's lap. He began pressing down on her before Lennox grabbed his left arm, twisting it up his back.

Dave was in no mood to let someone get the better of him. Letting out a thunderous roar, he propelled Lennox to the opposite wall.

The commotion drew nurses to the room, with Eric being the first to appear. He called out to Joshua, who ran to the room with a needle and a small bottle of a major tranquilizer.

Eric grabbed hold of Dave's collar, dragging him backwards and freeing Lennox, whilst Plough filled the syringe before plunging the needle into Hyde's right buttock.

"What the fuck?" spat Dave, swivelling around and just missing Plough's head.

Joshua was skilled at injecting patients in such scenarios, rendering Dave into a pliable mass of muscle and blubber. They accompanied him to his room, leaving the detectives with Melvyn, who was shaking wildly in his chair.

Wednesday watched Lennox light a cigarette in her garden as she waited for the kettle to boil. She was mesmerized by the furling smoke as it travelled skywards. Although her cravings were tempered by the new medication the smoking cessation clinic had prescribed, she still missed the connection she had with the cigarette. The intimate relationship she experienced in moments of angst, celebration, and total desperation, were all shared with a burning cigarette.

As the front door opened, and Scarlett called out a greeting, she knew she would not have the company of Lennox for long.

Gavin Roche thrust a brown envelope containing two thousand pounds into Sam Brass's grubby hand. Sam peered in before retrieving the notes and counting them out.

"Don't you trust me?" Gavin asked.

"I trust no one, and I suggest you do the same in this line of business."

Gavin shrugged. "Where's the stuff?"

Sam ignored him until the pile of notes had been counted. "In that rucksack," he replied after a few minutes, pointing to a tatty-looking bag propped up against the wall.

Stretching the top of the bag open, Gavin peered inside. Tiny, transparent plastic bags containing brown lumps lay at the bottom.

"Don't I get to sample some?" he asked.

"Nope, you can do that on your turf. Now get out of here, and only contact me on my mobile when you want to place an order."

Gavin slung the bag over his shoulder, gripping the handle hard, and headed home. If he had not been so cocky, he may have felt Sam's eyes boring into the back of his head.

Chapter 48

The kitchen light pierced the darkness of the early hours, as Wednesday sat hunched over the pine table, scraps of paper strewn over the knotted wood.

Creaking noises from upstairs disturbed her until she remembered how cooling air affected the floorboards. She was reminded of being alone, not like Scarlett who had driven home with Lennox in tow.

She studied the scrawled mind-map lying before her, scanning the names and their connections. The current way of thinking was getting her nowhere, so she decided to turn things on their head, and view the crimes from a different perspective.

Lennox poured the insipid coffee into a large mug. Wednesday watched from a distance before strolling up behind him and requesting his presence in her office.

"I think we've been looking at these crimes from the wrong angle," she said, spreading the new mind-map across her desk. "The tentacles of circumstance spread widely, and often towards people we never suspected."

"You obviously have someone in mind. Care to share?"

"Not just yet, I want to do a few more interviews and see if you come to the same conclusion.

Hunter stepped into Wednesday's office and sat down. Folding his arms, he fixed her with his stare until she felt pin-pricks of sweat dotting along her collar bone.

"How are things moving with this case?" he asked.

"It wouldn't surprise me if Doctor Manning's pissed a few people off along the way. He's arrogant, narcissistic, and a misogynist."

"Sounds like he's pissed you off."

"As a relative and as a professional."

"Enough to muddy your view?"

"Enough to see there's more to this case than meets the eye."

Hunter coughed. "Look Eva, if there's something you feel you should tell me, then now is the moment. I might be hard on you at times, but I am here for you . . . professionally, of course."

Wednesday could not remember the last time she witnessed Hunter's face go red.

"No need to clarify, Guv, and no, I've done nothing out of bounds."

"Good, good. Well, what do you propose now?"

"My mother is well currently, and I'd like to ask her about her time in the unit; who did what, when, who was liked and disliked. I will, of course, have Lennox present."

Hunter nodded. "How are things with Lennox and his son? Still in the YOI, I presume."

"Yes, and Lennox is finding it tough, but doesn't talk about it much."

Hunter stood up. "Interview your mother, and see if she can shed any light. But don't make this personal, Eva."

"I won't."

Wednesday banged on Lennox's office door. "We're off to see Joan Willow. I'm driving."

"Carey" by Joni Mitchell oozed through the speakers like honey through a mesh sieve. Wednesday tapped her fingers on the steering wheel, whilst Lennox watched the blur of poplar trees speeding past, blocking out the strains of Joni.

Chapter 49

Wednesday called out on opening the front door of her parents' house.

"I'm in the kitchen," Joan replied.

They found her sitting at an easel, enveloped in a shaft of sunlight coming through the window.

"You're painting again, that's a good sign. Where's Oliver?"

"He's in his studio. And yes, inspiration still manages to get through my med-fuddled mind. I hope it lasts."

Wednesday hummed a response as she walked towards the kettle.

"Good to see you again, Jacob. How's life treating you?"

"Not bad," he replied, fumbling with a packet of cigarettes in his coat pocket.

"If you want to smoke you'll have to go outside; I've given up again," she nodded in the direction of the back door; he needed no further prompting.

"What are you painting?" asked Wednesday, peering around the canvas.

"The garden as seen through the window. Seeing as you've brought Jacob, I can assume you're here on business?"

"I'm afraid so." Wednesday glanced at Lennox who was by the open door.

"We want you to think back over your time on the unit, if it's not too painful." She placed a mug of herbal tea on the table. "Perhaps you'll remember things more clearly now that you're home. Do you want Oliver with you?"

"Don't bother him, I'm fine. But I'm not sure I can remember anything worthwhile."

"I'd like you to close your eyes and focus on the days prior to Susan Roche's death. Sights, sounds, smells, people, and voices. Don't worry if it sounds trivial, we'll work out what we can use or discard."

Joan replaced her paintbrush in the jug of water, before picking up the mug and wrapping her hands around it. The steam misted-up her glasses.

"The first few days are rather sketchy; all my senses merged together."

"Move a few days forward. What can you remember about the last day Susan was alive. Did you see or speak to her?" Wednesday asked softly.

"I saw her in the lounge; she seemed different, more upbeat that morning."

"Who else was there?"

Joan inhaled deeply. "Melvyn was rocking in a chair near the door, waiting for his friend to visit, I think." She paused to take a sip. "Dave came rushing in at one point, screaming at Susan for stealing his cigarettes . . . I think."

"How did she respond?"

"She laughed, which was brave, I wouldn't have."

"Then what happened?"

"One of the nurses came in with tea and brownies, and Dave calmed down. Although maybe a nurse took him back to his room, I can't rightly remember." She opened her eyes and looked expectantly at her daughter, who smiled back patiently.

"Did anyone else visit that day? Did the doctor do his rounds?" Wednesday pressed.

Joan obliged, re-closing her eyes. "Not the doctor, but his wife came 'round. She listens if we need to talk."

"Olivia Manning, you mean. Did you talk to her?"

"I might have, I'm not sure. I've talked with her at one point, but I can't say on which day."

"Don't worry, Mum, you're being a big help."

"Am I, dear?" She took another sip of tea. "I wish I knew who killed Susan."

"Was she friendly with anyone, apart from you?"

"She never really interacted with anyone much. She would cry when her husband left the unit, but if anyone tried to comfort her she'd push them away; including me at times."

"Did they argue, was that why she was crying?"

"Not that I ever saw or heard. He always seemed pleasant in a misogynist way."

"What makes you say that?"

"He'd greet the men in a warmer manner, whereas we women just got a curt nod of the head."

"Susan included?"

"You could see he was making a deliberate effort to be nice to her, but the feelings were false."

"Was Susan aware he was having an affair?"

"She never mentioned it. Why, was he having an affair?"

Lennox stared at Wednesday. "Not that we know of," she lied. "Is there anything else that stands out in your mind? Did Susan have problems with any of the staff?"

"That charge nurse wasn't that caring to anyone, but I do remember Nurse Reilly showing a lack of compassion towards Susan; she never had any time for her, and would often tell her how badly she treated her caring husband."

Wednesday glanced at Lennox, pressing her lips together.

"Thanks Mum, I hope you feel okay after thinking about that place so hard. If anything else pops into your head, just let me know." Wednesday rubbed her temples, willing the thought of a cigarette to cease.

Lennox drained his mug and placed it by the sink. He could see Oliver Willow's pottery studio in the garden, and wondered whether he used it as a form of escapism from his everyday life. He watched Wednesday kiss Joan on the forehead before tapping him on the shoulder.

Lennox was pleased to be travelling in silence. Perhaps finally Wednesday understood how much he really detested Joni Mitchell.

Wednesday's phone rang on her desk. She listened closely before calling Lennox as he passed her open door.

"Barry Roche has returned home. Let's go and see what he has to say for himself."

Lennox pressed the intercom several times before Barry Roche's voice crackled through.

"What?"

"DS Lennox and DI Wednesday. Can we come up?"

There was no reply but the door latch buzzed. When they arrived on the second floor, the flat door was closed. Lennox knocked loudly.

"Coming, coming," he yelled over the barking dog.

He let them in as the dog excitedly greeted the pair.

"Mr Roche, how did Karen Reilly feel about you disappearing the way you did?"

He peered at her before shrugging.

"Did she want more from you after the death of your wife?"

Barry grabbed the excitable dog by his collar, guiding him firmly to the kitchen before closing the door.

"What is it you want to know, exactly?" he said, dropping into the armchair.

"Did Karen Reilly ever mention wanting your wife out of the way so you two could be together?"

He smirked. "You must be desperate if you still think Karen did it. She's too clever to do that; she'd get someone else to do it if she wanted that."

"What makes you say that?"

"She's a manipulative woman, and a very attractive one at that. She could make the Pope snort cocaine, if she wanted to."

"Did you ever tell her you two had a future together?"

"Not as such. She's a stunning nurse, why wouldn't I want to spend time with her. However, once Susan died, Karen became obsessed by wanting to move in together. I said it would look suspicious, but she wouldn't let up."

"Was your son aware of your affair?"

"No, I kept him out of it. Not sure he'd have been bothered, but I didn't want to risk it. He was embarrassed by Susan."

"Embarrassed?"

"How does a child cope with having a mother in and out of mental hospital? Kids teased him at school."

Lennox avoided looking in Wednesday's direction. "So Susan's death has perhaps done him a favour?"

"I'm not saying that. Jesus, you'll be saying he killed her next." He paused then looked between them. "You're joking, right?"

"This is a murder investigation; everyone around the victim is a potential suspect."

"Well you can leave Gavin alone; he's back at uni and making something of himself."

"Please don't leave again without letting us know."

"I *am* taking it seriously, but I'm innocent. I'm only guilty of having an affair."

They left the flat in silence, the subject of mental illness hanging over their heads, especially Wednesday's. Clawing, charred skeletal hands prodded at her mind and the grey memories caught within. With an exhale, she let the feelings go.

Chapter 50

Friday evenings were always busy in The Crazy Duck.

"I think I see a table," Lennox said. "You grab it, I'll get the drinks."

Wednesday threaded her way through the crowd, claiming the last table.

"Here," Lennox said, plonking a drink in front of her. "Cheers."

Wednesday smiled before taking a sip.

"Is there something you wanted to talk about?" he asked.

"Yes, but not what you imagined."

He frowned over the rim of his glass.

"I bet you think I want to talk about what Barry Roche said about mental illness in the family. But I don't."

Lennox's shoulders dropped as he took a large swig of beer.

"I'll be thirty-nine this year, which means I'm the big four-o next. Edging closer to a new decade has me thinking about the futility of trying to cling to the early years, and how we should appreciate each moment as it happens." She offered an apologetic smile.

"Very philosophical."

"It's to do with the advancing years."

"Forty isn't old. I dread the day fifty is upon me."

"*Don't.* Anyway, I want to break our rule and discuss Scarlett."

"I see." His neck muscles tensed. "This is going to be a big-sister lecture."

"When you didn't contact her over Christmas I was quite relieved. I thought I no longer needed to worry about the issue, but you seem to have taken-up from where you left off. Scarlett isn't strong enough to maintain a state of equilibrium through you treating her like a yo-yo. What's going on, Jacob?"

"I feel we've been down this avenue many times. What can I say that I haven't already said?"

"You can say the recent contact has been a mistake, and from now on you'll be nothing other than friends."

Lennox rubbed the thick hairs on his chin. "With all due respect, you're my boss at work but not in my personal life."

"I know, but I did warn you when you got involved with her in the first place, that it could cause difficulties between us."

"Our working relationship hasn't suffered . . ."

"I fear that could be about to change."

"Why, because I chose her and not you?"

Wednesday slammed her glass on the table, and people turned to look.

"I didn't mean that. Please, Eva, don't go."

Digby Hunter was clapping his hands in the Incident Room as Wednesday blustered in. Lennox was already there.

"Wednesday and Lennox, I want you to arrest Barry Roche for the murder of his wife. Damlish and Arlow, get down to London and arrest the son, Gavin, for perverting the course of justice."

As he disappeared to his office, Wednesday followed him.

"Am I missing something, Guv?" she asked, rubbing her temples.

"Apart from you being late, you mean? Due to your tardiness I took the call from the crime scene unit who have more results. Along with Barry Roche's skin cells on the dressing gown belt—which I know could be explained away—they found corroborating evidence of his finger and hand prints on the wall behind the toilet and on the ceiling tile moved to hang her from, in her ensuite. He can't explain those away so easily. I want them in to shake them with this evidence; see what they have to say."

As she turned to leave, Hunter stopped her.

"Is there a problem I should be aware of?"

"No Guv, I just slept badly, that's all."

She walked over to Lennox's office, rapping loudly on his open door.

"You can drive," she snapped more vehemently that she intended. But it worked. Lennox jumped out of his chair, grabbing his coat, and trotted after her.

Barry Roche was incensed as Wednesday read him his rights and Lennox cuffed him.

"You've got this all wrong; I didn't kill her," he protested.

"We've got evidence that says otherwise," Lennox replied, frog-marching him to the lift.

The lift was cramped with the three of them, and the sound of Barry grinding his teeth raised the hairs on the back of Wednesday's neck. Lennox bundled him into the car before they sped off.

Barry was put in an interview room to sweat a bit as Wednesday and Lennox gathered the paperwork. The pair watched him through the two-way mirror as he rocked back and forth, muttering to himself under his breath.

"Do you want a solicitor?" Wednesday asked as they entered the room.

"An innocent man doesn't need representation," he grumbled.

"Right then," she continued, sitting opposite him with Lennox by her side. "Finger and hand prints were found in Susan's ensuite on the walls and ceiling tile, in the exact places you'd need to put your hands to steady yourself to hang her body. The ceiling tile was moved to hang her from the pipe, remember?"

Barry rubbed his hands together vigorously, searching the floor for answers. He then looked up and peered straight into Wednesday's eyes.

"The ceiling tile was dislodged in one corner. Susan was paranoid someone was watching her when she was on the toilet, and she begged me to put it right. That's how my prints got there."

"Why did she wait for you to do it rather than ask the staff?"

"She said she didn't want the staff to think she was being irrational."

Wednesday raised her eyebrows. "We only have your word on that. You are, or were, having an affair with Karen Reilly, and that's motive enough to want Susan dead."

"I admit, I no longer loved her but I never wanted her dead. I hoped we'd divorce one day, I suppose, but I didn't really think about the future."

"Not even with Karen?"

"I've already told you my feelings about Karen. I swear I didn't kill Susan. I couldn't have, I'm too squeamish."

"So if we're to believe you, the alternative is someone is trying to frame you. Who would want to do that?"

"I don't bloody know."

"We're going to keep you here for a while, whilst forensics search your flat for more evidence. I suggest you consider carefully involving a solicitor. If they find other incriminating evidence you're going to be in serious trouble. We'll make sure your dog is looked after for the time being."

Barry bowed his head and stared at his hands. "You won't find anything."

"Is that because you've been very careful?" asked Lennox.

He looked up briefly before shaking his head slowly.

As they left the interview room, Lennox said he was going for a smoke in the courtyard.

"Don't be long," she barked, "we've got work to do."

Wednesday marched to her office and slammed the door. Hunter watched her every move.

Gavin Roche jumped as the police knocked loudly on his university dorm room. On opening the door cautiously, he toppled backwards by the force of Arlow pushing against it.

"What the fuck," he spluttered, eyeing the plastic wraps on his desk.

"Your father's been arrested," Arlow began. "And so are you for possession of drugs, as well as perverting the course of justice," he added, scooping up the evidence from the desk.

Gavin rolled his eyes. "They're not mine," he snarled, as Damlish cuffed him. "And why's Dad been arrested?"

"For the murder of your mother," Damlish said, swinging him around.

"Really? The old man's got more bottle than I gave him credit for."

He grinned at some students as he was frog-marched down the corridor. Suddenly, a fog of anxiety engulfed him as he wondered what Sam Brass would do to him when he found out about the arrest.

Chapter 51

Gavin nonchalantly tipped backwards in the chair, much like a naughty school boy in detention. Wednesday noticed his yellow-stained finger-tips on his right hand.

"You understand the charges against your father, and why you've been arrested. So do you have anything to say?" Wednesday asked.

"It's laughable you think my old man killed my mum. He's got the brawn but definitely *not* the brains."

"But you have, perhaps? Let's face it, you've profited from the life insurance."

The smirk on his lips dropped for a second before lighting up once more.

"You're fishing, you've got no proof."

"We do have evidence regarding your father's actions. Perhaps you had the idea, or put the idea in his head."

"Bullshit. I admit I didn't care much for her, but I thought she'd finally manage to kill herself one day. She tried enough times."

"That must have been difficult for you."

"Not really, it just meant she spent more time in a nut-house, which meant I could bring mates home after school."

"You couldn't otherwise?"

"Not with the mad old cow there. Never knew how she'd be around them; couldn't trust her. Once she flirted with my best mate, which everyone found hilarious, except me. I got bullied because of her."

"So you've more freedom now that she's gone."

"Not really, I'm at uni now, remember?"

"Talking of which," began Lennox, "the amount of drugs found in your room is more on the intention to supply scale rather than just personal use."

"I'm just looking after it for some friends."

"We're not stupid."

He shrugged, studying his fingernails.

Lennox got up to see who was knocking on the door. After a few moments of muttering, he re-entered the room and whispered in Wednesday's ear.

"We'll be back shortly," she advised before exiting with Lennox in tow.

Once in her office, she clicked on her computer and read the results for herself.

"How bizarre," she uttered. "Barry Roche never mentioned she'd visited the flat. Let's check with him then I think we should pay her a visit. We'll leave Gavin to the drug squad for now."

Olivia Manning opened her front door. "My husband's at work."

"It's you we've come to see," Wednesday replied.

Olivia's eyes did not flicker as she let them in, guiding them to the lounge.

"What can I do for you?"

"Have you ever visited Barry and Susan Roche's flat?"

She searched the ceiling for a few seconds. "Actually yes. Susan asked me to fetch a clean nightdress and some makeup. Why?"

"Why didn't she ask her husband?"

"Because he'd get it wrong."

"How did you get in?"

"Susan gave me her key."

"Do you often do this kind of thing?"

"It's the first time I'd been to a patient's home. She was desperate for her things to make her look and feel better; I took pity on her I suppose. Usually I'm just a sympathetic ear and provider of tea."

"I presume your husband's aware of this?"

"Of course, we have no secrets. Am I in some sort of trouble?"

"Your boundary lines are rather blurred. What's to stop you from telling your husband what a patient said to you in confidence?"

"I have a certificate in counselling. I know the codes and ethics attached to this kind of work. Only if a patient poses a risk to himself or others do I reveal the conversation."

"Why did you fail to tell us of your visit to Susan's flat?"

Olivia expelled a deep sigh. "I'm obviously in trouble otherwise you wouldn't keep hounding me with the same question. I suppose it just slipped my mind."

"Now would be a good time to tell us what you talked about with Susan, and what was her mood like on the day of her murder?"

"In a good frame of mind, considering her illness. Her only worry on that day was her son, Gavin."

Raising her eyebrow, Wednesday waited.

"She worried he'd fail his studies."

"What made her say that?"

"Fear, nothing more."

"Did she talk about her husband?"

She paused. "Yes, she wasn't always that complimentary."

"Could you elaborate," Wednesday urged.

"He wasn't understanding of her illness. He tired of her quickly, and always seemed keen to have her admitted to hospital."

"Have you been in contact with the husband or son since her death?"

"I considered offering them support after their bereavement, but I didn't think they'd take it up." She crossed her legs, slowly turning her slim ankle; an action Lennox did not fail to notice. Wednesday noted his interest.

"That will be all for now, but please remain available for further questioning."

"You mean don't leave the country," she giggled like a school girl.

Once in the car, Wednesday unleashed her anger; venom in her voice.

"I really wish you'd stop ogling every woman we question. You're beginning to look like a lecherous old man, not to mention you're supposed to be dating Scarlett."

"Firstly, I'm not *old*; I'm in my early forties. And lastly, I'm not dating your bloody sister, sorry, *half-sister*. We meet up occasionally."

Wednesday glared at him. "Don't cry when your world crumbles."

Back at the station, Hunter was prowling around waiting for progress. Gavin Roche was being interviewed by the drug squad, and Barry Roche was sitting in a cell refusing to eat or drink.

"So?" Hunter called out as Wednesday and Lennox entered the Incident Room.

"Olivia Manning had a plausible excuse for being at the Roche's flat," Wednesday replied turning her back on Lennox.

"Can I see you in my office? Alone."

Hunter waited for Wednesday to enter before closing the door.

"Right, what's going on?"

"Guv?"

"Between you and Lennox."

"Nothing to worry about."

"I am worrying. There's a distinct cold-front between you. You make a good team. Is this to do with your journalist sister?"

"It's not interfering with the job. And yes, Scarlett is partly involved."

"Well see it doesn't mess up this case, otherwise I'll bang both your heads together."

Wednesday left his office, chewing on angry words in her head. She jerked her head at Lennox towards her office, and waited for him to arrive. Pulling a chocolate bar from her desk drawer, she bit into it and pushed the chunk into her cheek, giving her a hamster-like face.

Lennox shut the door and stood in front of her.

"Sit, for god's sake, I'm not about to expel you from school."

He sat and half-smiled.

"Look Jacob, I can't pretend not to notice your attitude towards women or your on-off relationship with Scarlett. However, for Hunter to notice something's awry between us, we must assume we look bad to the whole team. So for the sake of a good working relationship, I suggest you don't mention what you're doing with Scarlett."

"And what will you do?" he smiled.

"I'll tolerate your company and your clothes stinking of tobacco."

"Thank you, Boss," he replied with a bigger grin, which he quickly wiped from his face as she shot him a fiery glance.

"Something's not right with this case," she said, before biting off another chunk of chocolate. "All the evidence is pointing to Barry Roche, but he's adamant he's innocent."

A knock at the door interrupted her flow.

"Yes," she snapped.

"Gavin Roche has just given up the name of his supplier. Does Sam Brass mean anything to you?" asked DI Boxer, from the drug squad.

"It does, and I want to interview him too." Pushing her chair back, she wiped chocolate from the corner of her mouth, before tapping on Lennox's shoulder to get going.

Chapter 52

Joni Mitchell's voice filled the void in the car as Wednesday drove to Sam Brass's home. Squinting in the sunlight, she pulled the visor down.

"Have you thought about quitting smoking?" she asked.

"Seeing how you suffer, I'm not keen on the idea."

"I'm *not* suffering."

"I beg to differ."

"All right, it's not easy. The tablets are working, but I won't be on them forever. I'm worried I'll relapse. Yet I'm so much happier being smoke-free."

"Well hold on to that feeling and remember it when you're tempted."

"You sound like you've swallowed a pompous self-help book." She pulled up hard outside Sam's house, jerking Lennox against his seatbelt. He thought better than to dowse her with another winsome cliché.

He rang the doorbell several times, but there was no reply. Wednesday stepped back from the door, looking up to the bedroom window in time to see the net curtain twitch.

"He's in. Get 'round the back," she commanded.

Lennox skidded on the mossy path as he ran around the corner and scaled the side gate, just in time to meet Sam coming in the opposite direction. Lennox lunged for him but Sam dodged his grasp before spinning around and running back into the garden.

Sam was fast and halfway up the back fence when Lennox caught him by the ankle. Yanking hard, he pulled Sam down, but not before Sam's right foot caught him in his face.

"Get down, you're under arrest," Lennox yelled through gritted teeth, rivulets of blood edging down his cheek from a heel-shaped cut.

Sam's legs flayed around wildly. Lennox was about to lose his grip when Wednesday arrived at his side, grabbing Brass by the other leg, and dragging him to the ground.

"Time to calm down," she said, snapping the cuffs around his wrists.

They heaved him to his feet and marched him to the car.

"What the hell is this about?" he spat.

"You're wanted by the drug squad, and we have some questions," Wednesday replied, opening the car door and tossing him inside.

Lennox sat beside him whilst Wednesday climbed into the driver's seat before slamming the door.

Sam sat grim-faced, refusing to talk to Wednesday and Lennox; he was still seething from his encounter with the drug squad. Lennox tenderly prodded the fresh dressing on his cheek.

"We've evidence of a shadowy figure going into the unit the night of Susan Roche's death. The height and build of the individual matches you," said Wednesday, sitting back in her chair, resting her gaze on him.

Sam fidgeted in his seat. "What if I told you Eddie texted me saying he wanted to see me desperately? It was after visiting hours, so I crept in. He's my brother, what could I do?" he shrugged.

"I'll need your mobile to verify that. What did Eddie want?"

"He was really low and fancied some chocolate; he's on a restricted diet. Anyway, Susan had wound him up saying he needed to lose weight to get a woman. He said he was gay, and she said he was using that as an excuse for being single."

"Did he say anything else about the victim?"

"No, he was too busy stuffing his face."

"Who else did you see that night?"

Sam leant forward, pressing his elbows into his thighs.

"I saw that bloke in charge, with that young student. Tried chatting her up once; she's a stuck-up cow."

"Where did you see them?"

"Nipping out for a fag."

"Did you see the other nurse?"

"The gorgeous one with the short blonde hair and blue eyes? Yeah, she was going to her car."

"What time was that?"

"About two, I suppose. Why?"

"Did you see if she drove off?"

"She did."

Wednesday left the room, asking Arlow for Sam Brass to be detained for injuring a policeman, giving them time to find Karen Reilly.

Karen Reilly answered the door, her wet hair plastered to her head, making her look bald. Clutching her dressing gown, she let them in without uttering a word.

"We've an eyewitness account of you leaving the unit the night of Susan Roche's murder. You failed to mention this," Wednesday said.

"I knew you'd find out one way or another; and I was so careful." She collapsed onto the sofa, her dressing gown parting to reveal blotchy calves. "I left, but only for an hour. I met up with Barry in the Premier Inn; he begged me to go."

"Have you got any receipts?"

She nodded, getting up and wandering over to her handbag. She riffled in her purse before retrieving a crumpled receipt and handing it to Lennox.

"Do you have to let my boss know?" she asked, looking at Lennox with her doe-eyes. "Of course you do," she whispered, seeing the look on his face.

Back in the car, Wednesday popped a mint in her mouth.

"This means Gavin Roche has no alibi for that hour. He would have had the time to rush to the unit, murder his mother, before getting back home. Barry would have been totally unaware."

"Perhaps we should see what Eric Knight has to say?"

"No better time than now."

Arriving at Eric Knight's home, they found the place empty. On contacting the unit they were informed he had taken a few days leave.

Chapter 53

Lennox scoured the pages on his computer screen, scribbling notes as he progressed through the document. He was consumed with the need to get back on an even keel with Wednesday.

With a satisfying sigh, he pushed his chair back and headed for her office.

"I've been researching skunk, and how it's much more dangerous if consumed, rather than smoked," he said, with a smile on his face.

"And?"

"What happens if Eddie Brass has been eating it rather than smoking it? There'd be no smell, and the side effects could be more intense and dangerous."

"I don't see how this is helping us."

Lennox stooped slightly, wishing they were working from the same page rather than completely different manuals.

"It's something to bear in mind."

They were interrupted by the phone ringing. She answered it with her back turned towards him, and spoke for several minutes before turning to face him once more.

"CSU have found leather glove prints in Susan Roche's room. There was a delay as they sent the prints to a leather specialist. This now points us to someone else being in that room who was trying to hide the fact. Maybe Barry Roche is being set up, after all. Who'd want to do that?"

"He doesn't strike me as bothering anyone that much."

"He must effect someone; someone we haven't noticed or thought about." She pushed the scraps of paper to one side, and took a clean sheet from her drawer and began doodling.

"How are things with Archie?" she ventured, without looking up.

"I'm totally out of contact with him. Hopefully once he's released he'll make contact with me."

"And Alfie?"

"We're communicating secretly via e-mail."

"Is that wise?"

"He worries his mum would ground him if we did it openly, and knowing Lucy, she probably would."

Wednesday shrugged her shoulders whilst drawing circles. Then a thought struck her.

"I'm going to visit my mother whilst you recheck Barry Roche's alibis."

Lennox watched her leave, aware they rarely separated to interview people. He wondered whether she wanted to see Joan alone, or she was just still angry with him. He suspected the latter.

Joan answered the door.

"On your own? You look troubled," she said, leading her daughter to the kitchen, where she switched the kettle on.

"How have you been since being home? Any of those nightmares you were having on the unit?"

"None thank heavens; they were terrifying."

"You said you never smelt cannabis being smoked, is that correct?"

"Yes. What's this all about, dear, and why isn't Jacob with you?"

"He had other things to do."

"Being mentally ill doesn't mean I've completely lost the ability to see what's going on with people around me. Have you two fallen out? Is it over Scarlett?" She tipped boiling water into the teapot then brought it to the table. "Your silence speaks volumes, dear daughter."

"Then hear me roar and concentrate on my questions."

"You seem very fixated about cannabis on the unit. I thought that stuff was bad for people like me."

"It is, according to a lot of research. It's just lots of relatives felt their family member was showing little sign of improvement. Even you had those horrendous nightmares."

"And why do you think that was?"

"Perhaps you were all consuming cannabis in some way."

Joan poured the tea and pushed a cup and saucer in her daughter's direction. "Why would someone want to give us that?"

"I can't answer that, Mum. If I could I'd perhaps see who would have the reason." She blew on the steaming liquid before taking a sip.

"You didn't all eat the same food, did you?"

"No, there was a menu to choose from; that was a plus side of the place."

Wednesday sighed, pushing her cup away, wishing she had made herself a coffee instead.

"Perhaps you should go back to the station and make it up with Jacob. You always let Scarlett interfere with your male friends and boyfriends. You're just as pretty, you know."

Wednesday laughed. "You have to say that, you're our mother. Anyone would say Scarlett was more blessed than me. But you're sweet," she concluded, patting her hand.

"You're the least likely to be mentally ill also, if I'm honest."

"What brings you to that conclusion?"

"Call it a mother's intuition," Joan replied quietly.

On returning to the station, Wednesday saw Lennox on the phone in his office. He was staring intently at his computer screen, unaware of her return.

Entering her office, her mother's words circled her mind; making ever decreasing circles that only served to make her feel nauseated and scared. Scared of potentially having a mentally ill half-sister, as well as a mother; both sapping her precious free-time and energy. Who would care for her if the worst happened?

Lennox was at her door.

"I didn't see you come back, Boss. Can I have a word?"

"Case related, I hope."

"Totally. I had a follow-up call from the forensic guys about the leather gloves. They narrowed the crime scene prints down to a golfing or driving glove. So I searched the crime scene photos to see if I could spot any—"

"And I've just remembered where I might have seen a pair. Let's run it passed Hunter, get a warrant, and go." she interjected.

Chapter 54

Elephant-grey clouds scudded across the sky, drenching the earth with torrential rain. Lennox peered intently through the windscreen as the wipers sloshed the water across the glass.

He pulled up outside the Mannings' house, pleased to see both cars parked out front.

"How do you want to play this?" he asked, pulling on the handbrake.

"Calmly, no need to heighten anyone's anxiety."

They dashed to the porch unable to prevent large drops of water from sinking into their coats. Lennox rang the bell and waited. Olivia opened the door with a look of expectation on her face.

"You bring good news?"

"Not exactly," replied Wednesday. "Is your husband at home?"

"Yes, come in."

She led them to the lounge, where Harvey was sitting reading a newspaper. He lowered it and peered over the top.

"How are you feeling?" enquired Wednesday.

"Getting better. Surely you're not doing house calls to see how victims of crime are recuperating?"

"No, but it would be remiss of me not to enquire."

Olivia beckoned for them to take a seat then announced she was making coffee.

"You might not want to do that when you realise why we're here," Wednesday said calmly. "We've a warrant to seize any driving gloves in the house or cars."

"Sounds intriguing. May I ask what we're supposed to have done with said gloves," he asked, folding the paper and placing it on his knee.

"You both have a pair?"

They nodded before Olivia left the room to make the promised coffee. Lennox followed her.

"Had you met with Susan and Barry Roche prior to her admission?"

enquired Wednesday.

"No, referrals come to me, then I sit with my team and discuss the cases. After that, we choose who to admit if there are too many referrals. And before you ask, I remember there being enough space for Susan Roche to be admitted."

"How did you find Barry Roche?"

"A typical husband who's at the end of his tether with having a mentally ill wife; not everyone copes as well as Oliver Willow."

Wednesday dug her nails into the palm of her hand, sitting rigidly in the chair. "So he was pretty stressed out? Did he actually tell you he'd had enough, or are you surmising?"

"A psychiatrist can read behind people's words, actions, and behaviours. Like you, for example," he said, turning his head towards Lennox re-entering the room. "You're always preoccupied with some personal issue whenever I see you. It's clearly weighing you down, and may start to affect your work if you don't sort it out."

Lennox scowled, and Olivia entered behind him with a tray of refreshments. Wednesday controlled her breathing.

"We've received new information hence our need to see your driving gloves."

"Here are mine," said Olivia, handing over her black leather gloves before pouring the coffee. "I'll get yours if you tell me where they are," she said, handing Harvey a bone china cup and saucer.

"I leave them in my car; but I'm not sure about giving them anything until I've consulted a lawyer," he snapped.

Olivia's face shone with a layer of sweat. "There's no harm, surely?"

"Firstly, I want to know why they want them, and secondly, are they asking other people, or just targeting us?"

He was speaking as though they were not in the room; another ploy to reclaim the power, Wednesday suspected.

"Everyone's being asked. We're here first as I remember you taking off a pair at the nurses' station."

"There you see, nothing to worry about, they're asking everyone," chimed Olivia, handing around a plate of biscuits.

Wednesday declined, so Lennox begrudgingly followed suit. She drank the percolated coffee quickly, keen to get going. Lennox sensed her haste and gulped his down.

"If we could have Doctor Manning's gloves, we'll be on our way," Wednesday asked.

Olivia rose and returned shortly with them.

Once in the car, Wednesday put the two evidence bags in her bag as Lennox switched on the engine and headed to their next destination.

Jordan Campbell opened his front door, eyes widening on viewing the detectives. He extended a clammy hand to greet them, as though they were visiting for dinner.

He took them into the tiny front room of the terraced house, where Fiona was seated in front of the TV. Garish colours and loud sounds of an advert swamped the small space, as Wednesday and Lennox jostled for room to stand.

"How are you doing, Mrs Campbell?" asked Wednesday.

Fiona's eyes remained fixed on the screen, until Jordan touched her shoulder.

"I'm okay thanks," she said faintly.

"Why are you here?" questioned Jordan, resting his hands on her shoulders.

"We won't keep you long. We have a warrant to collect any leather driving gloves belonging to people in this case. I remember seeing a pair on top of Fiona's handbag."

"They belonged to my father; they make me feel close to him," replied Fiona. "I don't want you to have them, they must stay with me."

"They have a warrant, darling. We have no choice." Jordan left the room, returning two minutes later with a large pair of tatty leather gloves. "They're too big for her," he stated, noticing Wednesday's raised eyebrow. "She just carries them around in her handbag as a source of comfort."

Fiona gazed up at them as Lennox put them in an evidence bag.

"They'll be looked after, and all being well, returned to you soon." Wednesday wanted to reassure her, sensing her melancholy saturating the room.

As they began leaving, Wednesday turned around. "Did you experience nightmares whilst on the unit?"

Fiona's eyes remained fixed straight ahead.

"I never dream. I saw things there; shadows brushing across my brain, scary faces . . ." she paused to sigh loudly. "I'm better now that I'm home, but I can't let Jordan leave me; I'm terrified of being alone. Night shadows scare me."

Wednesday looked towards Jordan, who was gently shaking his head. He knelt before her. "I'm here for you; you're safe now."

"Didn't you feel safe before, Fiona?" Wednesday asked. "Did you feel unsafe on the unit? Was somebody troubling you?"

"I sometimes felt soothed on the unit, but fear could quickly take over me at times . . ." Fiona began crying, and Jordan no longer looked affable.

"You've upset her," he said harshly. "Please leave and bring the gloves back quickly. What do you want them for anyway?"

"Just part of our ongoing investigation."

Wednesday shoved the gloves into her bag as they walked back to the car. She felt troubled about upsetting Fiona, whom she saw as a younger, more fragile version of her mother. She wondered if Jordan would cope as Oliver has done, or would he abandon her as her own father had Joan all those years ago.

"Let's get these back to Alex," she said, fastening her seatbelt.

Lennox switched the engine on and headed back, mindful of the small wall building between them; realising he had more to lose than just his partnership with her.

"Sam Brass is going to court with regards to his drug dealing. He's not a happy man, but his arrest was a bonus I suppose," Hunter said, walking alongside Wednesday towards the canteen. "How long will the glove results take?"

"Alex has given them top priority, shouldn't take too long."

They grabbed a cellophane-wrapped sandwich each and joined the queue.

"How do you find going home to an empty house, when your mind is crammed full of work, and you've got no one to share the misery with?" he asked, picking up a yogurt and studying the ingredient list.

Wednesday willed her mouth not to seize up or splutter out garbage. She inhaled discreetly to compose her thoughts.

"It's never bothered me. Even when Scarlett lived with me, I couldn't discuss work, so I'm used to it. If I'm really hitting a rough patch, Lennox comes 'round for a working dinner."

"Could you still do that with the current climate between you, or would you be better off without him?"

Wednesday handed over some money for the sandwich and waited for the change. She stood back and let Hunter do the same, giving her time to reflect on what he had just said. It had not occurred to her just how much she relied on Lennox, and how it would be if he was no longer around.

"Has he asked for a transfer?" she queried as they headed back.

"So you'd miss him," he mused, "just like all the other female staff in the building."

"No, I enjoy working with him, we complement each other. But as for being attracted to him, if that's what you're asking, then I see him too much as a colleague. Besides, he's dated Scarlett, in case you've forgotten." She tucked a strand of hair back that had begun springing free from the bun.

They mounted the stone steps and entered the building.

"I'm finding going back to an empty house quite daunting at times," he sighed, "but I suppose it's something you get used to, right?"

"You do, until one day you feel you'll never be able to share space with someone again. Space becomes a precious commodity."

Hunter held the door open for her to enter the Incident Room. She drew a sigh of relief as they parted for their respective offices; she found speaking with him an intense experience.

On opening her front door, the smell of burnt food assaulted Wednesday's nose, and the sound of sobbing made her heart sink. Scarlett.

Chapter 55

Scarlett was sitting at the kitchen table with her head in her hands, her pre-Raphaelite curls cascading over the table. The sound of her hiccups and sobs reminded Wednesday of the time Scarlett, aged seven, did a cartwheel in their parents' lounge, smashing one of Oliver's ornate tea-pots that was due to be delivered later that day.

"What's happened?" Wednesday asked, opening the back door to let the black smog dissipate.

"Niall sent me home from work; it's got to be bad for my boss to do that. Then I tried baking some cookies, and burnt the fucking stuff." Her voice was muffled, but the sentiment of despair was not disguised.

"Forget the baking, how about I make a pot of tea, and I'll open some biscuits?"

"Tea and sympathy, how original," she sniped. "I'd rather have a glass of wine."

"You know alcohol isn't going to solve anything."

"Oh stop arsing around, and open a bottle."

Scarlett's voice made Wednesday jump, but her determination not to allow Scarlett to rule the mood of the house, made her fill the kettle and slide it onto the hob.

"Have you heard when your appointment with the consultant is?" asked Wednesday, monitoring her tone of voice.

"It was yesterday."

Wednesday spun around. "We've missed it."

"You did, I didn't," she replied, easing herself out of the chair and heading towards the fridge.

The only thing Wednesday could hear was the rush of blood coursing through her ear canals. She steadied herself against the worktop and watched Scarlett removing a bottle of wine from the fridge door. A celebratory move perhaps?

"He was very matter-of-fact, saying it probably didn't come as much of a surprise, seeing as I've had a few episodes in my twenties; something we all chose to ignore." She paused to pour a large glass of white wine. "My diagnosis is bi-polar affective disorder. What do you think of that, then, sis?"

The room swayed, as Wednesday staggered to a chair. She focused on trying to breathe more slowly and evenly, but the screaming voices in her head were overpowering.

"Why didn't you say anything yesterday or last night?"

"I needed time to assimilate the info first. Besides, you've reacted as I expected, and I couldn't have dealt with that yesterday. I'm more sanguine today." She downed half the glass before topping it up. "Don't look at me like that."

"Sorry," Wednesday muttered, aware of heated pin-pricks on her eyeballs, threatening tears at any moment. She blinked rapidly. "Have you told Oliver or Mum?"

"Nope, as I've already said, I needed some head space before sharing the news. But now you know, you can tell them for me."

Here we go, thought Wednesday. "I can't take over your life, you have to be in charge, otherwise you're letting me and your illness define you."

"I can't face telling Mum. The self-flagellation she'll display will be unbearable." She drained the glass in a few gulps.

"That's something else you'll have to control; you know how mental illness and alcohol don't mix, or illegal drugs come to that."

"Good luck with that," she laughed wryly. "Although drugs have never been a hobby of mine, so you don't have to worry there."

"Worry," shouted Wednesday. "Worry, I do nothing but bloody worry. When I receive a call from Oliver, I instantly worry about Mum, and now I have to add you to the mix."

"Nobody's asking you to be the family saviour. Who's going to worry about you should you become ill?"

And there it was. The fear was out of the bag; the fear that haunted Wednesday most of her life. With Scarlett now ill, the fear was tangible, compressing her chest, and impeding her breathing.

"Still, as I've said before, your dad is sane; boring but sane. My dad, however, has a tinge of madness lying dormant in his soul. The only reason he stays sane is he knows they would spiral into decline; feeding stray cats instead of themselves."

The frayed image made Wednesday smile, which in turn moved to laughter. "I think I may be experiencing my own breakdown. My family are going to be the death of me." She sipped some tea. "No man is ever going to want to enter this family now," she smiled.

"Are you going to tell Lennox?"

"Do you want me to?"

"I don't know."

For the first time, Wednesday saw emotional pain transmitted through Scarlett's eyes. She had the look of a child who had just discovered dogs do not go to farms when they are old.

Moving to her side, she put her arm around Scarlett's shoulders. "Let's take one day at a time; but Mum and Oliver need to know." She gave her a squeeze before going upstairs for a shower, hoping to wash the stains of the traumatic day from her body.

Alex was hovering around Wednesday's office door when she arrived. He noticed dark shadows spoiling her eyes, but said nothing.

"You owe me for the speed of these results," he said, brandishing a piece of paper.

He followed her inside, waiting for a rush of her enthusiasm he normally experienced. Receiving only fleeting eye contact, he resigned himself to being disappointed.

"The gloves belonging to Fiona Campbell aren't the ones. She'll be pleased to get them back, by all accounts. However, the ones belonging to Olivia Manning do match the prints. I managed to get a partial fingerprint from inside the glove, so if you get me hers I could check to see if they match."

Wednesday clicked back into gear. "That's great; I owe you a drink for this."

"Now you know that will never happen," he smiled as he left.

She looked around for Lennox and saw him talking conspiratorially to Maria Jones. He saw her and sauntered over.

"They've found Eric Knight; they're bringing him in," he said.

"Is that what you were discussing with Jones?"

"No, that," he said looking around before stepping closer, "was about Hunter's birthday. She thought he might need cheering up, so she's arranging drinks in The Crazy Duck followed by an Indian. You'd be up for that, wouldn't you?"

She blushed. "Probably. Anyway, let's interview Eric Knight, and I want Arlow and Damlish to arrest Olivia Manning on suspicion of murder. We'll interview her after Eric."

Eric looked a former shadow of himself as he sat in the interview room. Stubble stippled his chin, and his usually pristine crew-cut was bushing out.

"Do you want a solicitor?" asked Wednesday.

"No need, this is all a big mistake."

"We'd be interested in knowing why you decided to disappear?" Wednesday asked.

"I needed a holiday."

"You'll perhaps be intrigued to learn we've arrested Sam Brass with intent to supply. He's looking at a long stretch. However, he's got a deal if he gives up the names of big buyers." Her eyes never left his face.

"What's this got to do with me?"

"He told us interesting stuff about the unit, and frankly, if you don't mention things before we charge you, it won't look good."

"You're bluffing, I'm not falling for this," he smirked.

"Okay, perhaps we're of little consequence to you; whereas the NHS action could affect the rest of your career."

"So I bought a little cannabis to relax at home with, big deal. I wasn't stoned on duty, so who cares?"

"The quantity you bought was undoubtedly for resale, we're not fools."

"You've no evidence."

"We've Sam Brass's statement, plus the THC levels in the patients on The Raven Unit backs up what he tells us." She paused before continuing, letting the silence weigh heavily in the room. "May I say as a DI and a patient's relative, your actions are despicable, and you'll undoubtedly be struck off the nursing register for this." She cocked her head trying to catch his eye.

"It kept the bloody mentalists quiet," he spat. "You try working day and night with paranoid, aggressive people. They get on your nerves. They needed controlling, and this worked a treat."

"But it had an adverse effect on some of them too."

"Of course, but that made the shift more exciting and fly by," he grinned.

"I always thought you were a bit eager to exert your authority with a needle."

"Oh come on, lady, don't tell me chasing and arresting people doesn't give you a buzz; why else would you do this crappy job?"

"There's the satisfaction in a job well done, and getting criminals off the streets."

"Bullshit, that's just poster talk. It's all about having power over people; that's what it's all about," he said, slapping his hand on the table.

A tap at the door alerted Wednesday to Olivia Manning's arrival.

"Is that what Susan Roche's death was about, power?"

He looked directly at her, fire in his eyes. "You're not pinning that on me," he snapped. "She was a pathetic woman, but I had no reason to kill her. Her husband's a better bet than me."

They left him for the drug squad to deal with as they prepared to interview Olivia.

Olivia sat in the interview room looking as demure as a character in a Jane Austin novel. A delicate smile graced her lips as they entered the room.

"Have you instructed a solicitor?" asked Wednesday.

"No need, everything's in hand."

"Really, because from where I'm sitting, you're facing a charge of murder, which is well outside any sort of comfort zone, and a solicitor would watch over your interests."

"This will look after my interests well enough," she replied, placing a hand-written letter on the table.

Wednesday picked it up by the edges and read it.

To whom it may concern,

I, Susan Victoria Roche, do declare that I instructed Olivia Darcy Manning to aid in my suicide so I didn't fail again. I chose when, where, and how it was to take place, and if you're reading this now, I can only assume that we succeeded. Thank you Olivia, from the bottom of my heart.

Yours faithfully,
Susan

"This is a little too convenient," Wednesday said, slipping the letter into an evidence bag. "This will have to be examined by a handwriting and fingerprint expert to corroborate your story."

"Whatever, I've nothing to fear."

"We don't just want your fingerprints for elimination purposes, we want them in connection with your leather gloves. The prints of your leather gloves were found in Susan's ensuite. Are you sure you don't want a solicitor now?"

Olivia's pinched mouth remained closed; her eyes gazing directly into Wednesday's. She inhaled deeply before speaking. "Of course you'll find my prints there, didn't the letter mean anything to you?"

"Tell me," asked Wednesday, sitting back in her chair, "why would you do this for her?"

"She wanted to die and I wanted Harvey's unit to fail. Two birds with one stone, if you like."

"I comprehend her desire, it's in keeping with her illness, but why do you want the unit to fail?"

"Because it's ruining my marriage. Harvey used to be an attentive husband in the first few years, then he opens the unit, and I rarely see him. He rushes there for any emergency, stays late, starts early. The unit's his mistress and baby all rolled into one."

Wednesday gazed upon the woman who was acting like a spoilt child.

"How did this plan come about in the first place?"

"I used to spend time with the patients, thinking it would get Harvey to notice me. I said this to Susan one day as she was bleating on about how uncaring her husband was. She suspected him of having an affair, and decided she no longer wanted to live, but she wanted to punish him."

"So you planted evidence to point in his direction."

"Yes, wasn't I clever?"

"Except for the prints from your gloves."

"It doesn't matter, this letter redeems me. It's assisted suicide."

"I suspect the bleach incident was also your doing."

Olivia blushed. "I wanted the poor image of the unit to keep growing. The bleach was just an inspired action to make the press interested again. Nothing bad came of it for a patient," she smiled sheepishly.

"Would I be correct in saying your martial arts expertise came in handy when you assaulted your husband?"

"You're smart, DI Wednesday; I like smart women. I wanted him to take the crimes seriously, and I thought that would do the trick. Plus, I was so very angry with him, so it was cathartic."

They left the room, leaving an officer watching over Olivia, and headed out for examples of Olivia's and Susan's handwriting.

Chapter 56

"You okay?" Lennox asked as he started the engine.

"A few things on my mind. Something about this case still isn't feeling right," Wednesday replied.

He coughed. "Lucy and boring Brian have put the house up for sale. She wants to move the kids away from London and the gang culture."

"I see. Do you know where to?"

"To bloody Wales. I didn't realise boring Brian was half Welsh; he's got family there."

"How do the boys feel about that?"

"Archie's apoplectic apparently, and Alfie thinks it'll be fun. He told me they plan on opening a cheese shop, as the London home would give them enough money for a house and starting the business."

"Has she told you this, or is it all in Alfie's e-mails?"

"Just Alfie," he replied, pulling into the Mannings' driveway.

Harvey answered the door promptly and let them in.

"Why have you got Olivia? Does she want to see me?" he asked.

"She's not requested it, nor has she engaged a solicitor," replied Wednesday.

"What does she need a solicitor for?" his eyes widened.

"It looks like she assisted Susan Roche's suicide, and attempted to frame an innocent man."

Harvey shoved his hands deep into his pockets, and looked up to the ceiling. "Is that serious?"

"Assisted suicide isn't legal in this country, and attempting to frame someone comes with its own consequences."

"There must be something I can do to help her."

"You could advise her to get a solicitor."

"What are you here for, then?"

"We'd like an example of her handwriting."

"Strange request."

He took them into the lounge and began opening drawers looking for something.

"I'm not sure what I can find for you, everyone uses e-mails these days. How about a shopping list?"

"Something longer would be better."

Several minutes later, he triumphantly held a sheet of paper aloft.

"How about a draft letter to the council, bemoaning the bin collection timetable."

Wednesday took it from him, glancing at it.

"This should do," she answered, placing it into an evidence bag.

"Are you returning to the station?"

"No, we've another visit first; you'll have to make your own way there."

"You were rather blunt with him," commented Lennox, pulling on his seatbelt.

"Call it a personality clash."

"The man's just found out his wife's been arrested."

Wednesday shrugged as she checked her mobile for messages. She could not decide whether the silence from Scarlett was a good or bad thing.

Barry Roche was waiting for them impatiently.

"You're late," he barked, brandishing a handwritten note to him instructing him on how to heat up his dinner. "I found this, you're lucky, I was throwing everything out that belonged to her. And if that makes me callous in your eyes then so be it."

"We're not here to judge you," Lennox said, aware of Wednesday's distracted demeanour.

"I hope you get this sorted out soon. Stop people whispering behind my back."

The handwriting expert was waiting for them at the station, eager to commence.

Lennox followed Wednesday to her office and closed the door.

"Forgive me if I'm speaking out of turn, but it's unusual for you to be so preoccupied. I hesitate to say this, but is it my fault, and if so, can I make it up to you?"

His caring words made Wednesday blink rapidly, and delve into her snack drawer.

"It's not you as such, but it is a personal matter, and I'm distressed to hear you think it's affecting my work."

"That's not what I said. I'm asking you as a friend, if you can consider us as that."

"I think this is a conversation for after we've solved this case, don't you?"

When her telephone rang, it gave Lennox the excuse to leave. However, she held him back after hearing who was on the other end of the call. She listened intently before replacing the receiver.

"That was the handwriting expert. The suspected suicide note wasn't written by Susan Roche, or Olivia Manning. I *knew* there was something not right about this case," she sighed.

"So if they didn't write it, who did? Do you have someone in mind?"

She shook her head. "We're going to need handwriting samples from everyone on the unit; patients and staff. I'll get Arlow and Damlish onto that. And before you ask, yes, I want a sample from Joan too."

That evening, Wednesday sat at her kitchen table pushing scraps of paper around. The sound of creaking floorboards from upstairs alerted her of Scarlett's movements; she was finally awake.

Getting up, she filled the kettle and leant against the worktop awaiting her arrival with trepidation.

"I thought you'd still be up," Scarlett said, entering the kitchen, wearing silk pyjamas.

"It's only eight thirty; of course I'm still up."

"Did you see Lennox today?"

"Of course." She monitored her tone.

"Did you tell him?"

"I wanted to, but there wasn't the right time. You're sure you want me to tell him? People don't have to know."

"It would explain a lot of my behaviour to him."

"And what do you expect from him after? Are you hoping he'll have a meaningful relationship with you? Because I don't see him doing that with any woman, never mind one with a mental health issue."

"Perhaps you'll have a better shot at him now," she replied bitterly.

Wednesday sighed, resigning herself to an evening of melodrama. "What about Mum and Oliver, they need to be told, and I don't think me doing it on my own is going to work. How about we go together? I'll try protecting you from Mum's histrionics. What do you think?"

"Whatever."

Wednesday bit her lip and made the herbal tea.

"It's amazing, you've had little sleep, not brushed your hair or washed your face, and yet you have an ethereal beauty about you that transcends any need for grooming." Wednesday looked at her, instantly recognising why men, and women, were drawn to her.

"I'd trade it all to be sane," Scarlett whispered.

"You've only just heard the news; give it a few days and you'll be bouncing around as you normally do."

"Have you ever thought that my bouncing around was me having a manic phase?"

A gentle smile lifted the corners of Wednesday's mouth, but prevented the words coming out; what good would it do?

"Drink your tea, then we can find a film to watch if you wish."

Scarlett turned her nose up at the tea. "No thanks, I'd rather take refuge under my duvet." And with that she was gone.

A couple of days later, Wednesday received a call from Alex Green.

"I've hit a snag with the fingerprints on the letter," he began, "I've identified the fingerprints of Susan Roche and Olivia Manning, as expected."

Wednesday groaned.

"No, but there's more. I've found some DNA on the letter that I can't identify. This means getting DNA from everyone around the case, I'm afraid."

She thanked him for his diligence, expecting him to request a drink together, but he just hung up. She missed his attention. Opening the drawer, she pulled out a packet of biscuits.

Wednesday updated Hunter, who in turn got a warrant set up.

"How are things between you and Lennox?" he asked.

Initially, she looked at him blankly, then realised what he meant.

"Fine, Guv, as I said it would be."

"Pleased to hear it. You make a good team, and I don't want anyone, including you sister, to get in the way of that."

She smiled feebly before heading for Lennox's office to update him. She then set Arlow and Damlish the task of contacting each individual to ask them to attend the station, to provide a sample of DNA. She knew some would vehemently object, but they would have no choice. She felt they were inching closer to the murderer; and time would reveal the answer like an eclipse eventually allows the sun to shine once more.

The reception area of the police station was clogged-up with everyone involved in the Susan Roche case. Certain indignant individuals were causing a huge fuss at being called to the station.

"You could have taken this from us at home," Karen Reilly said haughtily.

"Too many of you to get through," Arlow grunted.

One by one, a cotton bud was brushed against the inner cheek, until finally the mission was complete.

"What happens now?" asked Fiona Campbell, gripping her husband's arm.

"These will all be processed, and anyone of interest will be contacted," Wednesday said, mindful of Fiona's fragile demeanour.

Fiona and Jordan ambled away like an elderly couple, not the young couple they actually were.

"I won't sleep tonight," she whispered.

"Your meds will make sure you do," he replied, squeezing her hand. He knew that he, on the other hand, would have a restless night.

The following morning, Wednesday arrived at work and found Lennox surrounded by giggling female officers. She gripped her Styrofoam cup and retreated to her office.

"Can I have a word?" Alex asked, standing in her doorway.

"Good news I hope."

"Here are the results; I thought you'd want to see them straight away," he said, placing the paper on her desk.

"Perfect, you're a star," she smiled to his back as he walked away.

Picking up her bag and the Styrofoam cup, she removed Lennox from his adoring fans, asking him to drive so she could finish her coffee.

Chapter 57

Olivia Manning opened her front door, offering a meagre smile to the detectives.

"Is your husband in?" asked Wednesday.

"He's at work. Can I help you?"

"No, we'll go to him."

Harvey was waiting for them at the unit.

"Olivia said you wanted to see me; she's understandably anxious."

"We're here to take you back to the station for questioning. If you want a solicitor, you can phone on the way there," Wednesday said.

Normally, people protested at that point, but he quietly put his jacket on and left his office walking between them.

"I won't be long," he called to the nurses on duty as they left.

"So you think I should definitely get her a solicitor now, is it that serious?" he asked from the backseat of Lennox's car.

"It is serious, and yes I would strongly advise a solicitor, but not for your wife, for you," Wednesday replied.

Harvey lunged forward, restrained only by the tightening seatbelt. "Me," he exclaimed, "I assumed it was for Olivia. I thought you wanted me to corroborate her story."

Lennox pressed his foot down further on the accelerator.

"I didn't say that, but I did suggest you call a solicitor."

Harvey slumped back, rubbing the top of his head with his hand. He gazed out the window, watching carefree people walking along the pavement, couples hand-in-hand, oblivious to his woes.

They took him to the interview room, and sat opposite him.

"The suicide note your wife produced was found to have your DNA on it," said Wednesday, watching him closely.

"It would have if it were in our house; I may have touched it at some point."

"You never mentioned any knowledge of it before now. Anyway, at some point you sneezed on the letter."

"I have no knowledge of its contents. It could have been lying around, and I may have sneezed on it." His voice rose in desperation.

"The droplets of phlegm," she continued slowly, "were found underneath some the ink."

He straightened his back, breathing heavily through his nose.

"What I'm saying is you sneezed whilst you wrote the suicide note. But what puzzles me is why did you do this, and why does Olivia appear oblivious to your involvement?"

"I thought you detectives could deduce every aspect of a crime," he replied snidely.

"Officers have been sent to your home with a warrant; if there's anything else to find, they'll find it."

Harvey pressed his lips together, folding his arms tightly across his chest.

"But you're right, I have deduced more about this. Olivia did assist Susan in committing suicide, there's no doubt about that. But I believe they were trying to implicate Barry Roche, perhaps for having an affair. Now your involvement puzzles me . . ."

A knock at the door interrupted her, then an officer peered around the door. Wednesday rose and went to speak with him.

Harvey watched her as she returned and sat opposite him.

"They've found what looks like Susan Roche's original suicide note in your study. The handwriting will be checked out, but my guess is, it's the original one."

"You'd be correct," he replied.

"So the question is, why did you copy her note? Who would that damage? The answer is Olivia, isn't it?"

"Why would I want to do that?"

"Because she's trying to interfere with your precious unit. She calls it your 'baby.' I suspect she's jealous of the time you spent there; she's said as much." She placed her elbows on the table, placing her hands in a prayer-like position.

"She didn't hide the fact; she frequently moaned at me when I returned home, no matter what time it was. She was unsupportive and bitter."

"So by giving her a false suicide note, it would place her under suspicion."

"And it worked, didn't it?"

"Except it wasn't her handwriting, which only added to the confusion. But your DNA on the letter began to clarify things. Olivia's in the other interview room, so we'll get her half of the story and put them together; there'll be no more secrets."

Harvey sneezed before retrieving a handkerchief from his pocket. "Damn hay fever." He blew his nose before continuing. "Susan Roche had an appointment with me, where she confided that Olivia wanted the unit to fail. Susan then said she knew her husband was having an affair and she wanted to punish him."

"So you came up with a plan to suit you both."

"Not straight away. My bitterness towards Olivia fermented in my mind until the small shoots of revenge began growing."

"So Susan wrote a suicide note and gave it to you to copy. Then she gave the copy to Olivia, so she believed she was covered should the crime be suspected."

"You're good, but if I hadn't sneezed, none of this would have come to light."

"It would have, as we'd have taken handwriting samples from you all. Even when someone disguises their handwriting, the expert can still see the subtleties in the loops and pen pressure. We'd have still got you." She sat back, looking directly at him. "I wonder what Olivia will think when she hears this."

"I don't rightly care; this is all her fault. Anyway, I haven't done anything; I didn't touch Susan Roche."

"The planning and perverting the course of justice won't go unpunished. And I'm not sure what the GMC will think."

Harvey stopped smirking.

An undercurrent of excitement buzzed around the station, mainly caused by Maria Jones, the organiser of Hunter's birthday party. Those who were going congregated in the Incident Room, waiting for the birthday boy to emerge.

Hunter was greeted by a sea of smiles before they all headed for The Crazy Duck. Lennox was whisked away by two women latching themselves onto his arms.

"How does he do it?" Hunter mumbled, walking next to Wednesday.

"He oozes charm, Guv."

"It's Digby, we're off duty, remember?"

She smiled, aware of her cheeks glowing.

"So you've never been tempted by his charms?"

She laughed. "He dated Scarlett. Need I say more?"

"You don't like hand-me-downs."

"Precisely."

"Does that go for divorced men too?" He held the pub door open for her to step inside. "Well?"

She looked across at Lennox engulfed by a swarm of women. "Maybe I should relax my rules a bit."

Digby Hunter accepted a pint from Wednesday, allowing his fingertips to brush hers as he did so.

Acknowledgments

I owe my sanity to Jessica "Goose" Kristie and James Logan at Winter Goose Publishing. They bolster my (at times) flagging confidence, and James is an awesome Editor-in-Chief, from whom I've learnt much.

And to Peter Martin, for cooking meals whilst I'm knee-deep in editing.

About the Author

Hemmie Martin spent most of her professional life as a Community Nurse for people with learning disabilities, a Family Planning Nurse, and a Forensic Nurse working with young offenders. She spent six years living in the south of France, and currently lives in Essex with her husband, one teenage daughter, Rosie, one house rabbit, and two guinea pigs. Her eldest daughter, Jessica, is studying veterinary medicine.

9 781941 058305